Acclaim for Chase Webster's
EAT'EM:

"…this book is going to change an entire genre of writing and no one was even warned."
-Mary Duncanson (Author of Trouble Comes Knocking)

"…this never disappoints. You'll be happy you bought it."
-Jason Boyd (writer/journalist)

"YOU are the talent that walked into my classroom…I'm glad it's Eat'em's time!"
--Yvonne Jocks (author of OVERTIME series)

"I was laughing so hard on public transit that people were staring at me."
-Catie Anne Du Bruille

"Love it! It's a great read and just the type of book I look for."
-Mom

"Intriguing"
-Trey Kegley

"Sooooo excited"
-Patrick Rivers

"You had me at Jolt Cola"
-Jaime Bengzon

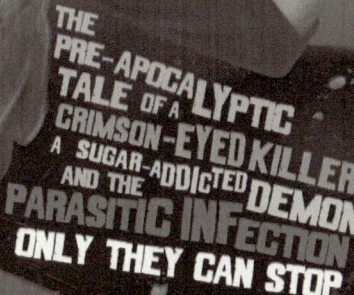

EAT'EM

THE
PRE-APOCALYPTIC
TALE OF A
CRIMSON-EYED KILLER,
A SUGAR-ADDICTED DEMON
AND THE
PARASITIC INFECTION
ONLY THEY CAN STOP

CHASE WEBSTER

ISBN-13: 978-0615977935 (Chase Webster)
ISBN-10: 0615977936

Printed in the United States of America
Typeset in Garamond and Big Caslon

Edited by Dallas Webster
Cover design courtesy of Milan Jovanovic
Title page courtesy of Benjamin Roque

This story is fiction. All of the characters are from the writer's imagination.
Any similarities to real people, aside from where specifically stated
otherwise, is entirely coincidental.

Facebook.com/chase.m.webster
Cweebs.deviantart.com

For Mom, Dad, Sissy, Dr. D, Auntie A, Little P,
Brookleberry, Monkey, Bug, and Bubba

Prologue

*L*ooking at the charges against me, it's easy to assume I had a terrible childhood. Twenty-one counts of first-degree murder, how could I not?

But I wasn't a weird kid. I wasn't awkward or abnormal. I ran track and played baseball. I liked to draw. I had friends. My family cared about me. I was an average student and did my best to stay out of trouble. I certainly wasn't a social outcast. Truth be told, I failed to stand out in any way whatsoever. Everything changed a few days after my fifteenth birthday. The day I met a demon. A demon I would come to know as Eat'em.

"Can I have this?"

The question stood contrast to my dreamless sleep. I startled awake and clapped the darkness away.

A small red creature stood on my end table, no taller than the Victorian lamp beside him. He held a bottle of Pepto-Bismol antacid tablets tightly to his chest. In his arms, the pink bottle looked cartoonish and large.

The creature had porcupine thick hair and a prehensile tail.

Bronze fur framed his large quizzical eyes – eyes icier than the most frozen blue, encapsulating triangular pupils as dark as the ocean's depths. I didn't immediately pin him for a demon. At the time, I was more interested in Animal Planet than mythology. He looked more like a simian to me, a word I'd learned from watching Planet Earth. Still half asleep, I figured he was a spider monkey of sorts.

"Human child," he said, shaking the bottle, "Can I have this?"

Perhaps I should have been more surprised, even scared of the imp shaking the bottle of antacids, but the creature could not have seemed less threatening. His piercing eyes, almost translucent, were captivating and hypnotic. I found myself more mesmerized by his presence than frightened.

"I'm sorry," I sat up. Tucking my blanket onto my lap, I said, "But, you can talk? I mean. What are you?"

"Me?" his eyelids blinked outward from the bridge of his flat nose toward his indented temples. It reminded me of some kind of reptile, like a tree frog or something. "I'm me. You. I'm asking you, yes. Can I have this container of small delectable candies?" He rattled the container dramatically.

"The Pepto?" I asked.

"The Pepto," he sighed and read the label. "Yes, the Pepto. This, yes. The candies. They're in here. I found them, yes. I found them here. You. You were sleeping. I found these. They're yours, yes? I want them. If I can have them. These. These Pepto. Oh... yes. If I can have them I'd be grateful, yes... I'd follow you. I'd follow you now until the day you die. From now until then, yes. I'd follow you and I would be your one true compatriot. The Don Quixote to your Sancho Panza, the Batman to your Robin, the Huckleberry Finn to your Nigger Jim. Yours. You. And... hm... yes. From then on I'd do what you ask of me. As your one true ally to do what you need. I'd be the best friend you have. Best. All I ask for, to be yours until forever, is that you bestow upon me these delightful morsels I have found of yours for my consumptive pleasure."

"Yes," I said, not thinking twice. "Take it. Eat'em."

"Eat'em, great," he said. "Yes. A strange name, but I like it. That's what you will call me then. Eat'em. Thank you for this." His long tail whipped around him and wrapped around the lid to the medicine bottle. He twisted hard, his face turning a darker shade of red. "What's this? A trick! You've bought me for a container that doesn't open? Oh... young human child, this is not becoming of you. No. Not. At. All. Bad start... bad start."

I reached for the bottle and he yanked it back, clutching it tighter to his chest. "It's a child lock," I said.

"Whoa there, child!" he said. "You gave this to me. It's mine. Mine, yes. Trick or not, I want it. It's mine."

"I'm just going to open it for you."

He squinted at me, the quills down his spine puffing out before relaxing back flat. "Okay," he said. "But if I don't get it back in... I don't know how long. How long it takes you to open and return it. That long. If that's not how long it takes to get it back. If instead it's longer, yes. Then the deal is off."

"What deal?" I asked as I opened the bottle and handed it back.

He looked into the open bottle, eyes wide with pleasure. "Oh, the deal where I'm indebted to you forever. Don't worry, no. That was plenty fast. Very fast. Oh... these are so worth it. More than worth it. I've been waiting all but the last ten minutes for these. I thought you'd never wake up... Then if you did... I was only half sure you would see me. And if you did, yes, I was only then about one-point-two percent sure that you would say yes to my having these. Which, one-point-two percent of half of never... wow. The odds were so stacked against, yes. But here we are."

The imp held up a couple tablets, they took up his whole hand. He smiled widely and popped them into his mouth and began to chew, crunching loudly.

"Oh, yes... yes... yes," he said. "The odds were so high against me ever getting these since I saw them ten... maybe eleven minutes ago. But fate had it that all those harrowing mathematical improbabilities would contradict the reality I had perceived which was you silently sleeping forever and me never getting these... Pepto. Which aren't very good, by the way. Not at all. But so worth it to defeat the odds."

He popped more pink pills in his mouth and chewed, then offered me one.

"No thanks," I said.

"You are missing out," he said before crunching loudly on another tablet. "To honor our new friendship, I will eat your share and my share, yes. Man, human child, you don't know what I had to go through to get these. I was behind this house and a huge beast. You. You have a huge dumb beast. Oh how I hate, hate beasts. They hate me though, yes. So that's mutual. And I had to hide in the dirt behind the house and the beast kept digging until, man... you wouldn't believe it if I said human child, but the odds are strikingly improbable. More so improbable than you waking to give me these!" He bit a tablet in half, chewed vigorously and continued. "That beast got yelled at for digging. Someone yelled, 'Reena!' and the beast went away."

"Reena?" I asked. "The neighbor's Chihuahua?"

"Yes, that," the imp said, "Horrible thing. It went away and I climbed through a hole in the wooden barrier blocking that house, this house, yes. Climbed through, and the door was open. All the doors. Every door, usually shut, all of them open, yes. Leading me to this. This bottle of Pepto! And you. And odds were good I'd be standing here holding the bottle and you wouldn't wake. Wouldn't see me. Wouldn't respond. And odds were against all the good things that had to happen. All the doors. All the waking and seeing and responding. Yes... I was going against all odds and so I bet it all. Bet myself to you. Oh man, human child, worth it. Worth it so much. Even if these. Pepto. Really bad, awful stuff."

The demon sold himself into servitude for a bottle of really bad, awful stuff. And as promised, he never left my side.

Perhaps he stayed with me because I saw him. Perhaps he

stayed with me because he was lonely. Perhaps he stayed with me because he needed me. Whatever the reason, Eat'em stayed with me. Not quite the Batman to my Robin, but he remained my invisible sidekick nonetheless. My not-so-imaginary best friend.

Seven years later, as I stand trial for the world to see, Eat'em remains at my side. After all, he's at least part of the reason I'm here.

It's easy for the media to point at me now and say, "There he is. There's the crimson-eyed killer of Texas. The Assassin of Arlington." Whatever they're calling me. I get it.

But Eat'em and I didn't set out to kill anyone. We meant to save the world from a threat only I could see. If we couldn't stop the apocalypse, we at least wanted to postpone it.

CHAPTER 1

July 2020 – Opening Statements

"Jacob is not the monster you've been told about."

The culmination of all I've done landed me here. My every action is under the magnified glare of countless eyes. Their emotionless gaze judges without compassion and without remorse. And for the first time in my life I'm not so worried about what I see as I am about what they see.

Them… The people… The State of Texas vs. Jacob Brook… The State of Texas vs. Me.

My past is a public autopsy and my future is dependant on a paunchy lawyer paid by the state.

"A lot of words have been thrown around about Jacob.

You've been told he's responsible for countless atrocities. Atrocities committed over the span of several years. Violent. Apprehensible atrocities."

My first look at the fifteen people on whose shoulders my life rides on and I know immediately... I'm screwed. I spent the last two and a half years in prison – presumed innocent. I would probably spend the rest of my short life there.

I would share my confinement with a restless red demon.

"Over the next few weeks you're going to hear from several interesting people. You're going to hear from friends of Jacob. Neighbors. Family. Renowned doctors and psychologists. Smart people. Very interesting. You're going to hear from a police officer. Jacob's arresting officer."

I feel the spiteful eyes as they observe the slightest facial tick. A twitch as I swallow back the taste of stomach acid. The repetition of the words "interesting" and "officer" bring about a sour taste to my mouth. My stomach lurches.

"It's all interesting because of what these people will have to say. What they will have to share with you. It doesn't support what you were told yesterday."

Mike, my attorney, walks around with his hands folded across his abdomen. He is like a cartoon character trying to keep his ascot from smacking him in the face. Yet, as helpless as I am at the mercy of a lawyer funded by taxpayers, he is slightly more eloquent than I originally feared. In conversation Mike is a stammering fool. Yet, somehow he manages to convey his point to the jury somewhat competently.

Mike gestures ever so slightly toward the prosecution, his hand gliding outward like a penguin that, just briefly, thinks it can fly. His counterpart, District Attorney Dale Gomes is ice. Gomes's eyes follow Big Mike around the room. He sees Mike as little more than prey. He's not entertained by Mike's presence. Nor does he look bored. He is simply attentive. He is studying.

"Now the defense is going to present you with stories. Stories of a man who hunted and killed innocent people. These stories are largely based on the observations of a single man. You will not be presented with DNA evidence… because there isn't any. One man. The testimony of one man is the only evidence you'll be told to rely on. Like a trail of breadcrumbs, the prosecution will piece together observations in an attempt to link my client to a series of events. Observations from a man who readily admits to stalking the defendant for months under the pretense of a hunch. I shiver to think of the conclusions someone might come to if they followed me around for several weeks, observing. Observing… That is a key word you see. The word they would prefer to use is witness. However, there is no witness. Therefore, you are going to be asked to trust without physical evidence."

I glanced at Lieutenant Bellecroix as Big Mike escorted me into the courtroom. His grayish skin is cragged with age lines and sorrowful sunken eyes. I am not the one he feels pity for.

"You've been told that - because the evidence is circumstantial. Circumstantial is a term you'll come to hear a lot over the course of this trial. There are also a couple concepts that were explained to you. Concepts I'm going to remind you of right now. These are concepts I want you to think about when you're hearing these testimonies. Concepts like 'burden of proof' and 'innocent until proven guilty.'"

Mike stabs his hand at the air as if these phrases are a magical weapon that dissolves prejudice.

I catch the eye of a middle-aged woman sitting in the jury pool. She wears a turquoise dress she most likely bought for the occasion. It's dark with moisture and sticking to her bosom. Her eyes match the color of her outfit, a piercing ocean. For a moment I feel lost in the non-blinking sapphires, tainted by heavy makeup and fake tan. I look longer than I should. She has decided I'm guilty.

Her head turns dramatically back toward Big Mike.

My pulse spikes. This room is purgatory. My last hope relies on a group of people that are just going through the motions. Hoping to score a free lunch before returning to their boring lives. I hope the blue-eyed woman is an alternate.

I hope she falls out.

"I think when you hear what these men and women have to say. When you hear their testimony. Facts. Science. Not opinions and conjecture. You'll come to the same conclusion I have. Jacob Brook is not guilty of murder. Jacob Brook is not the perpetrator here. Jacob Brook is the unsung hero."

Eat'em, my foot-tall demon, matches Mike step-for-step. He paces at his heel, his arm up and finger cutting through the air like a miniature Napoleon Bonaparte.

I shouldn't be so easily sidetracked with my life on the line. I should be trying to appear innocent. I should be attentive on Big Mike. I am lured by a swaying tail only I can see. How often do people wonder what it is I'm staring at? How often do they wonder who it is I'm talking to?

"To understand," Mike continues, "we need to stop trying to look into the mind of a killer and instead look into the heart of hero. We have to go back to these moments Mr. Gomes is going to say. He's going to say it's these moments that paint the picture of a monster. We're going to visit these moments and you'll surely agree with me when we do. This is the story of how one man is using his misunderstood gifts, gifts he received as a child, not to destroy life, but to save it. Contrary to the story of another man. A man whose story you'll come to realize cannot be trusted. A criminal in his own right who unlawfully began this misguided manhunt."

"This is the story of Jacob Caleb Brook."

Chapter 2

"Rise and shine, Jake!"

My Uncle Patrick.

Uncle Patrick much preferred to go by his middle name, Valentine. He flat refused to respond to uncle anything. He was actually two days younger than myself, a fact my parents both resented. Not much takes the wind out of a mother-to-be's sails like the grandmother-to-be sharing the same news. My dad swore up and down my grandparents did it just to spite them. He even believed my grandma intentionally postponed labor so Patrick Valentine would be the most celebrated of the two newborns. A picture of Val right out of the hospital has him in a 'World's Best Uncle' onesie. It hung proudly over the thirty-two inch plasma screen in our single bedroom apartment.

Val flipped the light on and I cowered deeper into the cushions of my parents' old leather couch.

"Seriously, Baby-Jake!" Val's chipper, *Every Morning is a Good Morning,* tone tended to conquer any other noise polluting the atmosphere. Silence wasn't something I'd experienced in some time. Calm was anything that broke through the storm, which Val could do without effort. "Come on, you lazy orphan, get up. Get up! Get up! Get up!"

Orphan for us Brooks more-or-less represented a term of endearment. We were both orphans. Mortality struck my dad first (Val's brother), and then it grasped its mangled fingers around the lives of my mom and stepfamily, finally, catching up to my grandparents within six months of each other. Val and I lived in our own apartment for only a few months. For his parents, death lingered agonizingly close for years, leaving me in the care of an uncle younger than myself. A cruel punch line to a joke only Val and I would ever be privy to.

"And could you put a shirt on, for the sake of humanity?" Val opened the fridge and rummaged around. "I swear to god, Jake-Nasty, I wake up early every morning, I'm tired of being rewarded with your Wicker Man physique. Plus, you're getting your damned nastiness all over my couch, Deadpool, so put on your costume if you're going to grind up on my stuff."

Eat'em pounced on the back of my head as I buried it into the security of a squished-to-mush pillow made out of some space-age memory foam; the guaranteed firmness of which gave out after a weeklong spell we suffered with no air conditioning. I futilely shoved fistfuls of mashed foam against my ears to block out The World's Best Uncle and my eager demon.

"Waffles, yes," Eat'em said. "I shall gulp the innards of Aunt Jemima, lapping plasma from her hollowed skull, yes. Imbibe her succulent fluids until she's empty once more!"

"Why can't you ever sleep in?" I shouted into a pillow.

"Because, Your Jakeness," Val skipped from the kitchen and stomped as he jumped into a squat in front of the couch. Then he sang in his best VeggieTales impression, "It's the first day… of the first grade!"

"No!" I grunted wearily.

"Yes!" Eat'em yelled.

"Yeah buddy," Val cracked the top on a soda. "First day of college. Wealth is no excuse to be an uneducated dolt." He sang Sublime lyrics, "Early in the morning, rising to the street."

"I'm not going."

"The Hell you aren't," Val kicked the couch and slapped the wall over my head. He trumpeted an off key version of Reveille with his face a few unintended inches from Eat'em's backside. "WAKE UP, PRIVATE STUPID! IT'S TIME WE LEARN YOU SOME GOOD!"

All my strength went into rolling over.

If one didn't know any better, they'd think Val and I were separated by years instead of days. His skin shone bright like my dad's once had. In fact, he could have passed for a younger, skinnier version of my father, with green eyes and fiery hair. Val's hair was unkempt and looked youthful. He never had to shave either, taking even more years off his complexion.

By comparison, I grew a tasseled bird's nest, crested with an ever-receding hairline that I'd been blessed with before stepping foot out of high school. Crests formed at the edges of my eyelids, burrows on my cheeks led from the sides of my nose to the corners of my mouth, and I'd been told my deep-set eyes resembled those of Steve Buscemi. Nobody ever said a *Young* Steve Buscemi... just I looked like Steve Buscemi.

The exception, of course, was my red irises. Sometimes I introduced myself thusly, "My name is Jacob Brook, and no, I'm not wearing contacts." The typical, "Okay..." takes up less time than when I waited for people to ask. Then they'd have to say, "Weird" or "that's cool!" "Were they always like that?" "Do you see things different?" And the conversation would lead to the scrutinizing of the rest of my features and eventually the inevitable, "Has anyone ever told you, you look just like that guy from the Adam Sandler movies," or "*Con Air*," or "*Boardwalk Empire.*"

Yes. Yes, they have.

"Soldier!" Val stood in mock attention. He held out a can of Jolt Cola directly over my head. "Hair of the Dog. You'll feel better after you've got some sustenance."

"I want some!" Eat'em shouted, standing rigid, at attention on the back of my head. "Sir, it's just the Jolt I need to slay that immortal hag Jemima."

"No!" I rolled over, tossing Eat'em to the floor as I did. I typically paid no more attention to the demon than I would a mole on my back. It's easy to forget I'm the only one who sees and hears the little devilish nuisance.

"You act as if I'm giving you a choice, Private Jake-Nasty." Val plopped the can onto my chest, using a deep scar on my right pectoral muscle as a makeshift coaster. "Hydrate or die!"

I grabbed the energy drink and sat up. A heartwarming desire to shove Eat'em into the garbage disposal gave my day new purpose. I shouldn't have stayed up watching movies. "Sure, I'll drink it," I said, "but it's not going to help."

"Just a sip, yes?" Eat'em tugged at my ankle. "One insurmountably insignificant ingested sip of said savory sensational liquid is all I request!"

"Just shut up,"

"Shut up?" Val asked.

"Yeah." When I needed to speak to Eat'em, I disguised it as a conversation between two parties. "I'll drink the Jolt and I'll go to school, but you got to stop the singing in the morning... and the soldier act."

"Yes sir, Colonel Jake."

I dressed, drank my breakfast, and snuck a couple more energy drinks into my backpack for my secret companion. A wired demon was a happy demon. I found the sugar-crash to be far more agonizing than the sugar-high. But if anyone had advice on how to wean a demon off anything a demon wants, I hadn't heard it.

I grabbed a wireless headset for my phone and slipped it over my ear before checking myself over to see if I'd forgotten anything. Val made a scoffing remark about my need for a headset when I don't have friends to talk to and I subtly waved for Eat'em to get out of the kitchen.

"Let's go, Crazy Jake," Val threw open the door to a sallow sunrise, which immediately overwhelmed the apartment in a blinding veil of white.

Valentine and I crossed the threshold into the bright sunlight, followed by a victorious Eat'em - an empty bottle of pancake syrup skittered behind us, lynched in the demon's tail.

Chapter 3

"Of course, I didn't think any of it was real either." I'm trapped in a box with Mike. My pudgy lawyer stares at me as I confess the existence of Eat'em like a grown man with an imaginary friend I never grew out of. "I didn't want to. I'd rather have been going through some schizophrenic phase than have accidentally adopted a foot-tall talking crimson porcupine-spider monkey thing only I could see and hear. From what I'm reading in prison, serial killers are often bed-wetters when they're a kid. That doesn't sound so bad in comparison.

"I get that it's hard to imagine how someone thrust into abnormal circumstances could simultaneously have a normal upbringing. But it's not that I didn't have more than my share of strange experiences. Not everyone's life can be humdrum boring, but that doesn't mean I'm automatically a psychopath. It's not like I chose to have the fantastic thrust upon me. And it's not like I didn't attempt to make it disappear."

Mike scrapes his palm across his five o'clock shadow. Microscopic flakes of dead skin flavor the air and float up toward an open vent. I wonder if the filter has been changed recently. He raises an eyebrow as he catches me staring, beckoning me to continue.

"See, I figured if Eat'em was real," my eyes drift to the demon sprawled out across the table, one arm dangling over the edge as he pretends to sleep, "a real life imp with the inability to be seen, or heard, or to shut up... then I should be able to kill him, right? What normal child, tormented by such a creature, wouldn't try to kill him?

"I have no history of killing animals or any of that crazy nonsense *actual* crazy people do. Killing things isn't in my nature. So, being the first thing I wanted off this mortal coil, Eat'em wasn't up against some grade-A natural born killer. He was up against a kid who just couldn't fathom his first date being chaperoned by an imp."

Mike stretches and squishes his face before he asks me anything. A hair bothers him from inside his nostril. He thumbs at it as he says, "So, Eat'em... he shows up. He gives you the impulse to kill things?"

"Not exactly." Eat'em pays me no attention. Our current circumstances bore him. "You got to give me credit for making it through the first four days before I began daydreaming about throwing him in the power wash or taking him out with the trash.

Days one and two were devoted to hiding him. I realized there was no point to that when my stepdad barged into my bedroom and didn't acknowledge the thing hunched atop my dresser like a gargoyle, drinking a family-sized tube of toothpaste. I started walking him downstairs on my shoulder like a pirate. I'd go to the fridge and he'd tell me what supplies to gather. Jolt Cola was our number one source of hydration those first few days. Eat'em would keep me up at night. I couldn't sleep. Halfway through my fourth night, that's when I decided to kill Eat'em."

"And how do you kill your imaginary friend?" Mike says without a hint of sarcasm. In his profession, I must wonder if he's no stranger to bizarre stories and excuses. I can't tell if his demeanor derives from belief, curiosity, or experience. Sweat builds on my palms and I wipe them discretely on my pants.

"The easiest way to kill a devil," I say and wait for a response from Eat'em before continuing, "especially one with a penchant for eating anything you give him, is to poison him. I figured it wouldn't be hard... He ate just about anything. Even things he disliked were impossible to pry from his tiny hands once he decided they were his. And almost everything inevitably made it into his mouth."

"Eat'em sounds like a child," Mike plays psychiatrist. He thinks he has me figured out. "Maybe a relic of a time you feel is missing? Stolen from you, perhaps?"

"Hardly," I go on, "I conjured up some potent combinations of laundry detergents and dishwashing fluids. I poured

20

him cup after cup of ammonia. I gave him bars of soap to snack on. All I managed to do was make my room smell as if a manufacturing plant for cleaning products exploded. Eat'em could chew the rust off a carriage bolt, wash it down with bleach, and brush his teeth with arsenic. Poisoning him accomplished nothing.

"My second strategy," I went on, "was to get one of my family members to accidentally kill him. They couldn't see him, so getting them to do the work was pretty difficult. I thought about waiting for Eat'em to sleep and tucking him under one of the tires of my dad's Prowler. Eat'em doesn't close his eyes for more than a few seconds at a time. I thought about somehow tricking him into standing in front of the riding mower. He may have swallowed thumbtacks, but even I couldn't think of a way to get the suicidal bastard to face down the John Deer."

"These are pretty violent thoughts, Jacob," Mike pulls the flab on the bottom of his chin and allows it to bounce back into place. He rubs his face to conceal some hidden emotion. Perhaps distrust. Mike seems too ready to accept what he hears. I don't know if that's good or bad.

"No, you see, I wasn't creative enough to think of a way to kill him." Eat'em wakes. He smiles at me. "I wanted to. But I couldn't. The prospect of just grabbing a kitchen knife and hacking him to bits never crossed my mind. It was too personal, and I'd have to live with it. Despite the fact that I questioned whether he was real in the first place, I wasn't some hardcore animal slaughterer. I just didn't think I'd be able to live out the rest of my life with him strung out on energy drinks. My very own blood-red addict."

Mike writes something down before laying a phone on the table and setting it to record. "What I want to talk about, Jacob, is the first moment you decided to take a life. I don't want to hear about your fantasies. I want to know the instant you decided to take a human life."

My gut lurches at the word *fantasies*. "I never decided to take a human life. Never decided to take a human life. Never. I've only ever wanted to protect human life."

"From what?" Mike asks.

"From the infection."

Chapter 4

The palpability of the Texas sun covered my skin like burning oil. Nothing prepared me for the dramatic change in climate when we arrived to the state by train two months prior. Even still, my body refused to adjust to the summer heat.

I sat in the back of Val's '04 mint-green Mustang to make room for our neighbor, a short guy named Isaac. Overdressed, Isaac climbed into the car, parting a suit jacket as he sank into the front seat. He always wore a vest and scarves, even in the hundred-degree heat. His dark hair swooped to the side with a cavernous part about an inch over his right ear. He was considerably older than my uncle and myself and seemed even worldlier than someone his age typically does. I suspected this was his second shot at college life. Either that or he'd taken a few years off after high school.

"I loathe this one, Jacob," Eat'em plugged his nose and pointed to Isaac with his tail. He crossed over the dash, hopped onto the center console, and leapt onto my lap in the back seat. He climbed my shoulder and whispered into my ear, "He smells funny, yes! Not the good kind of funny… but the bad kind. Like the kind of funny that makes you want to burn down a village to get rid of the stink." In reality, he smelled like mothballs.

I tapped Isaac on the shoulder and asked, "What kind of cologne you wearing?"

Isaac smiled. He had an awkward grin that bared his bottom teeth as much as the top, like a young child faking it for a family photo – warmer though, and more genuine. "I don't wear any… maybe you smell the starch. Does it bother you?"

"Not at all," I said at the same time Eat'em arched backward, holding onto my collar, and yelled 'YES!' I returned Isaac's sheepish grin. "I like it. I was just trying to place the scent."

"No! No! No!" Eat'em ranted. "You have to extinguish this fool from existence. Drown him in a bathtub, yes! Use lots of soap. In fact, if you care anything about the prolonged survival of your species you would get out of this car, stop by the gas station, grab fifteen gallons of bleach and a ten pound bag of Gummy Worms, soak this putrid moron in the bleach and give me the Gummy Worms, yes… and a slush!"

Val gave me the eye from the rearview mirror. Clearly, he agreed with Eat'em.

"Mind if I smoke in your car?" A cigarette stuck out the

corner of Isaac's mouth even before Val could answer. A few years would pass before smokers became almost entirely segregated to pits across the United States. At the time, the smoking section was anywhere your foot touched outside, unlike the designated areas that came into existence soon after, freckling the Earth in carbon monoxide clouds.

He offered the pack back to me, and I almost accepted, but declined when Eat'em said, "Blech! See, he's evil, yes! He wants you to smell like death, too."

Though Val and I share the same birth year, our academic achievements didn't quite compare. Having a demon willing to cheat on my behalf in return for some cheap culinary treats (as he sometimes called the junk food in the checkout line) gave me a unique advantage over other students. I was accepted into every college I applied to. Val had a lesser selection to choose from after high school. We compromised on UTA, a satellite of the University of Texas. Val would have to work full time for a year to earn enough money to enroll. I would be on scholarship. He wanted out of Virginia as badly as I did and so we landed in Texas.

We stopped in the front of a full lot. Val lowered his window as Isaac and I climbed out of the Mustang, followed by Eat'em, who crawled up my leg and found a perch on my backpack.

"You know where you're going, Jake-Nasty?" Val asked for the fiftieth time in the last couple days.

"Not really," I looked over the campus. It spread out like oil on a cloth, same as everything in Texas. Most of the buildings were only a couple stories tall – the space between, utilized only as a walking path, was wide enough to land a fleet of jumbo jets.

"I got you," Isaac dropped his smoke and smashed it into the curb. "I know this campus better than anyone. Don't even worry about it."

The second we climbed out of the car, the heat once again hit me like the open door of a sauna. Sweat dripped from my fingertips, my face, and my elbows. Isaac led the way as I left a trail of droplets in my wake.

"There is literally not a room on this campus I haven't been in," Isaac spoke so matter-of-factly, I didn't question whether he might be embellishing. As out of place as he should have looked wearing a suit under the Texas sun, he actually fit right in. He walked with a sense of arrogance, though his head canted forward and the jacket gave him the slightest appearance of a hunchback. Even with his squat stature, his awkward posture, and formal attire, he looked like any other student walking the campus.

Some girls walked by in pajamas and slippers. One had a sundress. A few people wore shirts with the university mascot, which was either a horse or a bull depending on the shirt. There were a few cyclists and a dude wearing a wife beater, swim trunks and flip-flops, gliding by on a long board.

"If you need to know anything I pretty much have my finger planted on the pulse of this place. I know what's playing in the theater, I know when the next basketball game is, I know where the best house party will be this weekend. Heck, if people are getting it on in the library," Isaac pointed to a large building to our right, "I know about it. Truth is, I've seen it all. I can tell you what's hot and what's not."

"He's a regular Van Wilder, yes?" Eat'em said from my backpack. "I hope he steps into traffic."

"There's a coffee shop in both the theater building and the library, sweet hangout spots, you can usually find me at either place reading the paper, which by the way, is Arlington's main local paper."

"Yay..." Eat'em groaned.

"Over here's the science building," Isaac pointed to one of the taller structures, "there's a couple science buildings, actually. This one's mostly for biology crap, if you like that stuff. They are in the process of planting a garden on the roof. There's also a building where they're researching how to convert water into power, like gas for cars, and I'm pretty sure that one has a garage where they build stockcars if you want to take a mechanics course. You can actually race them too, which is pretty fun."

"You've done that?" I asked.

"Yeah, man," he increased his pace a bit, "I've done everything here. Seriously, professional student! On the west side of campus there's a nanotech lab. They're making a microchip that's small enough to fit into the tip of a pen. South of that, near the theater, that's where you're going to take a lot of your English, history, languages are spread all over, but there's also photography, that kind of crap. Humanities. Do you like sports?"

"Sure."

"Well, I hope you don't like football," he pointed off in the distance to an ambiguous location blocked by countless buildings. "There's a football field and used to be a team, but it's gotten nixed. Still though, there's basketball, but they're in a gym that doesn't really have a designated court. Maybe someday, but even if not, there are sporting events all over Texas. The state is obsessed. Here though, it's about girl's volleyball. I've seen every game."

"How do you have time for everything?" Val asked.

"Patty," Isaac smiled, baring all teeth, "there's always time for girl's volleyball. Plus, I practically live here"."

Eat'em chimed in, "Does your grand tour include a shower?"

We followed Isaac into a set of double doors and down a hallway, where he grabbed a newspaper from a rack and kept walking. We passed a cafeteria on our left and entered a huge lobby filled with chain restaurants and a small shopping center.

"Are you a philosopher, Jacob?" Isaac took a seat, tossing his coat tails to either side, and opened the paper. "There are some great philosophy classes if you are into that kind of thing. They talk about how different people view the world. Some see us all as part, as one with the universe, whatever, all kinds of stuff. I find it fascinating. So many people with different points of view, different perspectives of the same events. I've often wondered what it would be like to see life through all of these different viewpoints. The world is becoming more connected all around us. It almost seems as if this should be the natural order of things. Together we can achieve much more than as individuals."

"Nut job!" Eat'em blurted. "Can we visit the soda fountain?"

"No," I answered.

"No?" Isaac lifted an eyebrow and again grinned like a whale eating krill. "I didn't mean that as a question. I definitely am not trying to start an argument."

I sat. "I just have to disagree with your philosophy. There's value in individuality. Historically, individualism has had some of the greatest contributions to cultural growth, right? I mean, our foundation is built by those who've denied societal constraints. Darwin, Edison, Jobs, Van Gogh…"

"Aren't you two perfect for each other," Valentine scoffed as he found a seat and ogled a group of passing girls.

"Merely men!" Isaac ignored Val, "And men are like cells. We're part of the bigger picture. The arm doesn't mourn when a cell dies. It just makes more cells. Yours is an interesting perspective, though. You should take philosophy. I think you might change your point of view. You're a smart kid…"

"A regular John Forbes Nash," Val said.

A ripple of excitement rushed through Isaac's face. "I like you guys. We should carry on this conversation again sometime after you've both taken a few classes. Maybe then you could teach me a thing or two. What kind of girls you like?"

"I don't know," I said at the same time Val answered, "What kind of girls don't I like?"

Dating would be impossible with Eat'em lingering. Even before Val finished the question, Eat'em belched and chirped, "Girls suck!"

"Well, find out and get back to me," he smiled. "I'm glad y'all moved in next door. You know how it is; us geniuses get all lost in our heads and get bored. Need other geniuses around to keep things interesting."

"Don't be his friend, Jacob," Eat'em pleaded as he leapt from atop my head onto the table. He stood between us, trying to block my view. "I don't like him. He's smelly? Check. He likes girls? Check. He has big boring conversations? Triple check! Yes? Yes! And he smells. I don't want you to be his friend… please? Please, please!"

"Sure," I said. "Geniuses stick together, I guess."

"No!" Eat'em yelled. "You fool! This is the beginning of the end! Put me in a box and ship me to wherever this isn't, because this sucks, yes. SUCKS!"

Isaac's teeth glinted in the dull light of the dining facility. "Good, man, now what do you got? What's your first class? I'll help you find it."

Chapter 5

MASS MURDERER'S IMAGINARY MENAGERIE. That's the headline that accompanies my reveal of the Grotesque Infection during my trial. The catchy title does a good job of making me out to look like a lunatic. The article itself is farce. The journalist, David House, wrote it as if I am suggesting a microbial alien invasion of fungus people landed in my backyard. It reads like a smug movie review. He even compares my defense to an M. Night Shyamalan film.

The jury is expected to remain impartial and not be swayed by the media. But the week after "MASS MURDERER'S IMAGINARY MENAGERIE" made the front page of the Star-Telegram the prosecution compares my every word to quotes from various silver screen killers.

Eat'em

Standing trial sucks. It's long and pointless and entirely unfair. I didn't get to go home and rest between court hearings. Which would make sense since I'm allegedly innocent until proven guilty. At Mike's suggestion, I explain everything to the jury except for Eat'em. They look at me as if I suggest I should be allowed into their houses at night to exterminate their children. My throat tightens and I stammer on, "The Grotesque Infection isn't caused by trees or plants or funguses or whatever. It's a bacteria or virus perhaps um… a little help?"

Eat'em paces on the desk in front of me, the lawyer I wish I had. He points at the jury with his tail and declares, "Grotesques belong to a phylum of the animalia kingdom known as Platyhelminthes. Some of the parasites in this…"

"Parasites!" I shout, cutting Eat'em off. "They're more like parasites."

"Parasites," District Attorney Dale Gomes leans back against the partition that separates the stand from an inappropriately sized audience of people with whacked ideas for entertainment. Some of them are students of law, or journalists. There are a few witnesses and some mourning family members I can't bear to watch. Lt. Hershel Thibodeaux Bellecroix holds his head in his hands at the back of the auditorium. He's sitting with a few other cops I don't recognize. Gomes looks at a clipboard and reads from it as if he's quoting me. He isn't. "Fungus, bacteria, viruses. You're so certain that this sickness needs to be eradicated; yet you're absolutely uncertain as to what it is. What makes you an expert on disease control?"

It can't be much more than sixty-five degrees in the courtroom and my shirt is all but soaked through with sweat. I want to scratch my face, but if I remember correctly, that's an admission of guilt. Maybe I saw that on a cop show, I don't recall. Still, I resist the urge.

"Doctors," the DA continues, "don't seem to share your opinion on the existence of Grotesques. None of your victims tested positive for anything. The only thing that seems to coincide with your story is other stories. Fiction, Mr. Brook. Movies. Video games."

"Objection!" Eat'em jumps onto the pulpit. "Objection, yes! I call mistrial. Leading the witness. This jury bores me! Jacob, come on, let's go… just plead guilty already!"

My little red lawyer doesn't quite understand what is at stake. Mike looks more interested in my answers than he does in defending me. I take a deep breath. "My life is at stake here. You want people to assume I'm a liar because of comparisons you've made to some bad zombie movie? Like *They Live* or *World War Z* or *Last of Us*? Well, clearly you stole your life from *To Kill a Mockingbird* and we can all assume you're full of shit too then, right?"

Judge Brentt, a string bean looking guy who ducks under doorways and walks with a giraffe's gait, likes to remind me I can be held in contempt of court. My outburst brings the courtroom to chatter, which the Honorable Brentt breaks up with a gavel. It plays out like a scene from *Law and Order* with the exception of the little demon humping the air and pumping his arm with an exuberant,

"Yes! Yes! Yes!"

The commotion dies down and I gather my thoughts. These eyes of ridicule, looming over me like hungry vultures. I've been through too much to die without them knowing. I search my soul for the perfect words to help them understand, but I come up empty.

Eat'em grows restless. He paces up and down the aisle going through purses and testing the gum stuck to the bottom of chairs for freshness.

What makes me an expert on disease control... My mind returns to the question that was asked.

"I don't claim to be an expert on disease control. All I can say is that whatever actions I may have taken were based on what I thought in the best interest of safety of others."

"Do you care to elaborate Mr. Brook?" Gomes is setting me up. He knows I have not thought this response through. We are boxers in a ring and he has me on the ropes, waiting for that wild haymaker so he can counter and put me down for the count.

"The 'victims' as you are calling them... I have come into contact with several of them, there is evidence of that. These people were infected. The infection makes them violent and dangerous, striking out at others, infecting others. If ignored, we're all at risk. These people..."

"People!" Gomes cuts me off. "That is an interesting choice of words Mr. Brook. Because that is exactly what you are on trial for. Killing *people*."

"They *were* people," I continue, "but once infected they are different. They are dangerous…"

"None of the people you've killed were expressing any kind of violence, though," Gomes raises both brows. "Is that not the case?"

Bellecroix turns his head away at this. He fidgets in his pew. I know he can feel my eyes on him, but he refuses to look up. He knows this accusation is bullshit. People are only violent until they die… then they're only missed. Someone could be a sociopathic jerk, liked by no one, but in death, they're tragic heroes. Nothing prevents people from mourning the lost except for the outcome of a "fair trial."

I shake my head and plead toward the jury. Eat'em nods back and forth from the jury to the judge, a lawyer through and through. "No," I say. "That's not the case. They know that's not the case. Officer," I shout to deaf ears, "Lt. Bellecroix! Tell them that's not the case!"

"If this infection spreads through bite," Gomes says, "Why don't the victims show bite marks? No such indications showed up in the coroners report."

"I don't know," I said. "The infected seemed to hea.." I stop myself mid-sentence as Mike gives me a cautionary glare. He is not ready for all the information to be thrown on the table or he doesn't want it coming from me. It would be stronger coming from someone else. I change direction. "My intention was never to kill people, my intent is to protect us from a parasite."

"You are not on trial for killing parasites, Jacob."

"I know, but…"

"You are on trial for killing people," Gomes raises an eyebrow and discretely cracks his knuckles one at a time – a challenge - implying nothing I say matters. Mike stares blankly.

"You understand the concept of burden of proof, Jacob?" Gomes rattles me with each word. Not only does he make me look the fool, he gives me a lesson in law while he does it. The burden of proof should be on him. He's the accuser. But I'm not on trial for what I've done, rather why I've done it. And his telling expression says it all. No excuse appeases my actions in their minds. "Nothing suggests any real threat to humanity. Nothing suggests anyone you killed was a risk to anyone at all." He lies. "Nothing suggests you're anything more than a common murderer."

"…but," I said.

"But nothing, Jacob," the only objection he gets comes from Eat'em. He lectures and berates me while the circus watches intently. "This morning we were presented with autopsy reports of several of your victims. Nothing lives in them. Nothing controls them or eats their brains. No parasites. *No bite marks.* Why should we continue to believe you when these reputable sources have shown there's no such thing as the Grotesque infection."

"Continue to believe me?" I belt out, "When did you believe me? Hardly anyone believes me. How can I prove to you what you can't understand?" I am no prophet, but I can relate to the plight. Still have to try… "I can't explain it, but I see things others can't. I can see the infection. Dilated pupils, quickened pulse…"

"Am I infected Mr Brook? Maybe I've been sitting in a dark room watching scary movies…" Gomes continues to mock me.

"No… That's not how it works. It's not that obvious. Listen, in this courtroom I cannot show you an infected if there are none here, but I can show you my ability. I can tell who in this room failed to wash their hands just by looking at them. And I can do that sitting right where I am. They just have to hold their hands up. You only want to believe what *you* can see, but I'm asking you to try to understand what I can see. I can do things that nobody in this room can do. I'll prove it to you and then decide if you choose to deny me. But it will be because you don't *want* to believe me. Is it too much of a stretch for you to think you don't know everything?"

I look out at the sea of faces. I've lost them with my incoherent rambling. They fear me. They think I'm a danger to their families. To them.

"Alright… Tell me, Jacob, have I washed my hands today?" Gomes holds up his hands briefly but continues before I can answer… "I fail to understand how the ability to assess a person's hygiene leads to the right to take a life."

Chapter 6

I sat in on a philosophy course instructed by Dr. Reeder. It surprised me nobody noticed I didn't answer during role call. Dr. Reeder didn't seem to care. Perhaps since he figured we paid out of pocket to be there, it made no difference if we were taking his class or not. Still, I welcomed anonymity.

Technically, I should have been in math, but five minutes in the class bored me out of mind. All I needed to do was show up for tests and have Eat'em read off the answers while I filled in the blanks. My teachers in high school thought my grades were a reflection of hard work, when truthfully I couldn't get through basic arithmetic on my own. I decided a better use of my time was to follow Isaac's advice. Philosophy surely couldn't be worse than redundant equations.

Dr. Reeder was a goateed man with blond hair and thick horn-rimmed glasses. He wore a black dress shirt and a brown leather jacket. His mannerisms seemed to reflect the behaviors of my invisible demonic buddy, from his inexplicable excitement for barely interesting subjects, to the constant affirmation he asked at the end of each sentence.

A direct conversation between Dr. Reeder and Eat'em would sound something like: "Critical thinking is good, yes?" "Yes." "Yes, yes?" "Yes, good, yes, yes, yes." Ad infinitum.

Eat'em sat on the edge of my desk, leaning far forward. The thick quills down his back laid flat and his large pointed ears perked up with every word from Dr. Reeder's mouth. Every so often he'd turn around, smile, and nod.

"Excuse me?" a shorthaired brunette with purple highlights pressed her hand to my shoulder. She sat directly behind me and I had to strain my neck to see her. The brunette's natural bronzed skin might have been more beautiful if her makeup weren't a couple shades too light. "Do you know what he's talking about?"

"Dr. Reeder?" the question sounded stupider with the addition of the crack in my voice. Her face mesmerized me, in spite of being makeup heavy. She must have been half Asian... maybe Japanese. A good mix none-the-less, with striking features that lacked symmetry. "Yeah," I continued, "Well, no... not really. Honestly, he lost me the third time he said, 'yes'."

"Me too," her cheeks blushed beneath the pale makeup. "I don't think I'm going to pass this class. If it's anything like this, anyway. I've heard his tests are impossible."

"I think you'll be fine," I turned to Dr. Reeder, whom paid us no attention. Whatever he talked about had him in another world. I probably could have flipped the desk without being noticed. "But, if you're worried about it, maybe I can help you. I'm pretty good at this stuff."

"Philosophy?" she asked.

"School in general," I said. "But yeah, philosophy too, I guess. We'll see."

She nodded and finally took her hand off my shoulder. "I'm glad someone is. What's your name?"

"Jacob."

"I like your contacts, Jacob," Instead of correcting her, I decided to simply say thanks. She touched her hand to her chest, where a tattoo of a black orchid seemed to grow from her fingertips. "My name's Dixie."

In addition to wearing too much makeup, she wore more perfume than she needed to. A strong scent of ocean mist wafted past my nostrils.

Dixie expended a lot of effort for attractiveness where none needed to be extended at all. She radiated natural beauty and covered it with distracting accessories and an overpowering smell. Part of her uniqueness spurned from a creative spirit, but something told me she hid a deeper secret beneath her bleached cheeks than just a pretty face.

Dr. Reeder lectured on, channeling the ever-attentive

demon, and I might have given philosophy a pass, except for the intoxicating aroma behind me, which I suddenly felt entangled with. The cool breeze from a rattling air condition unit brought me to a tropical beach with just a hint of Texas Dixie. I felt compelled to learn a bit more about philosophy than I cared to before.

Eat'em curled his legs up beneath himself, sitting on my abdomen as he clung to the side of my shirt. He bounced joyfully with my every step as I searched the campus for Isaac, Valentine and then hopefully our ride home.

"Gottfried Wilhelm von Leibniz said all of everything is *monads*, yes!" Eat'em pushed off my chest, digging his dexterous toes into my beltline. "Leibniz said monads don't die and we're monads so we don't die! Yes. Also monads are un-interacting Leibniz said, so I'm a monad and I'm un-interacting. You're a monad too, but by the miracle of a pre-ordained harmony, you're programmed by a different set of instructions governing your eternal *Self!* Communication between any two things first starts with the connectivity of monads as a reflection of the whole universe."

I imagined the Infinite Ocean and short, scissor-cut purple hair.

"See," Eat'em threw a sweeping gesture to a hallway of people paying no mind to the crimson-eyed eighteen-year-old and his even redder quill-covered companion, "they're all monads, floating in empty space, yes! Your monads and my Monads, they've met, so we met, yes! It all makes perfect sense. My Monads met the Monads of

---

the Pepto-Bismol and your Monads already met the Pepto-Bismol so then my Monads, your Monads, and the Pepto-Bismol's Monads make us all the same person!"

"I don't know what you're talking about," I found myself blindly strolling the middle of the campus, and half-listening to Eat'em regurgitate his version of the lecture we'd just sat through. A more pressing matter grew at the pit of my stomach as it became urgent I find a bathroom.

I entered a two-story building behind the library, which housed a large advertisement for a planetarium. My natural father used to take me to a similar learning center in Virginia. We took tours around the universe in domes filled with projected stars and moons. Constellations spanned out for as far as the eye could see in a room the size of a movie theater.

An empty Information Desk greeted all whom entered here. The lobby was empty and a poster declared the planetarium would open in just a few weeks.

Caution tape cordoned off the theater, but to my relief the men's room beckoned from just across the abandoned hallway.

I slid into the men's room, where I was greeted by an "Out of Order" urinal, a single sink, and a couple stalls. I could have scooped the stink from the air with a ladle. The bathroom reeked of stale urine, mildew, and something rotten. A large clear trash bag taped to the bottom of the urinal was filled with orange liquid to the point it looked about to burst across the sticky tiles. A dried out mop and bucket leaned against the wall, neither in serviceable condition.

"Ugh," Eat'em grunted as he dropped from my shirt. "I am not going in there. No. Yuck!"

I didn't blame him, but I didn't have much of a choice. I was raised to use a toilet when available. "I'll be less than a minute."

Rushing past the urinal and the stall nearest the door, I threw my backpack on the counter and opened the second stall to find it very much occupied.

Chapter 7

An elderly man held a woman in her mid-twenties around the waist, with her legs bent over his shoulders. The old man looked Mr. Universe ripped; like forty scrambled egg whites every morning for breakfast ripped. He wore a gray Deftones T-shirt and shorts too short with untied New Balance sneakers on his bare feet. The young woman hunched over in his lap was in a UTA polo with a giant atom and the word "Planetarium" written across the back. Supervision would have been happy to see their staff giving customers such a friendly welcome.

"I apologize." I began to slowly shut the door as the elderly Deftones fan lifted his head from the girl's neck.

His deep black eyes filled with confusion and distant recognition. A smudge of red climbed upside down from his upper cheek down to his pinched lips. Flesh hung from his mouth and a trail of sticky liquid led from his face to a gaping hole in the soft tissue on the inside of the girl's left shoulder. His eyebrows tightened, almost meeting in the middle. He spit little bits of skin and said the most heart-wrenching thing I'd ever heard. "Jacob?"

"Oh shit!" My brain exploded and I stood dumbfounded. I'd never seen the man in my life. There's little more disconcerting than an old man, mouth full of blood, saying your name. My world shut down.

Where am I? A bathroom. *Who is this?* Retired American Gladiator? *What do I do?* Two options: run or prepare to defend myself. *Act...*

I froze as the Deftones fan tossed the girl to the side and tackled me into the wall. An automatic hand dryer jammed into my spine. A meaty, calloused hand wrapped around my throat and lifted me up the wall. Thick fingernails dug into my skin.

The old man's eyes stared into mine like empty vortexes. "What are you doing here?"

"Oh shit, oh shit, oh shit!" I gasped and flailed fruitlessly.

"You're not supposed to be here." He said this as if he meant me specifically. Nothing about him seemed familiar. How could it?

My arm weighed half a ton, but somehow I managed to lift it to his face and thrust my thumb into one of his hollow eyes. I clinched my fingers in his tasseled hair and shoved my thumb into his socket.

He screamed, pulled me back and slammed me into the hand dryer with one hand.

The old man's mouth opened ungodly wide. He snapped his mouth at my side as if to take a chunk out of my abdomen. My knee instinctively found his throat and kept his face at bay as I threw a couple wild punches.

"Eat'em," I yelled between struggled breaths. "A little help would be nice."

I dislodged myself from the grip of the snapping grandpa and smacked hard against the moist floor. The overwhelmingly rotten air rushed back as I slid on my back, using my feet to shield me from the lumbering lunatic.

I pushed toward the exit, keeping my feet between the lumbering cannibal and myself. He grabbed my ankle and lifted me upside down. Everything flipped over. The bag of piss looked like a balloon clung to the ceiling.

I thrashed with my free foot, which he grabbed with such strength that gravity felt like it reversed.

The upside-down monster grimaced. "Why did you come in here?"

"To piss, dude," blood rushed to my brain. "EAT'EM!"

I looked over the bottom of the stall partitions at the bleeding girl that appeared to be lying on the ceiling. She looked so accepting; her eyes open, staring back at me.

"EAT'EM!"

"Eat what? Why are you yelling eat them?" asked Mr.

Universe.

My fist barreled into his groin and he threw me. My head crashed into the urinal and a big bag of nasty softened my fall. Careful not to pop it, I rolled under the first stall so I lied next to the bleeding woman.

The room rotated back to its normal orientation as I stared into her eyes. She looked young and lovely – her eyes crystal blue and familiar.

I rolled to my back as the old man pushed open the stall door and loomed over me, a giant. Clinched in his tight fist was the disgusting mop – a shit-water stiffened pad barely hung onto the metal rod. He lifted it above his head.

A sense of déjà vu came over me. Still, I had no idea who he was or why he was trying to kill me.

I rolled quickly under the stall, avoiding the crack of splintering wood and clash of metal against tile. Lifting myself up, I sat by the toilet opposite of the unconscious woman. The floor was covered in caked urine and twisted pubic hair from dozens of different dudes with a dire need of lessons in etiquette. In front of the toilet looked like some idiots had a pissing-for-distance contest not long ago.

My attention turned to the missing chunk from the woman's shoulder. The hole looked much smaller. At second glance scar tissue had already formed. It looked like she'd been bitten more than a week ago.

"What the?" the words fell from my lips.

"That guy looks like you," Eat'em said from somewhere outside the stall, bringing me back to the fight, "if you swallowed another you that had already swallowed another you. Yes. He's like the Russian Stacking Doll version of you! But with muscles."

"Thanks," relief spread through me at the sound of his scratchy voice. "Any advice?"

"Yes," Eat'em ducked under the partition. He made a face at the unconscious woman and continued, "buy a DeLorean and go back in time to remind yourself not to be such an idiot. And bring me a drink from the future."

"If I make it there," I said as the big guy slammed through the stall door, "I'll think about it!" I slid under both stalls, back toward the urinal.

"Who are you talking to, Jacob?" The brute followed me inside and outside the first stall as I rolled back and forth under the partition.

Did he use my name again? In my confusion I couldn't be sure. How would he know me?

I rolled out once more, planted both feet on the swinging stall door and kicked it hard into the brute. I stood and ran into the door, pushing hard against a force much stronger than myself. I rammed into it repeatedly as he stood there like an unmovable wall. When I felt him push back, I dropped to the floor and planted both my feet on his ankles as the door swung open above my face. He stumbled forward slightly before catching himself. I grabbed the bottom of the door and pulled it over me once more, smacking him hard in his face and he fell back into the stall.

On my feet, I ran toward the exit. I shoved past the bathroom door and crashed into one of the wet floor signs cordoning off the entrance to the planetarium. Balance lost, I stumbled and fell into the double doors, which flung open, toppling me toward a stairwell lined with theater seating. I held tight to a rail, spun on my heel, and momentum carried me headfirst into the stand for the projector.

I slumped down, out of breath.

"Disgusting, yes." Eat'em sauntered to my side, his tail waving gracefully behind him. "Absolutely grotesque!"

"Grotesque?" the word clattered against my skull.

"You didn't wash your hands," the little demon stuck out his tongue as he sat on the step beside me. "Just kidding, yes."

I stared up at the curved ceiling, the long tiles normally hidden by the illusion of space. Constellations formed from architecture instead of stars. No Big Dippers or Orion's Belts. No Pluto or Saturn. Those were a hallucination created by a small electronic box. Without it, the room contained no magic. My father used to love the planetarium, but now it wasn't anything that couldn't be reproduced with a cheap smart phone app. A device small enough to fit in my pocket could be pointed at the sky, day or night, and the universe would be labeled – zoomed in with a pinch. A telescope that could be used anywhere.

"This is magical, Jacob," Eat'em used me as a ladder to get to the projector. "Look at that, yes. Do you see that?"

Eat'em

I rolled over and crouched behind the projector stand. My throbbing skull would have to wait. Dread pressed against my heart. A dour aura pulled at my nerves and a change came over me. I pushed away my fear and gave myself to a feeling far more sinister. My hand searched the opposite side of the projector stand and my fingers found the plug.

"Hey!" Eat'em shouted. "Don't unplug it! I must know what it does, yes!"

The old man moved impossibly fast. Faster than anyone I'd ever seen. He leapt sideways through the open hallway, defying gravity as he jumped several rows of chairs. All of his muscles tensed as he leapt, flying toward me like a two hundred pound baseball. The twenty-pound projector was my DeMARINI baseball bat and I aimed for the stands.

Both the projector and the old man's skull shattered on impact. Fragments of bone, plastic, and metal shards exploded from my fists. Sour blood splattered from the impact as the man who knew my name crumpled into the back of a row of seats and dropped to the floor.

I should have felt remorse, maybe shock, but I felt powerful. I should have been afraid, but I was calm. I should have been confused, but I was clear-headed.

Adrenaline worked wonders in my system, and I knew it was only a matter of time before it wore off and I collapsed under the stress of what I'd done. For the moment, I had to disappear. And as

50

diverse as the crowd may be on campus, running around sticky with blood was sure to get me noticed.

I left Eat'em to mourn his shattered projector and hurried into the planetarium lobby to lock both sets of double doors leading into the building. The planetarium itself was closed, but I ran the risk of someone using the building as a shortcut to get from one class to another. The doors were glass, so I just had to count on nobody putting too much effort into looking inside.

On the opposite side of the lobby stood a supply closet and a small stand that sold souvenirs and UT swag, including mugs, pens, and a couple boxes. An open box of gym clothes beneath one of the shelves looked rummaged through. I grabbed a pair of blue shorts, a grey shirt, an orange hat with a mustang on it, a towel that matched the hat, and a container of hand soap from an open locker before making my way back to the bathroom crime scene.

I used the sink to wash up. Soap suds and blood pooled at my feet, as I scrubbed hard at my skin. I rinsed my hair over and over until the water ran clear. The clothes I brought went into my backpack, which I grabbed from the counter where I left it, and I dressed in my new outfit.

I looked like a college student. Or at the very least, I looked like Steve Buscemi playing a college student. I scraped what blood I could from my fingertips and ran the faucets with the drains closed until the water ran over, onto the floor.

"Can we get Frosties after this?" Eat'em sulked into the hallway from the planetarium. "I need something to take my mind off the magical box you took from me, yes."

"Sure," I didn't care. Hopefully, Val wouldn't mind the diversion, and if so, I'd deal with Eat'em's pouting then. "Whatever you want, buddy. You ready to go?"

"Yes."

I hesitated to look at the girl beneath the stall, but I couldn't bring myself to do it. As awful as I knew I would feel later, I left her on the floor as I took a pen from my backpack and very carefully punctured the nasty bag beneath the urinal.

Cleaning the bathroom wasn't an option. I knew nothing of criminology, or how easily they could separate DNA from the soapy tiles. As horrible as it was, I had to pop the bag.

The horrid scent worsened as foul liquid followed me into the hallway and quickly flowed into the open theater, pouring down the stairs.

I put my shoes back on in the lobby and waited until I felt certain all traces of my presence were hidden in filth. The sour aroma filled the room. Hidden in the horrid pool of body fluids was my DNA, but I could do nothing about it.

My throat tightened. I needed to move before I began to feel nauseous again.

"Let's go," I headed out, Eat'em lagging behind.

"What are you going to tell Val about your new outfit?" Eat'em met my eyes in the door's reflection.

"School spirit," I answered as we stepped into the sun.

Chapter 8

Val had a copy of the paper the morning after the incident. I ripped it from his hand, dreading the inevitable. No front-page headline declaring a murder on campus. I flipped to page two. Page three. Nothing. Then on the fourth page, a blurb so insignificant I almost missed it. The police blotter: "Vandal strikes Planetarium".

My eyes deceived me. It couldn't be. They had to have found the bodies. The search party had to have started. The school should be on lockdown. Where was the article I expected?

My heart wrenched as I thought about it, a cold chill travelled down my spine. I expected Val to ask why I looked so guilty, but he let me read.

"Yesterday afternoon the custodians arrived to find the

projection system in the planetarium in pieces. Vandals broke in and destroyed the 20,000-dollar projection equipment, leaving nothing but shrapnel in its place. In addition, a nearby bathroom was found to have suffered a similar fate as running sinks and urine flooded the floor, and several stalls were found dismantled. Police expect the same vandal is responsible. The planetarium underwent a huge remodeling and was set to reopen next month."

As I reached the end of the blurb I almost burst, "What about the girl?" But I caught myself at "Wha…" Nowhere was she mentioned. No bodies or missing persons mentioned in the entire paper. Why? No way did I imagine what happened.

I began to plan my trip back to the planetarium.

"Earth to Jacob!"

My kneejerk reaction was to think it was the mystery woman from the bathroom. Inexplicable sorcery helped her escape death and she knew what I'd done.

"JACOB!" a hand struck the table in front of me. "Wake up!"

The sweet smell of ocean breeze snapped me out of my daze. "Uh… Dixie?" my voice cracked sheepishly. "Hi."

"Hi!" She smiled broadly, her face pulling back in a fake display of shyness. She wore her purple-streaked hair in a bun. Her makeup seemed less harsh than it had been the day before. Still, she'd gone bold with eyeliner, giving herself the appearance of an Egyptian princess. "Are you OK? You weren't in class."

"Yeah," my gaze dropped from her face to her tiny hand, which still planted on the table in front of me. "I'm sorry. Yeah, I forgot what time it was. I haven't been getting much sleep."

"Oh whatever!" Eat'em yanked at my hair. His toes gripped my collarbone as he stood on my shoulders, leaning over the top of my head. "All you do is sleep, yes. I suggest we procure a Jolt Cola. You wake up long enough to say no, yes. I request the acquisitioning of a Standing Rock. You wake, say no, sleep, yes. I beseech, Jacob! The caroling warble of an ice cream truck! Wake, no, yes! 'Haven't been getting much sleep.' For crying out loud…"

"Well," Dixie pushed me aside with her hip and sat on the edge of the chair. Eat'em clambered over to my opposite shoulder. Dixie's hipbone pressed against mine. "What class do you have next?"

She almost sat in my lap. I felt her breathing on my cheek and the hairs on my arm tingled as her skin brushed against mine. The air caught in my throat. My chest squeezed out an answer. "Nothing."

"You're done for the day?" Her turquoise eyes glittered so close.

"Yep." I tasted her breath on my lips. "Got a few hours to waste until my uncle… uh… cousin gets off."

"Good!" she wrapped her hand over mine on my lap. I wanted to wipe my sweaty palms on my pants, but hoped instead she wouldn't notice. "While you're waiting on your uncle-cousin you can come to my class then? I have Biology… another hard one. Not for you, of course, since you're a genius, but for the rest of the world... it's a tough one. I have Kempter. She's an absolute science nut. Pretty much, if you don't like biology as much as she does, you can expect a big goose egg on all of your tests."

"Goose egg?"

"Yep," she raised her narrow eyebrows. The follicles where she plucked them were beginning to grow back. "A big fat zero."

Eat'em whispered in my ear as if anyone would hear him even had he marched up and down the library playing a small bugle and banging a snare drum against his head. "I don't like her, Jacob. Does she have to sit so close? Tell her to go away, yes."

"We wouldn't want you to get a zero, would we?" No greater confidence boost existed than doing the opposite of what the demon wanted me to do.

Dixie wrapped her arms around my neck, hurtling Eat'em to the floor. He landed with a thump and cursed loudly.

"Maybe afterward you can fill me in on what I missed in class today?"

"It's a date," Dixie smiled and stood, pulling me up behind her by the hand. "I sure hope Leibniz does it for you. If so, we're going to have a lot to talk about."

Eat'em perked up at the mention of Leibniz. He trotted up my side until he perched on my shoulder again. "Leibniz first, then she goes away, yes!"

I followed Dixie out of the library. The philosopher seemed as good a topic as any. Anything that could keep my mind off the missing planetarium employee and keep Eat'em quiet for a few minutes I'd meet with open arms.

Still the first week of school, the class was primarily a meet and greet, with a silly name game as a way to introduce ourselves to our lab partners for the semester. Professor Kempter noticed my name not on the roster and almost sent me packing, but instead offered to let me continue the class if I went and added the course "with immediacy." With Dixie pressing to be my lab partner, I couldn't say no.

Using the letters of our first names we had to come up with words that described ourselves. It went around the room with people using the same words over and over with little variety. It got to me:

"Just" – I believed in fairness. Justice.

"Arlington" – I was born in Arlington, Virginia… and, of course, I'm in Arlington now.

"Caring" – I don't know… Maybe "Copout" would be better. Everyone else seemed to be caring, so I guess I'm caring too.

"Obstacle" – Sure. Why not?

"Brave" – I must have sounded like an idiot. No more than anyone else.

"Daring, Intelligent, eXtraverted, Impressive, Earthy."

"Hey!" Eat'em stood stoic on the large black table that made up our desk. It was fitted with built-in sinks and Bunsen burners. Eat'em pricked up and growled at Dixie. "She skipped me! Yes! Ugh… Jacob. You got to get rid of her. I hate her so much, yes.

Eat'em

My name is Eat'em! Energy, Amp, Throttle, Emerge, Monster!" It might have sounded deep had he not just been listing the brands of his favorite energy drinks.

We continued around the room, learning how we were all a bunch of sweet, caring individuals and then we played a few more nauseating games to set everyone's names to heart.

After the grade school introduction, Kempter finally handed out the curriculum. It contained a range of material grouped by macro and microbiological studies. A month would be devoted to each of three fields, the last of which interested me most: Bacteria, virus, and parasitic infections.

I told Dixie I would see her soon and watched her out of the lab. Part of me wanted to follow her, but I knew I couldn't wait two months to speak to Professor Kempter about what was on my mind.

"Professor," I waited as the last student made his way out the door. "Mind if I ask you something?"

Kempter had a narrow face on a large body. A mug shot would make her look much smaller than she really was. Still, she looked pretty and young for a college teacher, maybe in her late twenties or early thirties. Her brow furrowed as she looked up at me, almost as if she were disappointed in my presence. "I usually only take questions from my students, Jacob, but since you promised to fix the issue, I'll make an exception. What is your question?"

"It's about bacterias."

"Bacteria," she corrected me. "Yes, we'll discuss bacteria and viruses in the last chapter. You've got a while."

Eat'em peed in the drain of the eyewash station at the corner of the room. He shouted over his shoulder, "Let's go! I'm scheduled for a battle to the death with a bottle of syrup."

I hesitated. With the planetarium incident still fairly fresh in my mind, I didn't want to say something incriminating. Then again, for all anyone knew it was merely an act of vandalism. Still, I felt I ran the risk of saying too much, that maybe she knew more than the paper suggested. "I've taken interest in the subject recently. I saw, uh, I saw an animal acting a little strangely and uh…"

"Strangely how?" Kempter puckered her lips, her face pinched in curiosity.

"Well," I relaxed, "I guess it seemed to recognize me. Like, it should have just ignored me, but it didn't. Instead it looked at me as if it'd seen me before."

"An animal?"

"Yeah," I scratched my brow, "a dog. I mean, had it been a person, he might have said I looked familiar. That's the look it gave. And it attacked me."

"The dog."

"Yes," I said, "the dog."

Kempter sighed. "Sounds like a regular dog to me. Maybe it liked your scent."

"When. Did. You. Get. Attacked. By. A. Dog?" Eat'em called out while banging his head against the door.

"I guess," I said. "I just figured it might be infected with something. It wasn't a wild dog, it seemed domesticated, but it was very aggressive. It bit someone. A girl. It looked bad…"

"Yeah, bad," Dr. Kempter interrupted me. "Did you call 911 or animal control? Where did this happen?"

Scrambling for words, trying to describe the assailant as a dog had dug me a hole I didn't plan on talking my way out of. "Well, no… I didn't call anyone. It happened so fast, the dog chased me away from the girl. I was able to beat the dog away with a tree limb. I figured the dog was sick. I went to, uh, check on the girl, but she was gone. I guess she must have healed quickly. I don't know who the girl was or if she went to the hospital or where she went or anything. The whole thing seemed weird, you know."

"Doesn't sound like any bacteria or infection I've ever heard of. Rabies maybe? Was the dog frothing at the mouth?" I shook my head no. Kempter threw her paperwork into a satchel and shoed me toward the door. She checked some equipment under the desks and went to turn out the lights. "What do you mean when you say the girl healed quickly? How much time passed between the bite and her disappearing? "

"Minutes," I said. "Seconds. I mean, I didn't get a great look at it, but it seemed like a bad bite. Not something you could just walk away from, but there was no sign of her. She was gone."

We stepped into the hallway. Kempter's berry-shaped frame filled the doorway as she passed through. "Sounds a little fantastic to me, Jacob."

"What if it was an infection? How would you tell?" I felt like a complete buffoon. "What if it's a virus that hasn't been discovered yet? Is there any way to know something is infected by looking at them?"

"Like the dog?" she asked. "What kind of dog was it?"

Eat'em shouted, "A CHIHUAHUA!" and I repeated the word, regretting it immediately. "Chihuahua."

"Sounds like a vicious Chihuahua," Kempter smiled.

Eat'em laughed and I shook my head shamefully, "It was."

"Well, Jacob, it wouldn't be too difficult to tell you if your friend was bit by a super-powered Chihuahua," She shoed me once more, leading me backward. "I just need a blood sample and if that dog is really that aggressive…" She paused. "Someone should catch it and put it down. Man-eating Chihuahuas running around… it's dangerous."

With a facetious "Stay safe" Kempter hurried off, moving faster than her beach ball body should have allowed.

Chapter 9

Kempter wipes a trickle of sweat from the side of her neck. Her eyes lock on mine and fill with dread. Her professional career rides on her testimony. A few days prior she told Big Mike about her concern in destroying her life by taking stand. She fears the public's response. She fears the hatred that's already filled her social media page. The threats. The defamation. The ridicule. Right now, her expression states it all. She fears me.

"Jodi," Gomes thumbs the collar of his shirt. "Can you tell us again your relationship to the defendant?"

It must be ninety degrees in the courtroom. The air conditioner spits warm air and dust. We just returned from a recess while some contractor worked to get the room back to its normal freezing temperature. Everyone remains soaked. The room reeks of body odor.

Kempter presses her sleeve to her forehead before finally breaking from my watchful eye. "He took my biology course." She says to the DA. "He was one of my more interested students. We began to do some extracurricular research which is not uncommon for university students. I pictured him becoming my graduate assistant after he completed his undergraduate work."

She seems rehearsed. Her mannerisms, gestures, the extra octave in her voice as she compliments me... it comes off as Shakespearean. Mike warned her to be genuine. Her nerves turn her into a caricature of her usual self.

Gomes hovers over her, a vulture preparing to swoop down and eat her alive. "Extracurricular research? Is this how you refer to Jacob's claims of an unknown virus? This so called 'infection'?"

"Yes and no. At first Jacob was just inquisitive. He asked vague questions about the behavior of dogs," she sighs heavily. "From his description, it sounded like he was talking about the behavior of dogs. His story sounded far-fetched."

Gomes tilts his head and nods for her to continue. When she doesn't, Gomes presses her. "So, you never requested a blood sample?"

"No, I didn't."

"But he did bring you a blood sample?"

"Yes."

"That didn't bother you?"

"No."

"Why not?"

"I teach science."

Gomes puts his back to the jury. Mike explained Gomes's method for handling witnesses as equal parts face-time for himself and whoever is on stand. "He's got one of those trustworthy faces, and he's counting on you to look like a blubbering fool. Don't look like a blubbering fool." Kempter looks like a blubbering fool.

"Do your students often bring you vials of blood?" Gomes asks.

"He didn't bring me a vial of blood. He brought me a T-shirt."

Gomes nods. "Do your students often bring you T-shirts covered in blood?"

"It was a small stain."

"You didn't think that maybe it was human blood?"

"No," Kempter says.

"Why not?"

"Because it wasn't."

"Are you a forensic scientist, Jodi?"

She shakes her head and licks her teeth, clearly insulted. "I teach forensic scientists."

"Did you know it wasn't human blood before you tested it?" With his back to the jury, Gomes gives a look of indignation. He smacks his lips. "Can you tell the difference between human blood and dog blood without a microscope?"

"Yes," Kempter rolls her eyes and the distain in her voice

overflows with sarcasm "that's one of the many powers I have as a science teacher."

Their banter goes back and forth as I study the jury. They don't nod or frown. If anything they look tired. I search their faces for hope, belief, disbelief, anything. All I see is exhaustion.

"The sample he brought was high in white blood cell count," she emphasizes the word sample. "Other than that, I saw no indicators common in an infection. Lots of white blood cells can be a sign that someone is sick, though. It can be a sign of leukemia. It can also mean nothing. What did surprise me, though, about the sample, was that it wasn't coagulated. The cells were healthy, moving around."

Gomes gauges her believability and upstages her. That's how Mike describes it. He paces away from the jury and once again turns toward them, giving them more face-time. "And you didn't call the police. Are living blood cells not an indicator that the blood is fresh? Did you not think the blood must have been put on the shirt recently?"

"No."

"Why not?"

"Because it had been four days."

"And how do you know it had been four days?"

Kempter looks at me again... the fear present, but less apparent. "Jacob brought the shirt to me on a Friday afternoon. I threw it in my desk. It was Labor Day weekend. My class is Monday, Wednesday and Friday. When I looked at the shirt it was Wednesday morning. It had been four days."

"And the blood looked fresh?"

"It was fresh," she says. "The cells were alive and well. Aside from a high white count, they seemed preserved... but they had been on a dirty T-shirt in a drawer in my desk. The stain should have been dried out. It wasn't. So I tested it."

Gomes nods, playing along. "How did you test it?"

"Looking at it, you wouldn't think there was much special about it," Kempter nods at me, "except for its behavior. I figured if there was an invisible infection, maybe I could give it to mice."

"And was there?" Gomes asks, "An... invisible infection?"

"Well, the first mouse showed no immediate affects," she explains, turning toward the jury. "I had been running maze experiments with my grad students to test the ability of mice to develop memory. I tested the exposed mouse with the mazes, and the results were typical of most mice. Nothing exceptional. Over the course of a few weeks the mouse was able to learn the maze and completed the maze in faster and faster times. At that point I determined that there was nothing special about the individual mouse and I returned him to the rest of my mice population. That's when I noticed something peculiar."

"And that is?"

"The mouse was aggressive," Kempter furrows her brow as she wipes away sweat on her upper lip. "Just at first. But it clearly bit another mouse. I thought nothing of the event at first. However, to be careful I placed the exposed mouse and the mouse he bit into solitary confinement. The bitten mouse had never been through testing. We were saving it as the control variable. However, when introduced to the maze for the first time, it ran it as if it had already learned the maze. As you can imagine, this compromised our entire dataset. It simply did not make sense for this mouse to know the maze."

"A coincidence…"

"Objection, your honor!" Mike's voice cracks as he shouts inches from my ear. "Leading."

Judge Brentt sustains before Gomes reframes his line of questioning. "Could this have been a coincidence, Dr. Kempter?" the DA continues. "Luck. Not a very large sample size to draw any conclusions from" Gomes implies.

"I thought the same… At first… On a hunch I introduced a third mouse. Also a control variable. This one bitten by the second mouse. It ran the maze even faster… as if it were memorized. All three could do it at the same rate. It was as if the first one had taught the other two. The same for a fourth and a fifth. Each one showed only the most temporary sign of aggression to any non-bitten mouse and each time it seemed the knowledge of the maze passed from one mouse to the next."

"What are you implying?" Gomes asks.

"It means they learned in tandem," she says. "It means whatever was in that sample allowed them to communicate as if telepathically. When one mouse learned something, they all learned it. This was very exciting, I began to plan many experiments and papers.

I explained my observations to Jacob. I was curious if we would be able to get another sample, however that's when things became concerning."

"How did things become concerning, Jodi?" Gomes asks.

"The third mouse died within the week," she explains matter-of-factly. "A perfectly healthy mouse had deteriorated incredibly quickly. In fact, every mouse bitten after the third mouse seemed to suffer some sort of mental breakdown. They turned feral. They became hostile and they forgot the maze shortly thereafter. Essentially, the blood sample, when introduced to the mice appeared to create a chain. So long as the links in that chain remained unbroken, the mice were smarter, stronger, faster and more agile than normal mice. If a link was removed. If a mouse died. The opposite became true."

"This is all very interesting, Jodi," Gomes finishes toying with her. He pauses before asking one final question. "And whom else did you report these findings to?"

She shakes her head, "Nobody."

Chapter 10

The planetarium reeked of bleach. In spite of the recent *vandalism*, the door remained unlocked and there were no heightened security measures in place. As much as I could tell, the only thing anyone had done in response to the incident was steam clean the floor and expand the cordoned area to include the hallway and bathroom.

A sign announcing the theater's imminent opening had been taken down from a stanchion in the lobby.

I pushed open the door to the theater. The carpeted stairs squished beneath my feet. Eat'em left a trail of foamy footsteps as he ran to the projector stand. The prints looked a cross between the fossilized feet of a small dinosaur and a humanoid primate. No matter how vivid they appeared to me, I knew nobody else could see them, and I wondered, as I often did, if they were just a hallucination. I wondered if my little demon were some elaborate rouse. Did I imagine the old man? Did I imagine the young woman? If I imagined them, what really happened here?

Eat'em climbed atop the projector stand as my mind wondered.

"It's gone!" Eat'em grabbed his tail in his tiny hands. He squeezed and twisted it in frustration. "It's still gone! What cruel joke is this? We come all this way so you may be redeemed for your destructive behavior and present me with this! Nothing, yes! What is this?"

I sloshed down the stairwell. "We're not here for you, buddy."

I expected for someone to have gone through great lengths to pick up all the pieces of projector. Most of the fragments still clung to the carpet. But there was no blood. The floor reeked of bleach.

"Why are we here then?" Eat'em sank onto the stand. His body slouched.

"I'm looking for something."

"YAWN…" He rolled onto his belly and swept his tail back and forth. "I'm already bored, yes. Let's get ice cream."

I knelt over the chair the old man collided with days earlier. One of the bolts holding it to the inclined floor was loose. The seat was noticeably looser than the two connected to it. Nothing else had ever been used and still looked pristine.

We headed for the bathroom and I snuck a peak in an

industrial trashcan, which held the door open. No splintered mop. The tiled floor squeaked as I ventured into the bathroom.

The urinal no longer leaked, but an Out Of Order sign scribbled on cardboard was taped to the flush handle. My arm tensed as I reached for the stall door. I pushed it open slowly.

"Where'd she go?" My question reverberated in the empty stall.

"Who?" Eat'em asked.

"Who?" I repeated. *Had there been no one.* "The girl!"

"Oh, yeah," Eat'em wagged his finger at the spot on the floor the blonde laid days ago. "Yeah, she left."

I sighed, "I realize. I just want to know where she went. What happened?"

Eat'em climbed the sink counter and made an exaggerated Puck-like gesture, sweeping his arm in front of him toward a grand audience of one. "Please allow me to illustrate the scene," He guided my attention around as he spoke, a true storyteller. "She stood from there…"

"Wait!" I interjected, "She stood up?"

"Yes," Eat'em pointed toward the theater, "You excused yourself without warning and she stood and exchanged a looooonnnggg stare with Mr. Big. And I'm like, 'Hey, disgusting right? He didn't wash his hands!' But they don't say anything. I pontificate, 'Attention ugly human creatures! Did you not see my acquaintance extricate himself from the commode prior to lathering his phalanges?' I slowed down, yes. I pointed to this sign," the sign above the sink warned washing hands is the number one way to spread illness and disease. "I said, 'he is spreading germs right now, people. Learn from his mistakes!' And then they didn't say anything again. Boring! So I went to see what you were doing and I say, 'Grotesque, you didn't wash your hands.' Not even you laughed. I even said, 'Just kidding!'"

I knew I saw her wound shrinking, but I didn't consider that she might have just gotten up and walked away. Why would she have? Why wouldn't she have told anyone what happened?

"THEN!" Eat'em clapped his hands, "BANG!!! My favorite thing destroyed in an instant! You had no regard for my feelings, yes! NO! You didn't ask me, 'Hey, Eat'em, is it okay if I smash your new thing on ugly number one?' NO! The human woman was upset too. She stood in the doorway there," he extended a finger toward the entrance the old man leapt through unaffected by gravity. "She was so mad her proboscis spewed bile. She screamed, 'Noooooo! Not my magical universe containing box!'"

"She didn't scream," I could almost make out a phantom of her, watching the muscled behemoth and me collide. How'd I miss her? I never missed anything.

Eat'em picked a nostril with his tail, "No, she didn't scream. But that's what she would have screamed! I know that box contains the universe, Jacob! I know it does. I confirmed it with the posters, Jacob! Confirmed, yes! There was the universe, I wanted it, and *you* smashed it! Are you happy now?"

"Wait," I stopped him, "What did you mean before, when

you said her probe-thing spewed bile?"

"UGH..." Eat'em feigned backward, his hands gripped to his pointed ears. "Her nose puked! You never listen... I'm talking about all of the galaxies in a little box waiting for me to explore and you're still asking about the stupid ugly human woman creature and her stupid nose! What is it with you and women?!"

We went back toward the lobby. "I'll make it up to you with a bag of Skittles later."

He huffed, "Well, if you'd have said that sooner."

The supply closet was the last place I'd been on our previous visit to the planetarium. A few cleaning products were missing, but nothing else had been removed. My attention dropped to the box of gym clothes. Still opened.

I closed the lid and almost turned to leave when I noticed a smudge on the top of the flap. Blood? I pulled the box out from under the shelf and squatted for a closer look. Tucked in the corner I saw fabric of some sort. It was crumpled, hidden behind boxes and junk. It felt moist.

"What in the?" I unraveled it. Dark stains covered almost every square inch of it; still I could make out a large logo in the middle. It read: Deftones.

"Great," Eat'em belched, "a shirt. Can we go procure the Skittles now? My stomach's rumbling."

Before I could turn to leave I noticed something that had fallen behind the box... A wallet. I shoved it in my backpack and left the planetarium.

Chapter 11

I hurried away from the science lab with Eat'em riding along in my backpack, just his head poking through the top.

"Don't you dare stop for her," the demon said, "Bros before hoes, yes Jacob?"

"Where'd you hear that?" I said under my breath in spite of the lingering crowd. College campus is the ideal location for any schizophrenic. Nobody cares much if you talk to yourself as it's a pretty common occurrence with most students. I'd avoid having a fist fight with Eat'em, sure, but I wasn't much worried about someone noticing me speak with him. Still, just in case, I often wore a Bluetooth headset. I rarely talked to anyone on the phone through it, and never listened to music, but perception is everything, and a well placed earpiece allowed me to talk to Eat'em unbothered almost anywhere.

"Uncle V, yo!" Eat'em patted me on the shoulder. "*Don't you know, B's come and go, not talkin' 'bout your bro, so drop your hoe.* Val knows what it means to be a friend, yes. Unlike you."

"Unlike me?" I stopped. "If he's so perfect, why don't you hang out with him then."

"He ignores me, yes. Duh!" Eat'em tugged on my collar. "You stopped. Don't stop! She's right behind us!"

"Hey, Handsome Jake," Dixie's hand grazed my elbow as I turned around. She swept a violet-streaked bang from her face and said breathlessly. "Why are you off in such a hurry?"

"YOU SUCK!" Eat'em screeched from my shoulder.

"I have to catch up with my uncle and Isaac," I said. "They're waiting for me."

"I could give you a ride."

"I'll poop in your shoes," Eat'em threatened.

"That's okay," I smiled my appreciation. "They've been waiting. I don't want to tell them they've been sitting around for nothing."

"That's right," Eat'em climbed from the bag, sat on my shoulder, and wrapped his arm around the back of my head. "Bros before hoes!"

"But next time," I said.

Dixie nodded, crossing her arms in a self embrace. The top of her floral sundress pulled down ever so slightly revealing the perfectly formed lines leading from her collarbone to her sternum.

She had more muscle and tone than her small frame should have been able to build. Growing from her chest and blooming on her right shoulder was the bright tattoo of a black orchid, with more than a slight resemblance to the art of Georgia O'Keefe.

I struggled to keep my eyes on hers and found myself staring at her blood-red lips at least twice.

"Or," Dixie smiled, "you might give me a ride one day."

"I don't have a car."

"I do."

"Then," my voice caught in my throat. I stared at her lips, but I could see her whole body perfectly clear like she was a centerfold pullout. She wore purple heels that matched her dress and her hair. Her legs were alabaster in cream stockings. I wondered if they were thigh highs or hose. I stammered. "Then, um, why do you need a ride?"

"You're hopeless." Dixie laughed and pressed a palm to my chest as if to check my pulse. She laughed before giving me a flick on my shoulder. "I almost forgot! Are you, like, having Jodi do your laundry now?"

"Jodi?"

"Miss Kempter," she said. "Did you not just give her a laundry bag from your backpack?"

"Uh, yeah," I said. My focus narrowed back to her eyes again. With the sun beating down on us they were almost another shade of twilight. "I mean no. It's for some experiment thing. Not a big deal."

Dixie hit my arm. "Are you doing extra credit without me?"

"No," I shook my head. "No, I swear. Nothing like that. It's just something I had a question about and I didn't want to have to wait until whenever we cover the material. It's nothing. Really."

"Whatever it is," she puckered her lips. "It sounds boring."

"To a dullard like you, yes!" Eat'em scoffed. "Zing! Yes, Jacob? Big Time!"

"It is," I said. "Pretty boring."

"Do you have a Facebook account?" Dixie asked, changing the subject once more.

"No."

She gasped, "How. Do. You. Breathe?"

"What's she talking about?" Eat'em asked.

I answered both of them at once, "I don't know."

"Well," she said, "everyone has one. So you need to get one. Social networking. Otherwise, how am I supposed to get a hold of you?"

"Morse Code?"

"What's that?"

"Nothing," I said. "Dumb joke."

"Me too, Jacob," she smiled sheepishly and pretended to tap out a message. "Beep. Beepbeep. Beep. Beep. That means get on Facebook so I can get a hold of you."

"Sounded more like *Shave and a haircut*."

"You," she said, "are a major dork."

"I realize," I said. "I'm sorry, I really got to go."

"Right, Valentine and Isaac," she said. "See you later... on the interwebs!"

She blew me a kiss and Eat'em belched in response.

Chapter 12

I didn't know why I hadn't thought of it. Instead of relying on an imagined sixth sense to track down the blonde, all I needed to do was surf the web.

Dixie, you're a genius!

Scouring page after page I dug through the profiles of UT alums. My first search brought up hits in the hundreds of thousands. People tagged themselves to the school dating as far back as the 70's. Some former students even used their thirty year old school photos on their profile, which made my search that much more difficult.

I narrowed the field to current students aged eighteen to twenty-five and the list became more manageable. Then it was just a matter of surfing until I found her.

Eat'em dug through the cracks in the couch on a quest for

day old chip crumbs, which he called consumptive loot. He pulled at the cushions, rummaged through my bedding, and shook the seats for whatever morsels he could find, grumbling as he went.

"This," he said. "Oooo this too, yes. Very salvageable. We'll put this one over here."

He added a handful of chip crumbles to a pile on the coffee table and meticulously picked out bits of lint. Then he scooped the whole mound into his mouth and washed it down with a bottle of A1 left out from Val's lunch – a Hamburger Mac Hot Pocket and microwavable French fries.

After finishing off the steak sauce, something I'd surely pay for later, Eat'em drug himself onto my lap and curled up in front of the laptop.

"Three, yes," he said, "definitely a three."

"Three?"

"Her." He nodded at the screen. I was on the profile of a Hispanic girl with drawn on eyebrows.

"She's a three?"

"Yep."

"Out of what?" I asked. "Five?"

"Fifty," Eat'em said. "Six percenter, yes. Ugh."

Laughing I asked, "How about her?" and clicked over to an Irish woman with fiery red hair and pools of freckles.

"Eight."

"Her?" I clicked to another.

"Two," he said, "No, no… One. One-point-five. No, one.

One's right, yes. One."

I looked at the oil-tanned brunette on the screen. She had long eyelashes, a slender face, pouty lips, and perfect skin. A botany major. She could have been a model for all I could tell.

"A one?" I asked. "You're giving her a one?"

"Yes."

"Out of fifty?"

"Hundred for her," he said, mocking a shiver.

"One out of one hundred?" I said, "Are you kidding? Who taught you this scale garbage anyway?"

"Valentine."

"Ha," I clicked to another picture of the brunette. A top-down shot, revealing a respectable amount of cleavage. "And you think Val would give her a one? Out of a hundred?"

"Oh no," Eat'em said, "he'd give her a perfect, yes."

I nodded, "Yeah, she looks pretty close to me."

"Well, you both have low standards."

"Alright," I said, "explain it to me then. What's wrong with her?"

Eat'em sighed and pointed out her flaws. "Her tresses are fake, yes. Her expression is fake, yes. Her mammaries are fake, yes. Fake. Fake. Fake. She conceals herself in blush and dye, she's ominous, she's small, and the picture is distorted to make her look even smaller, yes. Obviously, she's a one."

I minimized the window, showing Eat'em Dixie's profile. In it she sat half cross-legged on a carpet, with her head rested against her lifted right knee. She wore a pair of jeans and an oriental inspired shirt. Her hair was cut much shorter than she wore it now, still with her trademark violet locks. She looked relaxed, and natural, like someone caught in mid-conversation.

"How about her," I asked.

"Ew…" Eat'em shook his head. "I won't answer that."

"Why not?"

"Because," he said, "your heartbeat went up."

"No it didn't."

"Did so."

"It didn't."

"Yes it did," Eat'em grunted. "She popped up and you got all flustered, yes. 'Oooo she's so appealing.' 'Oooo she's a Virgo.' 'Oooo she smells like detergent.'"

"Stop," I said.

Heat rushed into my cheeks. It hadn't occurred to me and I felt completely foolish. Stupid.

"See," Eat'em stretched and thumped my chest. "It did."

I clicked the search bar. "I'm such an idiot."

"Agreed."

I typed 'planetarium' and hit enter. The page loaded with just more than a dozen results. Scrolling down, I checked each profile hoping to see the blonde.

No blonde.

"Damn it!" I rubbed my eyes. My head hurt from staring at the laptop screen the whole day. "I've got to put this down for a while."

"Yes, put it down. Social networking is for the anti-social, yes?," Eat'em shut my laptop and stood on it as I slid it onto the cluttered coffee table. "Keystrokes are a sign of the solipsistic lonely sort. Self-imposed solitary confinement, yes! You can't rip all them ones and twos from the screen, Jacob. Do you know what else you can't rip from the screen?"

"What?" I leaned back and followed a crack along the ceiling with my eyes. I couldn't remember seeing it before. Pretty much, I felt like the worst detective ever.

"Rip it!" Eat'em clapped for my attention.

"Rip what?" I asked, still fixated on the narrow crack.

"NO!" Eat'em said, "RIP IT! One for me. One for you. Yes? You're tired. I'm thirsty. Let's get your wallet and go procure us some rip its!"

"I should have guessed," I said. Then the epiphany crashed into my skull like a kid using bowling balls for skipping rocks. I spent all afternoon skimming the surface for the girl, when I could have plunged into the depths a day ago. "The wallet!"

I raced over to my backup and emptied the contents on the floor. There it was. A brown leather wallet, could it belong to the number one Deftones fan? I fumbled through the contents; a frequent meal card for a sandwich shop, credit cards, a couple dollars... and finally... a driver's license:

Louise Parsons

Sex: Male Height: 6'5" Weight: 235 lbs

His address.

"I like what you're thinking," Eat'em said as he climbed onto my shoulder and tapped the ID with the tip of his tail.

"Find him, find the girl," I said.

"Yes," the demon said, "that too. I was thinking more along the lines of having him pay for the rip its."

Chapter 13

"Of course I suspected him right away," Lieutenant Bellecroix scrapes a fingernail along the side of the pulpit. A nervous habit, perhaps. I imagine he was the type to carve his initials into every desk he sat at. "You can't take one look at the kid without being suspicious."

"Objection!" Mike and Eat'em sound off together.

"Sustained."

Bellecroix leans back and rolls his head toward the ceiling, intentionally avoiding eye contact with me. At the beginning of the trial he looked at me only with contempt, scowling at every turn, but now he just looks tired. His cheeks droop with sleeplessness. His lips crack from dehydration. His eyes no longer burn with rage.

"It's not how he looks," Bellecroix continues. "It's the way he looks. It's how he behaves."

"How does he behave?" Gomes asks.

"First time I seen him," Bellecroix says, "We'd gotten a lot of calls some kid is walking down Cooper Street covered in blood. And, I mean, he's head-to-toe covered. It's on his shirt, it's in his hair, it's on his shoes. I know spray patterns when I see them. I've seen enough, and I know, this kid was just involved in something bad. So, I pick him up and bring him in."

Bellecroix studies me the same way he did then. As if he never could get the image out of his head.

"I can't – *not* – bring him in looking like that," he continues. "In the car, he doesn't say anything. Just stares blankly out the window. I asked him if he's okay. I told him it wasn't an arrest. But he's just silent. Not shaken. Just silent. It's like he's coming up with a story to tell. That's the vibe I get from him."

"A vibe?" Gomes asks.

"Well, yeah," Bellecroix says, "I'm not a mind reader. I got a vibe. Now, I'm not thinking he necessarily did something bad. Maybe he was a victim. Someone's obviously really hurt. Maybe he was in shock. He ain't talking.

"We have our procedures. We start by interviewing him three different times. He doesn't get a word out with me, so he talks to someone else and then one more officer after that. Then we have him write out his account for the day, everything that happened in as much detail as he can. That's the first time he mentions a dog."

"A dog?" Gomes lifts an eyebrow toward me. "His dog?"

"Yeah," Bellecroix says, "He wrote that he had a dog get out. Run into some razor wire. He finds it and gets bloodied up when he's trying to get it out."

I remember the day. I remember the trail of lies I spun. I remember how hard it had been to fight the need to let someone in. The lieutenant seemed trusting... a deceiver in his own right.

Bellecroix continues, "I asked him what kind of dog. Mastiff, he tells me. Named General Lee. I tell him interesting choice in names and I ask him, like Dukes of Hazard, huh? He says, yes. He's relaxing a bit."

Gomes holds up a hand and says, "General Lee. That's the famous name of a Civil War general, isn't it? Sounds similar to another case you..."

"Objection!" Big Mike slams both hands on the table as he jerks upward. "Leading the witness."

Judge Brentt nods and warns Gomes to stay on topic.

"I was merely breaking ice with Mr. Brook," the lieutenant says. "Trying to get him to open up. At that point it was just important for us to find out if the blood he is covered in belongs to somebody that might need help or worse yet be dead. But when it came down to it, when we told him we needed to get DNA from his clothing, he said the fourth amendment protects him from unwarranted search and seizure. He said if we weren't charging him, he wouldn't let us take a sample. Said it was his right to not have police desecrate his pet more so than what'd already been done. There was nothing we could do."

"So your hands were tied?" Gomes asks.

"Our hands were tied," Bellecroix says. "He called his uncle to pick him up and that was it.

"How could I not be suspicious after that? Do you know how many people come into my precinct and have the Bill of Rights memorized? Recite the Fourth Amendment? To this day... one. Is it an important document everyone should know? Sure... but nobody does. Except for Jacob. Jacob, who is picked up from the side of the road after numerous phone calls from passersby all stating he's drenched in blood."

"Did his story check out?" Gomes asks. The slick DA appears disheveled as ever. He hardly bothers shaving anymore, and often smells of day old alcohol. He figures he won this case from the start and is simply playing the waiting game. His overconfidence bleeds into his demeanor.

"No," Bellecroix says, "but it didn't need to. We had nothing to hold him on. Being cut up and bruised and lying about a dog isn't grounds enough to force him to cooperate. The kid knew his rights and we let him go."

"Even covered in blood."

"Even covered in blood, absolutely," Bellecroix shakes his head. "There are countless reasons he could be covered in blood without doing what he did."

"Objection!" Mike slams the table again. His stamina in the case might be my greatest asset. He told me the goal was to outlast them. *A long trial is in our favor.*

"Sustained."

"It's not illegal to have blood on you," Bellecroix says. "And it's not illegal to lie to police – unless we're building a case and require your testimony. Sure, someone might get rung up for perjury charges here, but for me, only the evidence will tell me if you're lying or not."

He gnaws at a cuticle, looking at me only briefly before finding something else to be distracted with. Mike leans over and whispers, "Fidgeting means he don't believe his own words."

"I didn't have the evidence," Bellecroix says. "I didn't have the crime. We picked Mr. Brook off the streets and I believe we were right to do so."

What he didn't say on stand was that he took a swab of the blood from the chair I sat on during interrogation. It may be inadmissible in court, but I am not the only one who can play vigilante.

Chapter 14

Cooper Street lay shrouded in moisture – fog so thick I couldn't see my hand unless I held it a couple inches in front of my face. The midday humidity tasted grimy. Arlington disappeared in a looming cloud of grey and not even a blazing Texas sun could penetrate the palpable air.

Yet even with visibility near zero, traffic soared by at suicidal speeds. Early commuters refused to slow regardless of climate. An accident in this fog would easily result in an unstoppable pile up. Wailing sirens broke through the blinding mist, providing ample evidence in my theory of an inevitable collision.

A horn blasted as a set of headlights sliced through the fog and disappeared immediately – no taillights followed suit. The doomsday conditions consumed the car without second thought, allowing the driver to barrel down the road to tempt fate with reckless abandon.

Eat'em and I had walked a couple miles before the fog really set in. I considered backtracking to Val's apartment, but the low visibility might be to my benefit.

I knew where the old man lived.

Assuming the address on his identification was current, I would be there shortly. What I didn't know is whether or not the Deftone's fan would be there. Or if he was even still alive.

He lived on a cul-de-sac at the northern end of Cooper.

Eat'em and I rounded the corner toward Parsons's and searched for the one-story house through a wall of grey. I crossed a yard, tripped on a Texas shaped stepping-stone, and stumbled onto a wooden porch, almost toppling past a brick pillar and into an uncared for flowerbed.

The house number came into view over a doorbell panel with frayed wires snaking out from the hole where a button had once been. We'd come to the right place.

"My feet are tired, yes," Eat'em moaned. He yawned and stretched his legs from my shoulder, grasping onto the hair above my ear to keep from falling. "I want to traverse home."

"I know being shuttled around on my back all day is Hell on your feet, buddy," I approached the door, the porch creaking as I slowly stepped forward. "Maybe next time, you'll carry me, huh?"

"Huh?" Eat'em scoffed. "Indubitably, as always, your disregard for physics astounds me. You are a giant, yes... but your brain is sooooo tiny."

For a moment I considered knocking. Perhaps someone else would answer the door, a stranger, and I'd find out the old man never lived there. The heavy ball of mass pressing in my gut told me that wouldn't be the case. It was definitely the old man's house. I knew he lived there. I knew he was single and without kids. What eluded me was whether he still lived there. Had he crawled away after I presumed he died?

I rubbed my hand across condensation built up on one of the windows framing the front door. A small living room and formal dining room made up the front entrance. A bathroom or closet was to the left. And an open doorway led to a hallway lined with framed photos that were mostly black and white.

I checked the doorknob. Unlocked.

My legs trembled as I stepped into the empty living room. Breaking and entering took more guts than I normally had. We broke into an empty home, though. Louise Parsons was dead. I killed him. Now I just needed to find out how a dead man got up, changed clothes, and seemingly walked away.

The house barely looked lived in. A bookshelf stood in a corner with neatly stacked books all alphabetized. Beside a beige recliner sat a magazine rack. An old television with a built in VCR was by a fireplace. A cold shutter crawled up my spine as my eye caught the crude fireplace poker hanging above the open chimney.

I crept into the kitchen. It had a small island in the center equipped with hanging pots and pans. Above the sink, a window looked out to the vast grayness.

Eat'em ran to the fridge and pressed his face against it. He sniffed the air. "There's something in there!"

Two picture magnets were on the otherwise undecorated refrigerator. One picture was of a man crawling across the tops of an electrical wire meters above a thick canopy of trees. A helicopter hovered in the foreground. The other picture was of an old man and a mastiff. The dog wore a Civil War General outfit. The man wrapping his massive arm around the dog was definitely Louise Parsons. I was in the right house.

"Jacob," Eat'em tugged at my pants, "please open this, yes."

I reached for the handle and froze.

Behind me, reflected in the chrome freezer door, stood a lumbering figure.

I spun around just in time to brace myself for the rampaging Parsons.

Chapter 15

My face blistered above the scarlet stovetop. A bead of sweat rolled across my brow, down my bronzed cheek, and clung to my clinched jaw. It hung for a moment, too stubborn to let go. It fell and crackled as it splashed against the coils.

The large hand, which prevented my escape, belonged to the same beast of a man I encountered at the planetarium. His face, pocked with scars, was adorned with a brick jaw that looked more akin to Lou Ferrigno's than the former Louise Parsons's. His gnawed fingernails tore into my scalp as he wrestled my face ever closer to having a spiraled scar and one less ear.

My fiery eyes stared back at me in the reflection from the freezer chrome, decorated with the giant dopey-looking mastiff and a younger, less brutal version of the retired lineman.

Large veins wound up my forehead from the bridge of my nose. My teeth grinded and my cheek swelled. The first thing that would go would be my left ear, shriveling into my skull like a melted candle, leaving a charred black stub. Then my eye would dry out. Burst in its socket. My lip would curl away from my teeth; my skin would tighten, wrinkle, and flake away. I would need a graft.

So… that would suck.

"Welcome to my home." Lou turned up the heat with one hand as he held my head ever closer to the brightening coils. "Enter freely, won't you?"

My body flopped uselessly under his immense strength until my hand landed on an open drawer. I fumbled through the scattered contents. My fingertips, slick with sweat, searched for a weapon and my palm pressed hard to the bottom of the drawer to keep my face from turning to hamburger meat.

I found the hilt of a two-pronged skewer. My chin rebounded off the hot stove steaming with my boiling sweat and I drove the skewer into the soft tissue under Lou's brick jaw.

He let me go and I collapsed to the floor, momentarily relieved from the sizzle of cooked skin. I crawled around the island in the center of the small kitchen, creating what distance I could between myself and the very large, very angry, very alive sociopath.

"A close one, yes!" a small shrill voice cried out from atop the island. Eat'em dangled over the granite countertop, his tail wrapped around a hanging wok for balance. His red face burned with concern. He blinked his large triangular eyes and pressed an open palm to his tiny, puffed chest. "Jacob is off to a rocky start. Not Rocky Balboa or Dwayne 'The Rock' Johnson Rocky, yes. Rather he's looking horribly outmatched by the horrifically ugly Lou Parsons, whom may have eaten both Rockies before the match."

"Thanks for the help," the words escaped breathlessly. I had a severe case of cottonmouth and one helluva dry throat.

"Anything to motivate you," Eat'em held his arm up and sliced it through the air. "Ding! Ding! Ding! And now round two is underway. Can Jacob make up for such an embarrassing performance in round one? My money is on no!"

"Not now, Eat'em," I said.

"Who are you talking to, Jacob?" Lou rounded the island as he ripped the skewer from his lower jaw and tossed it skittering to the floor.

Again the beast said my name. This time I was certain. It rang, bitterly through my skull, which still felt a bit like hardboiled eggs.

He grappled me from the floor and lifted me above his head, ignoring an entourage of mule kicks and my slaphappy arm swings.

"It looks like Jacob is using the ol' Swing your appendages like a lunatic strategy," Eat'em held a ladel like a microphone. We really needed to stop watching so much television. "Will it work out for him?"

A wild elbow collided into one of Lou's droopy ears. He let out a guttural scream and threw me as if I were merely a large insect that had landed on his neck.

I tumbled across the kitchen, my body failing to defend itself from the harsh effects of gravity. I crashed onto a small mahogany table and slid into one of the miniature breakfast nook's three windows. The inside pane broke around me, showering me with flakes of jagged glass.

"Oohh," Eat'em leapt from the counter and crossed his arms at my side. "That's going to look brutal on the replay!"

Lou grabbed me by a leg. My other foot cracked into his jaw and I scrambled to my feet. He smiled at me and jumped forward as I sidestepped, grabbing a cast iron pot from above the island and bringing it down on the back of the big man's head.

"I did not see that coming," Eat'em said, hopping after us. "A pot to the skull? It's unconventional. It's against the rules. It's brilliant!"

I stomped hard against the lumbering Lou's kneecap. He stumbled face first colliding with a microwave built into the wraparound cabinets.

"It's unbelievable, but round two might go to Jacob!" Eat'em said. "Yes, I think he had a surprise round and I think everyone is in a bit of shock. Especially fat ugly Lou with his big dumb face, yes. But I don't think anyone is down for the count just yet."

I went for another go with the pot, just as Lou spun and grabbed my wrists. He lifted me, his nails digging into my skin. I dropped the pot. I kicked both feet into Lou's abdomen. He loosened his grip enough that my feet dropped back to the ground and I brought a knee hard and fast into his groin.

"Low blow," Eat'em bellowed. "Is it poor sportsmanship or thoughtful strategy?"

Lou shoved me.

Granite bore into my side. I did my best impression of Jet Li and flung myself over the island, knocking pots, pans, a napkin holder, and a robust set of knives to the ground with me.

I tossed kitchen supplies hopelessly. My pitch wouldn't have driven back a rodent at that point, let alone a feverishly angry muscle-bound jock, who somehow managed to be even stronger than he already looked. But I threw pots at him anyway, as Eat'em delivered a play-by-play for each toss. I crab-walked backward through the kitchen, hurling what I could find and keeping my feet between myself and the China Shop Bull, my hand searching blindly for something substantial to defend myself with.

The warm grip of a blade found its way into my hand. It was the damned bloody skewer. Still, I held onto it like I'd just pulled a sword from a stone.

I prepared for the raging lunatic, my hands behind my back, bracing for impact. He grabbed my collarbone, his thumb burrowing into the deep scar tissue on my shoulder. He lifted me from the floor. I swallowed back acidy bile that filled my throat and drove the skewer right between his eyes. The handle protruded from his dome, but he didn't relent.

"Inconceivable," Eat'em shouted into the ladle he whipped

around with his tail as he dodged the action. "Impossible. An act of God, ladies and gentlemen. Just when we thought this match had it all, we get a moment like this that truly shines. Jacob has created a unicorn out of the monster... A Lounicorn!"

At that, I laughed.

"Why are you laughing?" Lou pulled the skewer from his head and dropped it. "Is this funny to you, Jacob?"

"No," I caught a hold of myself and the fight continued.

"Weird intermission, that, yes," Eat'em followed us through the living room and into the hallway. "But the fight continues... Round three. And everything seems to be all tied up. This is anybody's fight. I, for one, am going to root for the underdog, yes. Because you should always chant for home team. Let's go Lou... Let's go!"

Eat'em trailed behind, cheerleading for the wrong guy. Again the demon fails to see what is at stake. We slammed into shelves, scattered books, body slammed a large empty kennel, and splashed a replica painting of a dog dressed like William B. Travis with blood and spit as either my head or his knocked the frame loose from the wall.

All of the black and white pictures lining the hallway were various historical figures portrayed by dogs. Travis as a Heeler, FDR as a German shepherd, some civil war general as a French poodle, and more politicians as pooches decorated the wall. I grabbed Abe "beagle" Lincoln and smashed it across Lou's face, which still carried the scars from our previous fight. Week-old scars that looked like

Eat'em

they'd been put there years ago. Even the two holes from the prong seemed faded.

Wood and glass confetti from Beagleham Lincoln rained down the hallway as I hit Lou until I had a fistful of splinters.

I dragged myself along the carpet. The cleanliness was immaculate – freshly vacuumed and steam-cleaned floors, perfect for bleeding out on. Still, the house had this musty smell the farther into it I crawled. Like someone hired a maid. Then died.

Bloody handprints followed me into a bedroom as I crawled on hands and knees, Lou slowly walking behind me.

"And this fight is almost over, people," Eat'em said from the hall, "Ugly Lounicorn is going in for the knockout."

I reached a king-size bed, which took up most of the room and halted at the floral bed skirt. Beneath the massive frame sat one of the most beautiful sights I could ever imagine… a glossy 9mm Smith and Wesson. Just within arm's reach, the beacon of hope renewed my love for the Lone Star State. I'd never been happier than I was seeing that pistol.

I grabbed the gun and rolled to my back.

"Whoa!" Lou's hands flew up in defense, "Jacob, you don't want to…"

My fingers wrapped tight around the cold grip. I squeezed the trigger. The resounding blast reverberated off my eardrums. I fired off three more rounds.

Eat'em rounded the corner. He might have cursed. He definitely yelled cheater. Lou dropped.

Chapter 16

When someone you love dies, it's as if the oxygen is sucked out of the room. Your breathing becomes heavier and you feel like you'll never get enough air. It's like surviving a plane crash in the center of the ocean. You don't know where to go, or what to do. You don't know if you'll ever be home again or if it'll ever be the same. You feel as if the world will swallow you before you ever again find dry land.

Witnessing the death of a stranger, even causing the death of a stranger, is hardly comparable. The faceless man beside me meant no more to me than the victim of a wreck that represents an obstacle for all those stuck in traffic with places to be. Even driving by a collision of immeasurable horror hardly ever elicits an emotional response; rather passersby simply pause long enough to soak it in – to keep a mental memento. Death can represent nothing more than a trophy used for bragging rights in drunken conversation.

Lou's final breath wasn't what sent my heart into a frenzy. My melancholy derived from the same deep seeded nightmare that consumed my sleep every night.

My chest pounded fiercely. I couldn't breathe. My ribs were prison bars for a heart that wanted out. Weighted pressure crushed against my cheeks. I could feel my face redden. My ears rang from the unforgettable sound of gunfire.

For a moment I was back in the ambulance, open wounds covering the entirety of my torso. I felt the needle pull from my arm as Eat'em snuck a drink from the IV. The vehicle raced through traffic, sirens blaring, and I heard myself ask, "Are they dead?" and the moment ended. I returned to Lou's carpet.

"Good job," Eat'em said, patting my hand. "I knew you would win. You shouldn't have gone so easy on him though."

From the safety of the floor I assessed my damage. I had some pretty decent cuts and some sore muscles, but nothing was broken.

I cradled the Smith and Wesson in my arms, thankful for its existence. Hesitantly, I wiped the gun as best I could and put it back in its rightful spot under Lou's bed. It seemed pointless. Blood and prints must have been all over the house. I promised myself Eat'em and I would lay off the cop dramas.

Walking out of that house, leaving a trail of bloody footprints, sopping head to toe in the wretched scented insides of who-knows-what, my gut churned and my heart felt heavy.

Eat'em followed close behind with a half-drank can of Jolt he found in Lou's fridge. I crossed the yard; kicking off my shoes, the red ring of blood stopped at the top of my pale feet. I wiggled my sore toes on the soft, manicured lawn.

The clouds dissipated and the sky cleared up once more. Texas weather was always so schizophrenic.

I almost fell back onto the dewy grass. I wanted to let the wet sod strip away the thought of having killed Louise Parsons… twice. Instead, I walked.

I drifted up Cooper Street as a ghost. My feet barely touched the sidewalk. Eat'em skipped quietly beside me.

I'm not sure how far I'd actually walked. It had to be several miles. I was lost in my own thoughts, trying to piece together the events of the last few weeks. I almost didn't hear the chirp of a siren. When I did, I thought it was only a fragment of a memory I ached to forget. Then the blue and white Dodge Charger skidded to a stop right beside me. That was the moment I met Lieutenant Bellecroix.

Chapter 17

"I've got some questions for you, Violent J," Val turned from the front passenger seat of his car. Isaac drove, which never happened before. Val would have to be passed out drunk in order to let someone else drive his Mustang, but there he was letting our neighbor drive us from the police station.

"Alright, Shaggy 2 Dope," I said, mocking his unintended reference to the band Insane Clown Posse, all the while ignoring Isaac's judgmental glare from the rearview, "I've got some answers for you. You go first."

Eat'em gestured for a semi-truck driver to honk and grunted at the lack of results. He held himself up by the ceiling handle behind the driver seat, pressing his tail against the seat to keep from swaying with each turn.

"Why are you covered in blood?" Val said. His temples throbbed, which they did when he ground his teeth, a habit of his when something angered him. His raised pitch was rife with accusation. "It sure ain't dog blood, like you told the police."

"It's ketchup."

"Ketchup?"

"Yeah," I said. "I was auditioning for a play."

"Don't be an asshole."

"Don't act like I'm a criminal."

"Look at you," Val said. "You look like a criminal."

"I'm not."

"What are you then?"

Eat'em dropped to the seat and threw his arms above his head. "The Champion!" he said in his best ring announcer voice.

"Misunderstood," I said.

We swerved and Eat'em fell into my lap. "HEY!!!"

"You look in over your head to me," Isaac said. He angled his visor to give me a better look. An expensive looking pair of Ray Bans hid the intention behind his eyes.

"I'm more worried about you being a victim," Val cut in. "You look like you got your ass kicked."

"Well," I said, "you should see the other guy."

I jolted forward as Isaac hit the brakes and pounded the horn. A car slammed to a halt in front of us and the driver flipped us the bird before running the red light.

"What a piece of shit," Isaac said. "I never understand it.

Schools of fish, birds, freaking ants can move together in a coordinated effort without near death collisions and chaos, yet the most 'intelligent' species can't make a 20 minute commute without nearly killing someone."

"Road rage much?" I asked.

"No," Isaac took off his glasses. His hazel eyes were bloodshot with fury. "I'm just not having the best day, alright? Your uncle having me pick you up from a prison sure isn't helping, and neither is the traffic. If everyone could just get on the same page, I'd be okay."

"Ah yes," I said, "the collective."

"Damned right."

"Hey," Val interrupted. "Quit changing the subject. I want to know what happened, Jacob. You can say it in front of Isaac, it doesn't matter, okay. I don't care what it is. I'm just worried about you. And if you're in trouble…"

"I'm not in trouble."

"You sure?" Isaac raised an eyebrow.

"Yeah, I'm sure."

"He's pretty much a badass, yes," Eat'em crawled onto the center console. "Right, Jacob?"

I grimaced. I didn't feel like a badass. Actually, the adrenaline from my encounter with Parsons ran dry hours ago and I actually felt like I'd come out the other side of a combine. Getting a better look at myself in the passenger side mirror only confirmed my suspicions. I didn't look like Iron Mike. But I looked like I'd met him.

"Isaac," I said, "can you drop me off at Dixie's?"

"Who's Dixie?" Val asked.

"A friend of mine."

"Girlfriend?" asked Isaac.

"Just a friend," I said. "She doesn't live far from the apartment."

Val gave me a crooked glance. "You might want to get cleaned up first, Hannibal Jakester."

"No," I said, "she won't care. I don't want to go home."

"Why?" Val asked. "You think we're done with the conversation?"

"For now."

"I'll take you to your girlfriend's," Isaac said. He seemed a bit cooler after getting his grief out on the other driver.

"She's just a friend," I reminded him.

"Can we meet this friend of yours?" Isaac asked. "Any woman who doesn't care whether you show up to her house looking like you slaughtered a man in cold blood is the kind of chick you want to lock down. Or does that go against individualism?"

"No," I said, "it doesn't."

"Would y'all knock it off with your philosophy shit?" Val asked. "Please and thank you."

"Well, can we meet her?" Isaac asked.

"No," I said again, "you can't."

Chapter 18

On the edge of Dixie's bed, I flipped a page on her biology textbook. She let me shower and gave me a fresh set of clothes – sweatpants and a hoodie. Not particularly appropriate for the schizophrenic weather, but at least they fit. Etched to the side of the sweats was the word 'Timberwolves!' which was the mascot to a high school about ten miles south of us.

She didn't say anything about my outfit or cuts and bruises. She just offered her wardrobe and led me to the shower. A shower tucked in a bathroom with a doorway stringed with beads. No door. Not that I ever had much in terms of privacy. But it was a little jarring knowing she could easily walk in on me at any moment.

I asked her afterward if we could study. I needed to be occupied by something other than the events of the last few weeks.

Super powered old men. Missing woman. And death. And police. Valentine. And Isaac. I wanted to think about Dixie, to be honest. It was a weird thought to jump in my mind only hours after shooting a man to death, but all I could think about was wanting to be with Dixie.

Eat'em clung to the front of an oscillating fan. He hummed as he drifted back and forth, back and forth. Every so often he would speak into it and his words would spiral mechanically through the room, only noticeable to the demon and myself.

Dixie sat dangerously close to me. Her crossed leg draped over my knee. She fluttered her toes against my ankle. I could smell her skin, scented with a lilac perfume. Her breath ruffled the front of my shirt.

It was a nice escape from my uncle's probing questions and my neighbor's prying eyes.

Clothes and knickknacks cluttered Dixie's room. She had a shelf lined with empty liquor bottles. Most of them were Asian brands I hadn't heard of. Sapporo was the only bottle with English characters. She didn't have a blank surface, as everywhere I looked were Post-Its with motivational quotes.

Whatever you are, be a good one. – Abraham Lincoln

I break away from all conventions that do not lead to my earthly success and happiness. – Anton Szandor LaVey

"*Be who you are and say what you feel, because those who matter don't mind and those who mind don't matter. – Dr. Seuss*" Eat'em read the last from a vanity mirror behind the fan. He laughed into the whirling blades and yelled, "You don't mind, yes? Do you, Jacob?"

My arms squeezed tight to my side. Dixie didn't have any deodorant for me, and I feared I might be ruining the flowery scent. She squeezed tighter to me and pressed her finger to the textbook in my lap.

"I don't get this at all," she said.

"It's tough," I didn't know if I agreed or not, but it felt wiser than saying it was easier than it looked. "I get stuck on genotype and phenotype. How one can have the genes for a trait they don't have... or show... or whatever."

"What about your red eyes?" I felt her breathing on my cheek as she leaned over to get a closer look. I tried my best to avoid eye contact. "Were those passed down to you? Think you'll have a red-eyed kid?"

"I don't know," goose bumps ran up my arm as it brushed against her. My chest pinched. "Maybe. I figure the devil gave them to me. They're awful for pictures, though, that's for certain."

"Do you believe in the devil?"

"I believe in demons."

Eat'em laughed a mechanical cacophony of 'Hahaha' and yelled, "I'm a demon, yes, Jacob?"

"Why do you say your eyes are horrible for pictures?" Dixie asked.

"I haven't had a professional picture done in my life where they weren't edited out. And now most cameras have built-in settings that automatically remove red eyes. So, I always look... normal." The further I pulled away the closer she pulled toward me. Her warmth intoxicated and suffocated all at once. "Most people don't see them as a spectacle. They see them as a bad omen. I get told I look like Steve Buscemi a lot. With horrible contacts."

She grabbed my chin and turned my face toward her. "I would have said you're more of a toss up between Benicio Del Toro and James Dean. You have Del Toro's eyes for sure... but more dangerous. Definitely have a James Dean thing going on."

"What is she talking about?" Eat'em burped into the fan. "Tell her you're done studying and done talking about stupid things, yes. *Time is better spent masticating than wasted copulating. – Eat'em.*"

My attention snapped to the oscillating demon on the word copulating.

"You don't have to turn away," Dixie's fingers wrapped around my mid thigh. "You're so shy."

I swallowed. The gulp seemed cartoony, but my mouth was oversaturated. I swallowed too much. And blinked too much.

My leg twitched.

I bet she felt it. My nervousness.

"Ew..." Eat'em dropped from the fan and climbed onto the opposite side of my lap. He pointed to her hand, gently squeezing my left leg. "She loves you, yes. She desires you. Offer her a progeny."

"I'm not shy," I pulled away and focused on the textbook. "Just, the things you say. Nobody's ever talked to me like you."

Words became jigsaw puzzles. The pages split into tessellations. I tried to blink it back into sensible structure, but I couldn't. I saw the threads and fibers that made up the paper and all the nooks the ink missed during print. Dixie's hand on my thigh seemed to dematerialize into living cells. The fine lines on her knuckles grew into caverns. Her freckles blew up into giant splotches. The thin hairs climbing up her arm were a forest with no canopy.

I looked out the window and felt like I could see across the city. "I killed someone today." Without thinking the words fell from my lips as if letting go of an untied balloon.

"That explains the clothes," Dixie said calmly.

"I'm not a murderer," I feared looking at her. I feared her judgment. I feared her hatred.

Unexpectedly, she drew nearer and squeezed my arm to keep it from shaking. "You don't look the type."

"I don't?" I searched her eyes for doubt.

"No," she said. "You're not plain enough to be a murderer."

"Plain?"

"Murderers are plain and boring. You're abstract. You are beautiful. You, Jacob Brook, are full of heart."

I smiled. "Abstract, huh? That's fitting, for some reason."

"Because you are."

"Yeah…" I said. "I'm also a killer. I mean, I'm not a killer, I guess. I only killed one guy… twice… kinda."

"Twice?" she cozied up to me tighter, stroking my arm, calming me. "This I have to hear."

"It's what I went to Kempter about," I said. "I think he had a virus. I saw him attacking a girl at the school. A blonde. He was… I don't know… I think he was eating her, maybe."

"So, like a zom…"

"No," I interrupted. "Nothing so crazy as that. I mean, maybe crazier, who knows. But he wasn't rotting or dead, just a normal guy… except fast. And strong. And he could jump like crazy. And pretty much he could heal instantly."

"Wow…" Dixie smiled, "…and you killed him?"

"What?" I asked defensively. "I don't look capable?"

"No, no," she said, "I'm sorry. I believe you. Just impressed. That's all. Go on."

She shook me and as I loosened up she draped her legs over mine in a way that she pretty much sat across my lap.

"It's just," I hesitated. "I don't know what happened to this girl. I thought she died. I thought *he* died before today."

"What if he gave her whatever virus he had?" Dixie asked. "What if they're already spreading it to others as we speak."

"They?"

"Him and her?"

"He's dead."

"Are you sure this time?"

"This time," I said, "yes, I'm pretty certain he's dead."

"I don't know," she kissed my cheek. "You might have to kill him again."

I couldn't tell if she was serious or joking, if she believed me or thought this was a joke. Either way, I didn't care, just talking about it seemed to lift a pressure from my shoulders, even if she didn't believe me.

"No," I shook my head centimeters from her lips. "No. Nonono. No. I'm not a murderer."

"No," she said, "you're not. But you did kill someone in order to save a pretty girl."

"I never said she was pretty."

"Was she pretty?"

"She…" I pictured the blonde's crystal blue eyes. "She was pretty, yes. I guess you could say she was pretty."

"See," Dixie said. "And fighting for a pretty girl doesn't make you a killer. It makes you a hero."

Her breath caressed my lips. I wanted to tell her *she* was pretty, but I froze, transfixed by her.

"I like you, Jacob," her mouth felt buttery; soft with Chap Stick. She kissed me. Our teeth clicked together and her tongue, smooth and rough all at once flicked the tip of my own.

Her fingers ran through my hair. Flakes of dead skin glided away from my scalp. The air filled with them. Swarms of discarded pieces of myself swam along the fan's current, pulling back as the air stilled.

"Ugh…" Eat'em bellowed, "I bet she tastes like raw meat."

She traced my ear with her fingertips. Through her purple locks I could read every Post-It as if at once. My peripheral vision widened. The world became too clear to cope with.

Her hand dropped to my jawbone, ran down my neck and found my collarbone.

"Barf!" the demon bemoaned. He leaned onto my arm, propped on the biology book. I tensed under the prickle of hundreds of tiny quills. They were more hedgehog-like than porcupine, the tips couldn't puncture flesh, but they were imposing enough to ward off curious animals. "You're going to get a disease. Herpes. Gonorrhea. AIDS. Chlamydia. Syphilis."

He proceeded to describe images we'd seen a few years earlier in a sexual education seminar required for my high school. That's when he first decided women were disgusting.

Dixie inhaled deeply through her nose as our lips remained locked. I'd stopped breathing. I couldn't breathe. I was going to suffocate. Part of me wanted to suffocate. To die pressed to her lips would be the best death of all. If not for the demon.

"Pustules and swollen lymph nodes, yes" Eat'em rattled off.

Dixie's thumb found the cavity on my shoulder.

I could hear the sirens start up again. My mind started drifting. Screams. Gunshots. I'm sixteen again.

I should have been lost in the kiss, but instead I was lost in my nightmarish memories.

Somewhere in the house a window shattered. I scrambled under my bed accompanied by my pipsqueak demon. My stepfather yelled. A gunshot. My mother screamed. Another gunshot. Another. Silence. Agonizing silence. An eternity passed. I crawled out of my room and slowly moved toward the stairs. My mother sprawled out on the living room floor. She breathed slowly. Her face frozen in fear. I smelled the blood before I saw it – metallic and sour – a hint of something that smelled like fire.

The twelve steps descending into the living room were higher than they'd ever been. I braced myself with against the wall as I approached my mother, listening to the shrill sound that escaped chest with each rise and fall. I knelt beside the fireplace and tried to touch her hand. I tried to say something, but I couldn't. A man came out of my parents' room.

He had sunken cheeks, pale eyes, and disheveled black hair. His face was placid and emotionless. He had a gun.

I grabbed the fireplace poker and gripped it with two hands. He laughed. He could have shot me. Could have taken my life. Instead, he reached for the poker. And I let him grab it from my shaking hands. I remember the icy sting as the first thrust punctured my ribs and cracked my shoulder blade. And my mother's eyes as I collapsed beside her. I blacked out shortly after the second stab. I woke in an ambulance to Eat'em drinking my IV fluid. My neighbors had called the police. The intruder was gone. Made off with some jewelry and the contents of my mother's purse. They never caught him.

Dixie pulled herself closer and kissed me passionately.

I wanted to enjoy this. Part of me did enjoy it. The taste of her tongue. The smell of her skin. The softness of her touch.

I fought back the memories, trying desperately to come back to the present. I read the notes of encouragement surrounding us as Dixie hand caressed my ravaged body, wounds new and old.

All that is necessary for the triumph of evil is that good men do nothing. – Edmund Burke.

I never fought back before. Maybe it was a second chance.

"The only cure for this is castration," the grating voice I couldn't get rid of. I have to admit, his timing is impeccable. "Yes. You will most likely have to live in a Eunuch colony. It won't be so bad, huh? No more girls!"

"Stop." I pushed Dixie away. "STOP!"

The world was an intergalactic map of particles. I felt like I could push through the floor. That ebb and flow of atoms that made up Dixie's bed shouldn't be able to hold me. Dixie stood. I couldn't make out her expression.

I searched for the crimson demon in the sea of visual noise.

"Jacob?" Dixie's tender cadence.

"No," I pushed her away, "I can't. So long as he's in my life, I can't." I squeezed my eyes shut, trying to make the swirl disappear into blackness. "I can't take it anymore! I can't take YOU anymore! You're a burden, Eat'em! You're a burden I can't handle! I can't have a life or a girlfriend or just five minutes without you ruining everything! I renege. I don't want you as a friend or a servant or an ally or any of those things. I don't want you climbing around in my head when I just want a normal life. Go away! GO AWAY! I don't want you around anymore! Eat'em, just go away."

The room spun. And when it came to a halt I finally opened my eyes.

My eyesight returned to normal. The outer edges, once again, a discernible blur. Dixie sat on the edge of the bed. Drawn away from me. Her face mottled in confusion.

An uncomfortable silence fell over the room. For the first time in over three years, Eat'em was gone.

"I'm sorry," I felt the breath come back to my lungs. As if I'd been in a vacuum the moment Dixie started kissing me and the air finally returned. I wondered how long I could have gone on feeling so breathless. Part of me wanted to try again…

But she looked afraid.

"I'm sorry," I repeated. "I have to go."

I left. For the first time ever, by myself.

Chapter 19

The bathroom blonde's name was Carrie Gerberich. Her stretched image on the restaurant's flat screen couldn't replicate how piercing her eyes were in person. The sapphire blue dulled on the display. Her milky skin washed out.

I ditched class to avoid an embarrassing conversation with Dixie. Confessing to her was stupid. Part of me wanted to hide in Val's apartment, but without Eat'em the quiet would drive me to madness. Instead, I settled for the chaos of Buffalo Wild Wings, a sports bar in the Arlington Highlands. The commotion from Rangers fans camouflaged my solitude.

High definition flat screen televisions decorated every wall. At least fifty sets played baseball. A few others aired either soccer or various college football games. And one, the one I found myself glued to, silently displayed a melancholy newscaster and Carrie's photo in the top right corner.

The ticker read "College student slain by police after violent attack, leaving two others fatally wounded…"

It was her. Miraculously back from the dead, only to have died again at the hands of police. I bit my lip to keep from hyperventilating.

"Excuse me," I yelled at a waitress to be heard. She spun around, her miniskirt staying perfectly pinned to her upper thigh, just low enough to keep her covered. "Are you able to turn up the volume on this?"

"Sure honey," she leaned over my lap and hit the volume up a couple notches, just loud enough to hear over the uproarious screaming. "Would you like anything to drink?"

"No," I returned her smile, if only to be polite. "No, I've got a couple years on me still."

"How about a soda?"

I shook my head, holding up a half-drank glass of water. "I'm okay. Thank you."

"Let me know."

She hurried off. I could tell she wanted to clear up the seat. There was a line at the door and all I had to eat was a complimentary basket of tortilla chips. The news of the blonde kept me glued to the chair, unwilling to make room for more guests.

"…investigating a series of similar events to happen over the last couple weeks…" A cropped and blurred photograph replaced the image of the blonde. It was two pairs of legs. A man's and a woman's. They laid motionless on a sidewalk. It could have been a cropped photo of a couple spooning had it not been for the streaks of blood. The tableau was shot so beautifully one might have titled it "Lover's Quarrel" and sold it at an auction. Yet in big bold letters the local anchorman sat in front of a piece of art simply titled "DEAD."

"DAMMIT!" a shout rang through the restaurant followed by jeers and boos. "That's what happens! THAT'S WHAT HAPPENS! You get rid of Hamilton and you might as well throw away the franchise! Sonofabitch! THAT'S WHAT HAPPENS!"

The anchor continued on with more details behind two violent outbreaks.

Police found Carrie cannibalizing on a homeless man outside of a RaceTrac gas station. The man, a Mexican migrant worker, lived in a field behind the convenience store with a community of vagabonds who used the lot for a place to stay at night. A clerk called police after discovering the girl eating the throat of the unnamed victim.

"She tore his neck clean out," a woman with a jagged yellow grimace said between missing teeth. "Had his throat all droppin' down like this," she made a pantomime gesture as if she stroked an invisible ZZ Top beard. "Blood's all ovah. I says to this guy, 'I ain't touchin' her. Got rabies. Seen it before. Rabies. Not touchin'. They got him in there callin' the cops."

The woman's English was broken more due to poverty and ignorance than a product of a second language. The channel censored most of her words, but reading her over exaggerated facial expressions left little to the imagination. Still, they gave her subtitles with the slang and swears clarified as if she were a Disney Princess speaking some foreign language from a distant far off land.

"Though officers at the scene have stated this is unrelated to the violent attack that occurred over the weekend, many aren't so quick to dismiss the similarities in the two incidents," another image flashed of a familiar house. Shattered pictures of the Canine Civil War and a single bloody handprint blew up on the screen.

Frozen corpses along the climb up Everest couldn't imagine the icy pangs that ripped across my flesh. Bumps raced across my arms and a cold sweat danced above my brow. Officer Bellecroix shouted accusations around in my skull. He'd remember. There was no way he wouldn't remember. It'd only be a matter of time now. The next image would be of me. The bloody-shirted suspect. I tried to push the thought out of my head. The anchor said they were unrelated. Unrelated. But… I knew there was no way he would have forgotten. The time. The day. My name and suspicious behavior. He would have to remember.

"It's difficult not to draw a comparison between the two tragedies, which occurred just one week apart," the anchor read deadpan. "Violence of this nature conjures images from such movies as World War Z and 28 Days Later, where mankind falls prey to a virus that turns men and women into cannibalistic hordes of zombies."

Straight from my mind to the screen, Lieutenant Bellecroix

took center stage at an impromptu press conference. The APD emblem shone behind him framed by an American flag on one side and a Texas flag on the other. Bellecroix barely hid the annoyance on his face from an unseen reporter.

"It's not zombies," he said bluntly. "I can assure you there is no zombie outbreak ravaging this state or any other. What we have here are two separate incidents that share a common theme. What that theme is, we don't know at this point, but we will find out. We're looking into the possibility of synthetic drugs. The word bathsalts is bouncing around. It's a possibility. We still don't know. But we'll find out."

An outburst from the baseball fans almost sent me out of my chair. I grabbed my water to keep from knocking it over and waited impatiently for more information.

"Unlike the attack last night, two suspects were found at the home of local resident Louise Parsons," I shook my head and almost blurted my confusion before regaining composure. The TV continued, "The two men shot and fatally wounded Parsons before commencing in what Lieutenant Bellecroix described as ritualistic cannibalism. In neither situation did any of the attackers respond to police request to stop."

What is going on? Could this be part of the infection? Is it making people cannibals? It almost sounds like it could be rabies. Who were these other two men found at Parson's? Are there more infected? My mind filled with questions.

The scene cut back to a reporter standing in front of the

RaceTrac where Carrie Gerberich had been shot only hours ago. A group of men and a couple women stood near the dumpster, smoking cigarettes and drinking from cans hidden in paper bags. The yellow-toothed Disney Princess nuzzled up to an old man in an Australian duster and a camo hat.

"A spokesperson for the Arlington Police Department said an investigation will be underway to see exactly why non-lethal means of apprehending Miss Gerberich were not utilized and stated she doesn't believe police acted in any way contrary to how they were trained," as the reporter spoke, I saw a familiar figure emerge from the dumpster behind her. Eat'em. He crawled from the depths of the garbage, dragging a large bottle, wrapped in his tail. He sat on the edge, his legs dangling over, sniffed the contents, stuck his tongue out and threw it back into the dumpster. The reporter continued, "We'll keep you updated as new information unfolds."

Was that live? I looked at my phone for the time and back at the screen. Yeah, it was.

I dropped five dollars onto my table and headed through a crowd of irate ball fans as they screamed, "Come on!" "No!" and a variety of colorful outbursts.

At one point in my life, I dreamt it would be me on that field. By the sound of some of the threats made by the Rangers' fans, I may not have been much better off.

Chapter 20

Finding the gas station took longer than I'd hoped. I walked for more than two hours before recognizing the dumpster from the television.

No police tape marked off the area like I thought it would. The place looked the same as it probably did any other day, still open for business in spite of the gruesome deaths that had taken place earlier in the day.

Dusk fell over Texas by the time I arrived. Various shades of pink and purple painted the night sky and a crescent moon smiled just above the horizon. The lights the city threw back at the heavens masked the stars. Soon it would be too black for most to see. Fortunately, my night vision surpassed most.

Crossing a gravel walkup, I peaked around the corner at the

empty lot behind the RaceTrac. Not a single square foot of the massive field remained unoccupied by sleeping bags, blankets, and makeshift bedding, all concealing individual mounds of misfortune. The smell could only be compared to that of a twice-worn, long-forgotten sock Eat'em once discovered in the threshes of Val's bedroom closet.

I hustled back to the dumpster and lifted the lid, careful not to bang it against the brick wall of the convenience store.

"Eat'em," I whispered into the darkness.

He wasn't there.

A sudden commotion brought my attention to the field of sleeping migrant workers and down-on-their-luck bums.

A man screamed *What's his name?* repeatedly while someone else shushed him and told him it'd be alright. My skin crawled, but as he drifted back to sleep, my nerves slowly subsided.

I closed the lid and headed into the store. A bell jingled to announce my presence, but nobody greeted me behind the register. I could hear someone poking around in a small room marked Employees Only. It sounded like he was dragging boxes around. Probably late night inventory work or something, even though it wasn't particularly late. Just a little before nine.

I drifted from one aisle to the next, hoping to see my demon friend with a faceful of chocolate, or nougat, or ice cream, or candy, or anything. I imagined him in the fridge, shot-gunning a rip it, his small gut protruding over his lap.

My heart began to sink lower and lower. Eat'em made me

mad, but I didn't mean to be so harsh with him. It wasn't like me. I prided myself in my infinite patience, and now my impatience for my one true ally left me with nobody else to confide in.

I found myself adrift by a shelf full of condoms and feminine products and rows of assorted medications. A single bottle of Pepto-Bismol chewable tablets sat alone on a row otherwise comprised of Tums and cold pills. I picked up the bottle and sighed.

When I looked up my heart almost dropped. A friendly-faced, blood-red, spiky imp leaned over the top of the rack, his tail swaying gently behind him.

I smiled and said, "Can I have this?"

"The Pepto?" he asked.

"The Pepto, yes," I said. I fought back the pressure at the back of my eyes and the urge to grab Eat'em and squeeze him. Instead, I said, "If I can have them I'd be grateful. I'd follow you now until the day you die. I'd follow you and I would be your one true compatriot. The Sancho Panza to your Don Quixote, the Robin to your Batman, the Tom Sawyer to your Huck Finn. I'd do what you ask of me. As your one true ally. I'd be your best friend. All I ask for, to be yours until forever, is that you bestow upon me these delightful morsels."

"You're paraphrasing, yes?" He said.

"A little."

"Yes," Eat'em smiled. "Take it, Jacob."

I opened the bottle and poured out a handful of pink tablets, which I popped into my mouth and chewed. "These aren't very good, by the way."

"I know, right?"

"But they're worth it. Worth it so much. Even if these. Pepto. Really are bad, awful stuff."

Eat'em leapt over the shelf and onto my shoulder. He kissed the side of my face and for a brief moment everything was once again right in the world. What is man without his demons?

"I missed you, buddy," I said.

"I thought you never wanted to see me again, yes," Eat'em thumped his tail joyfully against my back as he took his place once more on my shoulder.

I offered him a tablet and said, "A pact is a pact, pal. What's Robin supposed to do without Batman?"

Together we finished off the bottle of pills, gulping down our bitter-sweet friendship one awful tablet at a time.

"You got a stomach ache there, guy?" I hadn't heard the clerk come in from the back. He watched from the counter, as I finished the last bits of antacids.

"Yeah, sorry," I said, reaching for my wallet, "I'll pay."

Eat'em and I approached the register as I took out a couple bucks for the medicine.

The clerk kept his head buried in the computer screen. He fumbled around the keys, searching for the right input for the bottle of medicine. He said, "Just one second. It's my first time using this thing. Takes a while to figure stuff out."

"New computer?" I asked.

"More like a new brain," he said coldly, betraying his put-on smile. "You ever wonder what it would be like to be a god?"

"I'm sorry," I said. "Come again."

He looked up, his eyes black and vacant.

We shared the same sentiment.

"Oh shit!"

Chapter 21

The infected clerk moved faster than me.

Before I could react he shoved the register in my direction with enough force to knock me off my feet. I crashed into an overpriced rack of decade old DVDs, knocking it to the ground, scattering movies across the floor. Eat'em abandoned ship as I fell to the ground.

I sprung back to my feet in time to catch the clerk disappear into the back room.

Adrenaline flowing through my veins, I ploughed through the RaceTrac, leaving Eat'em to catch up.

I expected a massacre when I rounded the corner to the small storage room in the back. My imagination had the clerk chewing some poor girl to the bone. I thought of the blue-eyed woman who'd been here earlier in the day, devouring a homeless man as if he were a chicken potpie.

All that greeted me were shelves and boxes and an emergency exit opened wide to the field of vagabonds.

The clerk ran atop a fence line, like a sprinting tightrope walker, leapt into an adjacent parking lot and ran until he was out of sight. I stood in the doorway, blocked by sleeping arrangements packed tight as landmines. The clerk must have topped out at about twenty miles-per-hour give or take and that was while running across a picket fence. I had no idea how fast he was on land, but fast enough that if I had a clear track from here to wherever he disappeared to, it would take several minutes to cover the ground he covered in thirty seconds.

"Some hero," I said aloud.

At least I had confirmation. Whatever Lou had, spread. First to Carrie and two others, then to the Jackie Chan of convenience store employees. No way police wouldn't find out about it soon enough. A guy hightailing through the city at half the speed of traffic couldn't go unnoticed.

Why did he run?

I returned to Eat'em by the front counter and checked a computer monitor for some sort of clue as to who the guy was. Their system was aged, probably twenty or so years old. It consisted of a green background and white blinking letters. It reminded me of the old MS DOS screen used to play 8-bit text-based games like House of Horrors and King's Quest. I couldn't find a keyboard, but I doubted it was of the touch screen variety used at most everywhere else. It looked like it just scanned an item and popped open the register, leaving most of the math for whoever ran it. There definitely wasn't any useful information on it as I had hoped.

"What are you doing?" Eat'em asked, peaking out from around the monitor. "You're going to rob them, yes?"

"No, I'm not going to rob anyone."

"But you deserve retribution!" he kicked over a box of breath mints. "I understand you're not much to look at, but to vacate in hysterics is cowardly, yes."

"Thanks," I said.

"Obtain the contents of this drawer," Eat'em tapped the register with a curled finger. "Utilize its power to acquire Lottery Tickets, yes. Oh, yes. Then with those we secure even more of what grows from the magic drawer. Everything here becomes ours. When crazy legs returns, you discharge him! Better yet, detain him for abandoning his post."

"I don't think he's coming back."

"Then let's feast upon these delectables."

"Go for it."

Eat'em swung from the counter, running for the junk food.

Receipts I found in a receptacle beneath the register contained nothing more useful than the store name and items purchased. I looked through some drawers for a log book, anything that might have the guy's name on it, but came up short. Just pens, paper, and an even more archaic system that required some ancient form of printing; a combination of charcoal drawing and cave painting by the look of it.

I checked around for a calendar and after a minute found something better. Beside a filing cabinet a row of slotted shelves contained a half dozen clock-in cards. They were simplistic – the kind that receive a hole-punch each time you show for work. Each one had an employee name on the top along with the shifts they were scheduled to work, either days or nights, Monday through Sunday. Tonight's shift belonged to Trevor Schrekengost. Couldn't be many of them in town.

"Hey look!" Eat'em shouted from the front of the convenience store, "Val's here."

Outside, shining vibrantly beneath the light of one of the four pumps, was the unmistakable lime Mustang.

I dropped behind the counter.

Damn it.

"It's a party, yes!"

"No," I shouted. Damn it. Damn it.

I don't know much about divine intervention. For all the bizarreness I dealt with in having a demon living with me twenty-four seven, I never put much thought into a deity. It's not that I didn't consider the existence of a higher being, I just had more supernatural than I could handle. But Val, choosing to fill up at that exact moment at that exact gas station was nothing short of serendipitous.

My back pressed to the counter, I shifted to peak around toward the wall of windows, which provided no more cover than a few advertisements for cheap beer, cheap cigarettes, and ninety-nine cent ballpark franks.

All I could think was to manifest all of my energy into psychically keeping my uncle from coming inside.

It didn't work.

Using the counter as cover I cringed at the sound of the tiny bell, heralding his entrance.

"Hello," Valentine said. "Anyone here?"

I tried to block out the excited imp, gleefully cheering for me to get up. But I couldn't hear Val move. He just stood in the doorway, taking in the toppled shelf and whatever mess Eat'em might have made.

Silence.

Then I heard him rummage for something in his pocket.

"Get up, Jacob," Eat'em yelled, "Let's the three of us rob this place."

More silence.

My chest cramped. *Oh no!* Hiccups. They kicked in with urgency. I hate hiccups. To make matters worse, they always seemed to be violent when I had them. Not the quiet, somewhat cute, hiccups others seemed to be blessed with. My hiccups burned oxygen like miniature explosions keeping air from getting into my lungs. When I hiccupped, my whole body hiccupped.

I swallowed back, managing to muffle the "hic" as best I could. Val didn't notice it.

"Hello," I heard him say. "My name is Patrick Brook. I

would like to report a possible break in."

Of all the times to be a Good Samaritan, Valentine. Come on. Just steal some gum or something and get out.

"I'm at the RT on Cooper just off the interstate and nobody's here."

I held in another *hic*.

"The same one as what?" he said, "No. Sheesh, I don't know. I don't know anything about that. I'm just getting gas and came in for some drinks. No. I didn't hear. It's just empty."

I held my breath for as long as I could and exhaled slowly through my nose. I've heard hiccups are psychological. A sudden scare or change in stress levels can bring them on just as much as they can bring them to a halt. Every fiber of my being concentrated on making them go away. I relaxed and counted backward slowly from ten.

"Yeah," Val said, "Yeah, I can wait here. No, that's fine. But I'm going to wait in the car if it's all the same to you."

Nine. Eight. Seven. Six

"I'm in a green Mustang. So please don't shoot me."

Five. Four. Three.

The bell chimed and a cool breeze rippled through the store. He held the door open for a second longer than comfortable. Using my newfound psychic powers I attempted to push him out the door and the hiccups out of my chest.

Two.

For a second it seemed to be working. The door slowly

closed. My hiccups disappeared.

One.

But then I farted.

Chapter 22

I'm not talking about a little suppressed toot. I'm talking about a fart so poignant and palpable it could be removed from the surrounding atmosphere with an ice cream scoop. At that very moment, with nothing so critical as my keeping silent for an extra two seconds, I ripped ass to such a degree I would be forcibly removed from libraries, shunned from family gatherings, and ogled by every ten-year-old boy with an affinity for gaseous undertakings. Had a leer jet and a thousand foghorns gone off at that same second, Val still would have heard my offensive gesture.

And there I sat, basking in the horrid stench of broken wind, actually praying that Val's sudden awareness of my presence would send him cowering back to the vehicle. I mean, this fart was of Arnold Schwarzenegger proportions, and it stood to reason Val wouldn't want to stand toe-to-toe with a man whose sphincter could bring down gunships.

But instead of leaving, Val decided it was in his best interest to learn the identity of the Convenience Store Farter. The door closed, but with him still inside. He walked slowly toward the counter, stealthy as a grizzly on a trampoline. And the thought crossed my mind to knock him out.

I mean, I actually considered attempting to knock him unconscious. As if I possessed the roundhouse of Chuck Norris and the speed of Mohamed Ali. That I, Jacob, could render Val comatose with one swift motion and somehow he would wake up with no recollection. That'd be nice.

But I figured if the repugnant odor didn't put him out cold, my fists didn't stand much of a chance. At least not without beating him mercilessly first. It wouldn't go over well when he woke up.

Truth be told, I didn't even have a clue how much fight Val would have in him. He ate all Hell for food and didn't hit the gym as far as I knew, but he still looked as youthful as ever. And, in spite of my active lifestyle, my athleticism never really showed. When we were younger and we would fight, Val would have me on my back just as much as I would have him on his. That wasn't so long ago that I didn't fear the same result if I surprise attacked him in a halfcocked plan to not be caught behind the counter.

After considering my other options long enough to shame both our mothers I decided my best bet was to wave a white flag.

I slowly peaked above the counter and said, "Hey Orphan."

"J.B.?" his mouth dropped and his hand uncurled. His pale face turned a deep shade of pink. "What the Hell are you doing?"

Val meticulously spread a creamy layer of peanut butter across the top of a toasted English muffin. After spending the last couple hours talking to police while I sat in the passenger seat of his car, he'd worked up a bit of an appetite. He'd made up a story about meeting me at the gas station to pick me up after class - just enough to give me an alibi for being at the wrong place at the wrong time.

I sat on the other end of our small dining table, sans dunce cap, and watched his every deliberate knife stroke as he coated the bread, first with peanut butter and then adding a thin layer of mayonnaise.

"That's twice I've lied for you," Val said without looking up from his concoction. "Two times now I have lied to police."

He squeezed a glob of honey mustard onto his plate only after giving up on a frustrated hunt for steak sauce. Eat'em salivated at his side, waiting for the crumbs to start falling.

"Police, Jacob." He dunked the English muffin into the puddle of mustard and bit off only the part with a perfect blend of all three toppings. "And yet," he continued as he chewed, "in spite of my covering for you, you continue to lie to me."

"I'm not lying."

"Shh…" he said before taking another mustard dipped bite. "You'll get your turn to speak. Now is my turn."

"I'm not five," I said.

"You're still my nephew."

"Yeah, okay," I said, "and since when did we ever have a normal uncle and nephew dynamic?"

"Since always," he said, "now shut up."

I sighed. Our little kitchen was claustrophobic. I could feel the walls sweat as I grew nervous. We didn't even have a humidifier, which was stupid because we could afford it. We could afford a much bigger place too, but Val insisted on living like young adults. Like I would miss out on some valuable lesson if I lived more comfortably, with stuff that worked.

Val unshelled a hardboiled egg, peeling it a little bit at a time. He scooped the yolk out and in its place put a wad of minced tuna mixed with more mayo and diced pickle relish. "I'm curious as to why you think we don't have a normal uncle and nephew... dynamic, right? What makes us so different?"

"For one," I said, "I'm older than you."

"So what?" he said. "Have you ever had an uncle that was older than you? No. Have you ever had any other uncle than me? No, you haven't. You know exactly shit all about what a normal uncle and nephew dynamic is supposed to be. And..."

He swallowed half the egg and followed it with a bite of English muffin.

"And," he continued. "I'm doing the best I fucking can, Jacob. You know that?"

"Sure."

"No," he said, "you don't. You don't know. Either that or

you clearly don't give a shit."

"I do," I said.

"Then why haven't you been going to school?"

"I have."

"Mmm…" Val said, eating the other half of his egg. "You just can't help but lie, can you? You're pathological."

"I've been going," I said.

"Do you want to know who stopped by today?" he swept his wild red hair away from his face. He ground his teeth as he paused for an answer. "Your girlfriend. Dixie. She came over to talk to you."

My heart dropped. "What'd she say?"

"Enough that I know you haven't attended class in a while," Val said. "I invited her in for a cup of coffee and we had a good long talk."

"Here?" I asked. "You let her come in here? Like this?"

"And now I'm a pig?" he shook his head. "Well, you know what? I'm pretty sure she didn't care. And above all else, she lied to me too."

"She did?" I didn't realize I'd been holding my breath.

"Yeah, she did. Relief ain't it? It looks like you have more than one person willing to lie for you."

He coated another piece of bread.

"I don't know what to do, Jake," he said. "I think, man, I should be in mourning. Both my parents died this year. I never mourned though, right. Because as hard as it was for me to lose my mom and dad, I knew it must be hard for you to lose a second set of parents. And I'm all you have left. I know that because you're all I have left. That's it. The Brothers Brook. You said we don't have a normal uncle/nephew relationship, and you're right. We don't. You're not just my nephew, damn it. You're my brother. You're my best friend. You're fucking everything to me and I'm losing you and I don't know why."

"Val…"

"It's not your fucking turn to talk, Jacob." He took a deep breath. His eyes reddened with fought tears. "I don't know why you're walking around covered in blood. I don't know why I find you in the middle of the night in a gas station that looks like it's been robbed. You said you weren't robbing it? Fine, I believe you. That much I believe. But what in God's name were you doing in there, Jacob?"

"I was…"

"Uhuh, no," he said, "I don't want to hear another lie. You don't want to tell me the truth and that's fine. But I'm sick and tired of all the lies. It's as if the only person that will be honest with me is Isaac. He's worried about you too. We all are. And it's great that you have Dixie to go to, sure. She seems like a great chick."

"She's awful!" Eat'em barked at his feet.

"But when it comes down to it," Val fought back a lump in his throat. "I want you to be able to trust me, Jake. That's all. I've always got your back and I just want to know you're safe. I want to be a good uncle, sure. But more than that, I want to be a good friend. I'm worried about you."

He pushed his plate to the side and we sat in silence for an agonizing minute.

When I could take no more, I said, "May I talk now?"

"Go ahead."

"I appreciate what you've said," I stood, "but I don't have the luxury to tell anyone the truth. Even you."

Chapter 23

"Jacob is a murderer and a liar!" Bellecroix built up a bit of rage during the lawyer transition.

The transitions come off as chaotic scene changes in Broadway dress rehearsals. The witness sits idly by, twiddling his or her thumbs while the lawyers organize notes, straighten their suits, and make sure their hairpieces are nice and neat. Mike's a hundred times worse than Gomes. Where Gomes might straighten his tie, Mike presses the knot so it fits perfectly within the recession of his collar, every wrinkle smoothed over, his jewel embedded bald eagle shaped tie clip tugging his argyle tie so tight that if he bent over it would decapitate him before the courtroom. Where Gomes brushes his shoulders before approaching the stand, Mike uses a lint roller. Where Gomes goes through the minimal effort to make sure his shirt tucks in the front, Mike tightens his leg garters so his twenty-dollar buttoned-down baby blue GAP shirt looks like he ironed it to his rotund little body.

After glancing at his teeth for debris left over from whatever Hot Pocket he ate for lunch, Mike stands as boldly as a cherub in front of the stand, hands in pockets, and simply asks Lieutenant Bellecroix what he thinks of me. To which the officer replies I'm a murdering liar.

"Let's stick with the murdering part for now," Big Mike jiggles a set of keys as he walks. He calls this "putting it in drive" as it rushes the witness with a false sense of anxiety. Mike names many of his odd behaviors, making them seem like he pulled them straight from his law school textbooks. "My client isn't being charged for his honesty or lack thereof."

"The honesty of a suspect can make or break a case."

"Undoubtedly," Mike says, "and there are many reasons people lie. Especially to a police officer such as yourself. It's also important to understand that lying is not necessarily a measurement of guilt, is it not?"

"Yes…"

"Good," Mike says. "We're on the same page. Now then, shall we talk about murder?"

Bellecroix shifts uneasily and bites at a hangnail.

"Do you know how the state defines murder, Lieutenant?"

"Of course," Bellecroix says, his cuticle still pressed firmly to his lips. "Unlawful premeditated killing."

"It's the unlawful killing of another human being with malice aforethought, yes." Mike turns his attention to the jury, taking his hands from his pockets as he does so. This is "bringing it back to neutral" as he puts it. It's unsubtle and difficult to tell whether it's affective. "The emphasis here, Lieutenant Bellecroix, is on the words *malice aforethought*. We have different words for other reasons for killing. Words like Manslaughter. Homicide. Self defense. Each of these comes with varying degrees of punishment, ranging from time in prison to community service, license revocation, and no punishment at all. Do you know what the punishment for killing with malice aforethought is, lieutenant?"

"I do."

"What is it?"

"In most cases," Bellecroix says, "it's life in prison."

"But what is it in this state, lieutenant?" Mike jingles his keys. "It's the death penalty, ain't it?"

"Capital punishment," Bellecroix says, "sometimes, yes."

Mike tugs on the underside of his jaw, pulling his round face taut. "Capital punishment. That's a pretty heavy punishment for a pretty heavy accusation. You're essentially stating that without a shadow of doubt my client not only killed, but he did so with intent. He not only killed, but he did so after deliberation, planning, and thoughtful execution."

"Yes."

"But that's not in accordance with my client's confession."

"Your client," Bellecroix reminds us, "is a liar."

"There you go again," Mike says, "It seems to me that we have to base our accusations off this presupposition that whatever Jacob says is a lie or else this case falls apart at the seams. Is that right?"

"No," Bellecroix says through clinched teeth. "We know Jacob is a liar…"

"We know…" Mike interrupts. He matches the officer's intensity, both men almost snarling at one another. "…Jacob has lied. Who hasn't lied? And in his unique situation, who wouldn't lie? What we don't know is if Jacob premeditatedly and unremorsefully killed anyone. And you've supplied us with no such evidence that he has."

"Phone records," Bellecroix says.

"What about them?"

"We have records of Mr. Brook searching for home addresses, places of work, days… hours before killing his victims," Bellecroix says. "These are people with no prior correspondence with him, and yet he sought them out, tracked them down, and murdered them in cold blood."

"And what of the case of Louise Parsons?" Mike asks.

Bellecroix refrains from hitting the partition before him. His knuckles whiten with pent-up anger. "That wasn't Jacob," he says, "It was two drugged out cultists. It was all over the news. We've gone over this. The man's lies go beyond what he's done. He lies about the things he hasn't. He's nothing short of imaginative and his fight with Mr. Parsons is nothing short of an imaginative flight of fancy."

"His description of the house was fairly spot on."

"As anyone's would be who'd watched the news."

"And the handprints?" Mike says, "Jacob claims they were…"

"They weren't," Bellecroix says.

"Please do not interrupt me, lieutenant," Mike says calmly. He finally stops rattling his pocket. "Do you have the handprints on record?"

Bellecroix clicks his teeth and looks from me to Mike and back. "Mr. Brook had nothing to do – *nothing* to do with the Parsons case. Of the blood we found on Jacob's clothing? It was more likely that of another victim. Mr. Parsons was found days after we brought Jacob in the first time and every indication showed he had only died within hours of first responders. That doesn't make Brook innocent. That just means he had nothing to do with that one incident. What we can tie him to… we know he was assaulted at a convenience store. We have video of him entering and having an argument with the clerk. We know the clerk ran from Jacob after the confrontation."

"After he assaulted him," Mike says.

"Surveillance shows the night clerk, Trevor Schrekengost, running from Mr. Brook in terror," Bellecroix says.

"How do you know he was in terror?" Mike asks.

The lieutenant ignores him, "It then shows Mr. Brook return to the store. He goes through the waste basket and several drawers before collecting and pocketing Trevor's clock card. His intention wasn't to steal. It was to kill."

"Or maybe it was to find out who the guy was that just

shoved him across the store instead of allowing him to make a purchase?" Mike adds. "We watched the video. We watched it over and over. It's heavily scrambled at parts. Tears across as if recorded on old film instead of the digital camera that was actually used. Why do you think that is?"

"I don't know."

"It's weird, though, isn't it?" Big Mike asks more to the jury than to the stand, "The footage scrambled in front of Jacob as he grabs some medicine. Again near the front of the store as Jacob searches for the identity of his attacker. If I was a betting man, I would say it looked altered, wouldn't you say?"

Eat'em. The little demon sprawls out on the table in front of me. I see Eat'em in the convenience store footage, but all they see is grain. Mike refuses to use the demon as a part of the case, whether he believes me or not.

"It wasn't altered," Bellecroix says. "There's nothing in that footage that anyone would have reason to alter. The confrontation is still in plain view. We see Patrick Brook enter, call police, and upon discovering his nephew, he puts money on the counter to pay for gas and Pepto-Bismol. And again, we have both family members lying to police and not even hours later, according to phone records, we have Jacob Caleb Brook searching for the address of his next victim."

Chapter 24

I checked the address one last time. Trevor lived in an apartment near Arlington Memorial Park. The complex faced the enormous plot of overgrown lawn and beautifully crafted statues, but unlike the park, it had a certain radiant glow, beckoning all to live across from the masterpiece shrouded in darkness.

I sat on a bench in front of a tribute to the fallen soldier. A table set for one had a placard on it that read POW-MIA. A chair, leaned forward on two legs, rested at the end of a delicious looking meal; Eat'em discovered it to be a wax doppelganger rather than the small Thanksgiving feast it appeared to be.

Closer to the center of the park stood a larger than life bronze sculpture of Jesus of Nazarene on a stone cross. The mound of his final resting place lie surrounded by smaller sculptures depicting each stage of his crucifixion.

Normally these statues would be brightened at night with carefully angled spotlights connected to gas-powered generators. Even at two in the morning the park shone like a football field, and the lawn was cared for pristinely. Tonight it hid under a sky so bleak that not even the small sliver of moon cast enough light to create a shadow. We climbed a small gate to get in; it was marked with a sign with an apology over the government shutdown and a promise to open again when the situation cleared.

Aside from the closed off artistry, the park contained a disc golf course and was home to an incredible duck pond surrounded in a thicket of evergreens. Without daily care of the grove and the running fountain circulating the water, the east end of the park was left feeling tepid; no longer the lively environment I ran around when Val and I first moved to Texas.

"Are you ready to see what's in there?" I asked to myself more so than I asked Eat'em.

"It can't be worse than here, yes."

"Always the house demon," I said.

"Ugh…" he agreed, sticking out his tongue. "Nature."

We stalked across the street and walked the apartment grounds, searching each building for the address I found for the fence-running night clerk. I didn't know if he'd return here, nor did I know what I'd do once we found him. Still, I knew I had to. Whatever ailment inflicted Louise also inflicted Trevor and I needed to find out what it was. Whether he'd sit down and have a chat with me seemed highly unlikely. And I somewhat doubted I could force information out of him. I'd been lucky when I paid Parsons a visit — as I drew ever nearer to the clerk's home, I hoped I could manifest that luck again.

Beyond the external presentation of the complex, the inner upkeep didn't have the same welcoming glow. Pavement was riddled in cracks, window screens were torn up or missing, graffiti covered several walls, and an overflowed dumpster was surrounded by discarded furniture, including a three-legged computer desk and a filthy dogtooth fabric couch with a split frame and half-ejected foldout bed.

The sour smell of diapers followed us as Eat'em and I found Trevor's building adjacent to the spilled-over garbage.

His apartment was on the second floor with two stairwells leading up and two entrances getting in. The front entry wasn't much different than most other apartments I'd seen in the area. At the top of the stairs, a narrow walkway broke off into two directions, a room on the left and another on the right. An open hallway split the two lower rooms, allowing anyone to cut through the building to get to the backside without going around. Another set of stairs climbed up to the rear door, which opened up to the kitchen. These stairs spiraled and provided less maneuverability than the front. Based on the dipping wood patio, the back of the building was the last part not to receive the modern upgrades that the rest of the complex enjoyed. Much like the entire development, the further back you lifted the veil, the more the beauty gave way to disrepair.

I circled the building a couple times, considering my approach.

The man who lived behind those doors could run a mile in just over three minutes. He could outrun the most surefooted Olympian while sprinting across a tightrope.

Me?

I could catch a baseball.

We weren't exactly evenly matched. Even still, I encroached on his territory. Not confident, but not as scared as I should be. For – for whatever reason – he feared me. As it was him that ran from me. Not screaming, but panicked. Not as one might run from a wild beast, but as one might run from a confrontation that surely had no desirable outcome.

But what outcome that might be, I had no idea. I wasn't even positive I wanted to find out. I just knew whatever I found in Trevor's apartment would make the dark chill that crept up my spine seem like a blissful warmth by comparison.

I climbed the spiral staircase after deciding the safest approach would be the one less visible from the decaying parking lot. Closing in at three in the morning, I figured there wouldn't be anyone in or out for a couple hours, but precaution was in my best interest. I noticed a pair of headlights rolling in not minutes after I arrived at the complex. Probably a late night bartender returning from a busy night of appeasing Arlington's drunken masses. The last thing I needed was someone calling the police to report a prowler.

The early morning provided no light for the splintered deck, enveloped in uncertain darkness.

My spiky companion clung to my waist, uncharacteristically quiet as I skulked one creaking footstep at a time, until I reached the glass backdoor with blinds drawn tight.

I've always had extraordinary night vision. When I was a child, my mother reprimanded me every time she found me drawing in my room in what she referred to as complete darkness. I told her it helped me focus only on the page, which it did. And – full disclosure – I never liked carrots.

A small window peered in over a small sink in a kitchenette kept perfectly clean. I looked for signs of movement. The apartment, what I could see of it, appeared organized. Rustic dining chairs and an ornate chandelier gave it the impression of a country log cabin. And from the heavy fragrance that tickled my nostrils, the occupant was particularly obsessive with bleaches and detergents and other cleaning products without the added scent of sunflowers or lilies or ivory springs.

Frustration swelled in my throat and I attempted to swallow it back. What if Trevor moved? If that were the case, I might never find him. The tidiness. The scent. The furniture. From the looks of things, I was looking into a model home.

I let out a long sigh, both from disappointment and relief.

Then. As I turned to take the long walk back home. A shape on the floor of the living room caught my eye. It was bent and twisted in an unnatural position. Bent this way and that as if wrung out and tossed to the side.

It was the body of a young man. And it was clear from his tortured posture...

He was dead.

Chapter 25

The jail has a visitor center for those of us who can't post bail and haven't been convicted yet. It's a combination of a nuthouse lobby and the play area at most dental offices. The biggest difference is the number of security guards hovering around the exit, with its mocking neon sign and condescending poster that states "prisoners not permitted past this point."

A vibrantly colored play set with twisting plastic tubes like a tiny roller coaster for large beads sits on a jigsaw puzzle play mat on one side of the room. A guard armed with a pistol and pepper spray stands to the side near an empty table with miniature chairs designed to accommodate visiting children.

One could mistake this room for a fortified daycare.

I'm the only one without a gun. All the protection is for me, of course. More accurately, it's for whoever is behind a set of electronically locked doors. They are receiving a brief just to see me. As if I could spring a trap capable of disarming half a dozen police officers with nothing but my bare hands.

Though I'm fortunate enough to be out of cuffs in this room, it's still disconcerting to see chains locking every piece of furniture to the floor. Maybe it's a precaution; however, from my short stint here, I wouldn't put it past someone being unable to resist using anything in sight as a possible weapon.

I rest my head on my hands and watch Eat'em slide beads back and forth along the twisting tracks of the child's toy. Each time he reaches the end he triumphantly declares himself the winner and starts on a new set of beads.

The armed guard looks like he'll doze off at any minute. He pays neither Eat'em nor the self-propelled beads any attention.

My mind drifts along a sea of contemplation as Eat'em plays with the winding rods and various spinning blocks. What if my demon is from an alien planet? Maybe his planet and ours take up the same physical space. They collided eons ago, but instead of one destroying the other, they passed through one another. I think Eat'em and I must be stuck between these two worlds, seeing into both, but each of us can only affect one or the other. We're the last remnants tying the two realms together.

"Jacob," a familiar voice breaks me from my daydream. "How are you?"

Professor Kempter squeezes between a couple officers and

floats her way toward me. She's got the grace of any runway model and dresses the part. Her lavender skirt hugs her full-figured hips in such a way that advertises her appearance as something more than a man might be able to handle. There's elegance in her step, even as her weight shifts her side-to-side, and it all brings her a certain intimidating – might I say – sex appeal.

"Hanging in," I say. "You got a haircut."

"You noticed."

"You look great."

She takes the seat in front of me and scoots as far from the table as the chain will let her.

"You always look great," I say.

"Well," her cheeks struggle through a half-smile. "You look horrible."

"It's the outfit," I say. "But I thought you liked orange."

"It clashes with your eyes."

I laugh. "You're full of shit."

"You're modest."

"And you," I say.

"Have no reason to be." She bats her eyelashes.

Our relationship was never so flirtatious before I found myself locked up. It's not that bars made her more attractive. Only a fool wouldn't be captivated by Professor Kempter (She calls it *The Three B's: Beautiful, Beneficent, Buxom*). It's more that nothing quite takes your guard down so much as being surrounded by actual guards.

Her plum cheeks pale as her mood sombers. She nibbles on

her lower lip and huffs before saying, "I'm doing everything I can."

"I know," I say.

"I'm doing everything I can next to bringing in a mouse."

"I know."

"Showing them," she covers her mouth with her hand. "Showing them what happens."

"You don't need to do that."

"I could," she says. "I could break one of their legs. Let them see it heal for themselves. I could show them violent behavior when the chain is broken. I could show them just how connected they are... the common conscience. Moving together like synchronized swimmers..."

"You can't." We've had this conversation before. Pain swells in my chest each time. It's like the air goes bad and I can't fully exhale.

I look to Eat'em and his beads for comfort. He smiles back at me, announcing loudly, "Won again!" I flash him a quick grin, letting him know I see him.

"You can't, professor," I say.

"Jodi."

"Jodi," I repeat. I shake my head and released the words with the painful breath of air. "They took everything."

"I know."

"You have nothing to give the mice."

"I know."

"Nobody is going to let me go collect a sample for you," I

say.

"I know," she nibbles at her lip again. "But if you could somehow tell me. Tell me where I can find him. Maybe you wouldn't have to."

The thought is preposterous and my answer comes without consideration.

I shake my head and say, "No."

Chapter 26

My first instinct upon seeing the dead body was to dial the police. I punched 911 into my phone and stared at the glowing screen. But no matter how much I wanted to press the call button, I couldn't. I couldn't risk being questioned.

Even if I called anonymously, part of me feared my phone could be traced. And if it couldn't, I would still surely be questioned about it once the apartment was linked to the deserted gas station. I needed to avoid being caught up in too many coincidences. Until I knew what was going on, until I could prove what was going on, until others knew what was going on, I couldn't tie myself to it.

Something told me I was more than a mere curiosity to law enforcement. I was a suspect. And I couldn't afford to be one.

I turned off my phone and tried the doors. Of course they

were locked. Probably deadbolted. The only other way I could see in was to climb through the kitchen window. Breaking the glass was hardly an option, not with the potential of a light-sleeping neighbor, so I worked to jiggle it free of the small hook that kept it shut tight.

After a few tries it worked. The window slid freely and I pushed it to the top of its track and climbed in after my demon, who was all too eager to explore the contents of the dozen or so cupboards.

I snuck through the dark, careful not to touch anything. Fortunately, my short search confirmed the apartment was vacant, other than the body in the living room. I flipped the lights and squatted beside him.

The ambiance conflicted with the dead man. Not just that it was too pristine to house something as morose as a corpse, but he felt misplaced. It wasn't the kind of home you would expect a man such as him to live or even visit. Nor was it decorated in a way that I figured a convenience store clerk might set up his home. It was the home of obsessive compulsion. Everything had its place, organized for efficiency more than comfort. And without a single sign of struggle this man, who was not Trevor Schrekengost, lay displayed across the floor of the immaculate home – his arms and legs crooked as if he collapsed without a hint of warning.

"It can't be?" Eat'em shrieked from the kitchen. "The evil hag has a sister!"

I looked up in time to witness a bottle of Mrs. Butterworth maple syrup soar from the kitchen, smacking into a wall before plopping onto the carpet. Eat'em leapt behind it, wielding a steak knife like the sword of Achilles in defense of Troy.

"You pursue me for the last time, Hell Spawn!" Eat'em shouted. "Now you face the same fate as your sister, Jemima, yes. What say you?"

He plodded toward Butterworth and lifted her from the carpet with his tail so they stood eye-to-eye. The thin spikes along his brow stood on end as his face drew into a grimace.

"Nothing, yes," he said. "Your silence will win no favors from me. Remember this day, Butterworth. For it is your last."

With that Eat'em struck the syrup bottle with enough force to send it toppling to the floor. He pounced on it and their battle commenced – the demon's only upper hand was the bottle's inability to fight back.

"Damn you, Butterworth!"

I turned my attention back to the body before me. He was around my age. Eighteen. Nineteen at most. Skinny with curly brown hair. His eyes were brown and stared at nothing. His face was neither frozen in fright nor gripped in surprise. Rather he looked trapped in a scene of serenity like a Buddhist Monk who'd spent a lifetime in meditation.

A sudden impulse came over me to feel his neck for a pulse, like I'd seen hundreds of times by made-for-television cops. The gesture proved pointless. The man was dead.

Still, his chest gave the impression of a gentle rise and fall. I knew my mind only played tricks on me. I experienced the same phenomenon at my parents' vigil. If I could only shake them, they'd awaken. The mind often sees what it expects to see. Sometimes what it wants to see. But it rarely sees what is actually there. It must have been why the world was so closed off to seeing my crimson demon in his plight to rid the earth of the evil that was the maple syrup sisters. And it was why, no matter how I tried, I couldn't see the dead man as an empty vessel incapable of breathing.

Yet, with no time to react, I too found myself suddenly breathless. The realization I locked myself in an inescapable deathtrap only hit me as I heard the unmistakable sound of a key sliding into the outer lock of the apartment's front door.

"You listen here, Butterworth. If I hear a single peep out of you... oooo... I'm going to destroy you to the likes which have never been seen."

Eat'em shushed the bottle of syrup from a shelf above me. I hid amongst coats, starched and pressed, in a small linen closet that faced Trevor's front door. I tried to keep my nerves from rattling me. Claustrophobia didn't have the same affect on me as massive crowds, but I feared making the slightest movement, that the pitch-blackness would amplify any miniscule noise, changing it into a riotous clatter.

The closet provided no light, nor did it allow for any visual of the room beyond. I was left to nothing but my hearing – a sense not as finely tuned as my eyesight, as I'd spent most of my life trying to ignore it.

I listened to the apartment's new arrival. Footsteps

clamored one way and another. They were neither angry nor pacing. Nor did it sound like a search for whoever left the kitchen window open. This was the clomping around of busy feet. Whoever it was, he was cleaning.

He moved back and forth through the small apartment. Spraying. Scrubbing. Dusting. Vacuuming. Until everything fit in whatever idealistic chaotic harmony he imagined. Cupboards opened. Closed. Then the footsteps stopped in front of the closet. The handle turned. The door opened. And once again I stood before the gas station clerk.

Chapter 27

Trevor stood between six-foot-four and six-five. He maintained the five o'clock shadow of a grizzled vet and a shaggy mess of dark brown hair. He looked in tip-top shape and could have passed for any of the runners I once competed with. Except he could run on fences and probably had no intentions of another foot race.

For the briefest moment his expression held no emotion. It was the face of a sleepwalker, his consciousness elsewhere. When his cognizance returned his jaw flapped open in the same dumfounded expression I must have had on my own face.

He expected a row of garments equally spaced along the rod to the accuracy of a measuring stick. Instead he found an equally flabbergasted Jacob Brook. And I hadn't put enough thought into my plan of attack to do anything more than land a pitiful karate chop on one of his too-broad-to-care shoulders. It was meant for his face, but he ended up being a foot taller than I remembered him when he lurched over the register.

Unlike any number of Russians or treacherous Brits unfortunate enough to be on the other end of a strike from the MI6 operative James Bond, Trevor didn't collapse into the cataleptic ball of dreamland I hoped he would. To be honest, he didn't fall, stumble, or even react in any manner that would be considered worthy of mention. He stood, statuesque, bewildered and unamused.

"I really like what you've done with the place," I said. I made an attempt for the door, but stopped under the pressure of a grip too strong for the hand that made it.

He pulled me close and grabbed my face with both hands. His fingers bore into my cheeks as if he were a blind man assessing my attractiveness, except his touch was more menacing. Violent. He peeled my eyelids down with his thumbs as he wrenched my head ever closer to his, until the tips of our noses almost touched.

"What..." he said. "Do. You. See?"

"I don't understand," I tried to push away, but he held firm. Eat'em remained still on the closet shelf, reassuring the syrup bottle that it would be okay. It will all be over soon.

"Don't play coy with me, Jacob," Trevor yelled, prying my eyes wider, staring into them with empty vortexes. "This is a coincidence? You're just a home invader, huh? You happened to choose my homes?"

"Your homes?" He said my name. He knew my name.

"My homes," he said. "Mine!"

"I don't know…"

He squeezed my skull. A burning sensation scorched my temples. It felt like my head might crush under his firm grasp. The sensation stayed even as he let up. He said, "This is not by chance. You see something. These. Eyes. See something. What is it? How is it that you know when nobody else knows?"

"Know what?" I screeched as his fingers dug into my scalp. "I don't know anything. I swear I don't know anything."

Trevor's mouth fell open and he snapped at my neck. I thrust my arms between his and grabbed his chin, forcing his face away as best I could. With him pulling my face closer and me pushing his away, for a second I felt like I'd fallen victim to the world's least comfortable slow dance.

"I swear," I wailed. "I swear I don't."

He relented, but kept hold of my cheeks. "Then why are you afraid? If you are so oblivious, why is it that I am able to taste your fear?"

"Oh, I don't know," I said, "maybe it has to do with the dead man on your floor?"

"Ha," never had there been a more humorless laugh.

Trevor dragged me into the living room and shoved me to the floor in front of the dead man.

"What do you see?"

I saw my mother. The haunting image of her death still haunted me. Her exuberance robbed from her.

"Nothing," I said. "A dead man?"

"Wrong!" Trevor shouted. "He is not dead..."

"He's not dead."

"No," he said, "he lives in me."

The dead man blinked. Had I blinked, I might have missed it. But I didn't. His porcelain like eyes rolled back so far they looked like the eyes of a man blinded with cataracts. When they oriented to their proper position, they no longer appeared lifeless. Color returned to his nose and cheeks. His cracked lips parted, forming a bear-trap smile.

Both men spoke together, "I live in him."

I fumbled in my pocket, gripping the handle of the steak knife I'd retrieved from the demon cowering in the closet with his frienemy, Mrs. Butterworth. All of my fear rose into my throat and I knew I would never breathe again until they couldn't. I had to strike.

"What do you see now?" They asked at the same time. "Tell me, Jacob, do you see death? Or life?"

Their question answered with a knock at the door.

Nothing could have been more serendipitous than the three loud thuds. *BANG! BANG! BANG!*

Trevor and his back-from-the-dead roommate looked up at the same time. They spoke in unison, "Who did you bring...?"

With a sideways thrust that would bring tears to the eyes of the most experienced swordsman, I shoved the serrated blade into Trevor's chest plate until bone obstructed hilt.

I threw the other man off me and ran to the closet.

"Eat'em," I said, "let's get a move on."

"You're alive?" Eat'em said. "Terribly unexpected, yes. Mrs. B., I guess I owe you ten dollars."

"You were betting on me?"

"Against you."

"With a syrup bottle?"

"Yes," Eat'em said, "And I'm going to need to borrow some money. Do you have ten bucks?"

"No, what?" I said, "Never mind that, we need to go."

Bang! Bang! Bang!

I turned back to the living room, ready to brace myself in case the dead man had found his footing. He convulsed on the floor, writhing, bleeding from his nose and eyes, bile pouring out his lips.

"Okay, Eat'em, say goodbye to your lady friend," I said. "Come on, buddy. With haste."

"She's not my lady friend," Eat'em said. "I'll have you know, Mrs. Butterworth has agreed to marry me. She will now be Mrs. Butter'em."

"Fantastic," I said, "bring her with you. We'll have a wedding. Just get down and let's go."

Bang!

"Okay," Eat'em said. "You hold her." I grabbed his newlywed spouse and Eat'em climbed onto my shoulder.

"Jacob!" It came from outside. It was Val. "I know you're in there. Open the door."

"Shit," I said.

"Mrs. Butter'em does not approve of such language," Eat'em said.

"Screw Mrs. Butter'em."

"Hey!"

"We've got a bigger problem."

All we needed to do was go out the backdoor. We could go home and tell Val he must have followed someone else. Maybe that would work. Why in the world would he follow me anyway? Now, I had to worry about him putting himself in danger. I had to worry about bloodletting Trevor all over the apartment too. Perhaps I should burn it down. Pretend like it'd never happened. I mean, all I really had to do was get out, lure Val away, convince him something happened that didn't actually happen, and somehow cover up yet another crime scene from APD.

But there was one giant roadblock preventing our salvation.

The risen-dead roommate rose in front of the doorway. Blood poured from his face and his eyes turned a spidery red from rage and madness. He lurched and let out a guttural scream. Then he came toward us.

Chapter 28

His face wet with gore, his eyes filled with hate, his hands outstretched before him like a starving kid watching a donut roll down a hill, the crazed man lumbered toward me with a quickness only thwarted by the coordination of the dead. The terrifying howl that roared from his gaping mouth had the same shrill tenor of a wolf ringing the dinner bell. From the looks of things, I was the intended course.

Val continued to bang on the door as I prepared for the incoming assault.

"Double or nothing, Mrs. Butter'em," Eat'em said, "yes?"

I don't know if I did it because I was angry at the demon or if I couldn't think of anything else to do, but I wound up and threw the bottle of syrup with the intensity of the best pitchers in the business. My accuracy at the mound kept me from throwing fastballs in the game, but at ten feet I hit my target with enough force to send him toppling over backward. Meanwhile, Mrs. Butterworth, or Butter'em, exploded in a cascading fountain of maple syrup. The mournful cry from Eat'em, if audible to anyone but myself, would have been heard from all the world.

"What have you done?" he bounded to the floor. "My love! My sweet, sweet love!"

"No," I said, "Not now buddy, we need to get out of here."

Eat'em crawled on his knees, he turned from his downed darling and lifted his hands dramatically above his head. Golden brown topping ran down his tiny arms and dripped from his elbows.

"What have I done, Jacob?" he said. "What have I done to deserve this?"

The drooling maniac began to climb back to his feet and Val slammed into the door hard enough I heard the frame buckle and crack.

"We were going to go to Maui," Eat'em cried. "France. Guam. The Cayman Islands!"

As the feral curly haired freak clambered to his hands and knees, I kicked him hard across the jaw, turning him once again to his back. He screeched, twisted, and struggled to find the proper way to defeat gravity.

"We had so many plans," Eat'em continued. "You ruined everything."

"Jacob!" Val yelled as he kicked the door, further cracking

the frame. "Open the damned door! I know you're in there. Open the door." He kicked again. "I heard screaming, man. Do I need to call the police?"

"NO!" I yelled. Damn it! No hiding it now. I couldn't pretend it wasn't me that answered. Damn it. Damn it. But maybe I could still steer him away. Why'd he have to follow me?

I kicked the freak again. This time he grabbed my leg. As I tried to pull free, I stumbled back and tripped over Trevor's limp body, the steak knife still protruding from his chest. I grabbed the handle and attempted to yank it free, but couldn't dislodge it before the snarling freak was on top of me.

"Then open the door, Orphan," Val said.

Hands grappled for my wrists, yet I managed to shake free of his grip before his face came barreling down toward my throat. I grabbed his face, shoving both thumbs hard into his eyes. He growled fiercely as he tried to bite his way past my grip. Blood, drool, bile and upchuck fell from his lips and onto my face. I turned my head and tried to block out the smell of copper, acid, and what I'm pretty sure was a tuna melt.

"I can't!" I screamed at Val as I wrestled the snapping six-foot pile of vomit. "I'm predisposed!"

"With what?" Val said through the door. "What is it? What's going on in there?"

"Only that he murdered the love of my life," Eat'em wailed.

"Is it drugs?" Val asked.

"No," I said. The freak's teeth clicked maniacally above my

mouth. I attempted to force him to his side, but he proved too strong. And blindness didn't seem like too big a deal to him. "Val..." Sticky, wet, bloody puke rolled down my cheek and onto the back of my neck, sopping into my hair. My arms began to shake. "...I'm being attacked!"

"Hold on!" Val yelled. His foot slammed against the door. Again. Again. The frame cracked and the wood around the knob began to splinter.

Part of me wanted to send him away. But the desperate part of me. The part of me that was tired of being alone with a Jolt-addicted demon and a secret not even I understood – that part of me – knew I needed Val. Whether he believed me didn't matter. If he didn't break open that door in the next few seconds... I was certain... I was going to die.

"Val," I yelled. I covered the freak's mouth with the palm of one hand and shoved a couple fingers into his nostrils to keep my palm from sliding on the liquid pouring from his face. I felt his teeth drag across the heel of my thumb. "Hurry, Val."

"Have you. Ever. Kicked open. A door?" The door cracked between each word. The deadbolt shook loose with each flurry of kicks from the other side.

"The back window is open!"

"I know, dumbass," Val said. "I saw you climb through it."

I pushed a knee beneath my attacker's chest to make more space. It wasn't much. But it was enough to quickly change my grip from his mangled eye to his throat. He gargled, but continued to snap ferociously, as if no amount of physical pain would get him to withdraw.

"Use it!" I yelled.

Eat'em wallowed, "Mrs. Butter'em!!!"

Val said, "I got it!"

The door gave in to his last kick. Wood particles and bits of metal flew across the room.

Val didn't hesitate. He screamed, "Get off my nephew, bitch!" and tackled the freak from the side. The two of them rolled into the antique dining set, smearing blood, syrup, and who knows what throughout the carpet as they did. Val threw a couple solid punches and the thing snapped aimlessly at the air.

I stood, planted a foot on Trevor's abdomen and ripped the knife from his chest. A spout of blood shot from the open wound, and I paused long enough to make sure he wasn't going to magically revive and even the playing field.

Val sat on Monster Ray Charles, pinning his arms beneath each knee. Every time the beast clicked its teeth together, Val answered it with a vicious right hook to the side of its skull; yet, surprisingly, it kept biting and hissing.

"Move, V." I said, nudging Val to the side.

He punched the freak one last time and when he moved to the side I plunged the knife into its neck and ripped it free. I stabbed it again and again, not caring where the knife struck, over and over, without remorse, without feeling, without consideration... another stab and another. Until it no longer moved and until I no longer could lift my arm.

Val grabbed my hand on my last downswing. There was no longer a blade connected to the handle.

Crimson covered everything. My hands. My clothes. My uncle. Everything was red with blood. Streaks of gore so vivid I could count the cells swarming with in it.

I collapsed into Val's arms and began to sob.

His narrow fingers ran through my hair as he stroked my head. "Orphan," he said, "It's going to be alright."

Chapter 29

"So it's the apocalypse?" Val said. "Gee, and all this time I just thought maybe you had a drug habit. This is much better."

We finished loading the second corpse into the hollowed out dumpster couch and shoved the cushions on top of them to conceal their presence. It was my idea to get the foldout bed from outside and use it to conceal the two bodies, but that was the last good idea I had. Just getting it up there, detaching the frame, and getting Trevor and his roommate inside was exhausting enough to take the wind out of us.

We plopped down on either side of the sofa and soaked in the view of our macabre crime scene. Blood and pancake syrup soaked every nook and cranny of the small apartment.

Even the bathroom looked pulled from Hitchcock's Psycho,

as we took advantage of our hosts' hospitality, cleaning ourselves up, and borrowing some of their clothes. Our new outfits hung a bit loose, but came emblazoned with a couple nifty sayings. Mine read "Honey Badger don't care!" His: "I stole this shirt from a dead man (Why he had this shirt, I have no idea)."

We spent a good deal of time looking over our wardrobe options, and figured these were the most suitable of the bunch. Appropriate for the occasion.

"I think I'm sitting on someone's face," Val said.

"Most likely."

"Now what?" He asked.

I shook my head. "No idea."

"Well you better come up with an idea, Killer-Jake. You got us into this mess, you damned well better start thinking about how to get us out."

After a minute of silence, I finally let out a long exasperated breath and hopelessly said, "I don't know."

"Great," Val said. "I find out my little nephew is a murderer and he doesn't know squat about getting away with it."

"I'm not a murderer," I said.

"This is what," he said, "three, right? That's what you told me? Three? Maybe you're right... you're not a murderer. That's enough to make you a serial killer, ain't it?"

"I'm not a serial killer."

"What then? An assassin?"

"No!" I said, "I'm not an assassin either. I'm none of those things."

"That's right," he nodded and leaned back, staring past the ceiling. "Because they're infected, right? I gotcha. Like zombies. End of the world. Zombies are fair game."

"They're not..." I glanced over at Eat'em. He'd plucked a couple dandelions while we were retrieving the couch. He now placed them by the half empty bottle of syrup. He sniffled as he watched me from the corner of his eye. He'd undoubtedly try to get something out of this. "...I don't know what they are," I continued. "But you saw him. He wasn't right."

"Well, you did gouge his eyeballs," Val said. "He was probably pretty upset."

"You can't be serious."

"Of course I'm not serious," Val turned to me. "He was a flippin' zombie. I'm just trying to add levity to the situation is all. Shit. Jake-Nasty, we got to get moving if we're going to have this mess of yours cleaned up by sunrise."

"He wasn't a zombie," I said. "He talked, Val. Him and the other two. They knew my name."

"Fine, then they're psychic zombies," Val stood up and readjusted the cushion before turning his back to me. "Do I got blood on me? Am I still good?"

"You're fine," I said, "and they weren't psychic zombies either. They're fast, man. Can jump at least twenty feet and run on fences. Definitely not zombies."

"That thing definitely," he paused. "You going to get off

your ass and help me?"

"Yeah," I got up, "Where we going?"

"Out," he said. He grabbed one end of the couch and gestured for me to grab the other. It weighed more than it did coming in. Val went on, "That thing that I saw definitely wasn't running on fences or jumping any twenty feet. That. Jacob. Was a zombie."

"Like I told you," I said. "He wasn't like that before. I mean, he was on the floor, like he was dead, but he woke up and he talked. Then after the other went down, Trevor…"

"Because you killed him."

"Yeah," I said, pulling my end higher to grab underneath. "After that. That's when the other started seizing and that happened to him, you know?"

"Typical zombie behavior," Val said. "They die. Come back. Start trying to bite your face. He didn't bite you, did he?"

"No," I hefted my end around so Val could go through the door first.

"Oh, I gotta walk backward, huh?" he said.

"I will if you want."

"No," he said, "I don't care. You're just an asshole."

"Yeah, thanks."

Eat'em yelled, "What about Mrs. B?"

"Hold on," I said, dropping my end.

"Dick!" Val dropped his side and shook his hand. "A little warning next time would be nice, Jaker."

I grabbed the bottle of syrup, holding my arm down just long enough for Eat'em to climb up. "Sorry," I said to Val. "Can't have a funeral without all three bodies accounted for."

I grabbed her cap and resealed her as best I could before joining her with the two bodies and lifting my side.

Val grunted as we backed the sofa through the open door. "Next time you drop a futon while I'm helping you carry it – for a freaking bottle of syrup – I'm going to lose my mind."

"Note noted," I pulled the door shut behind us and followed Val toward the stairwell. "Where we taking this thing? Just back to the dumpster?"

"Great idea, Einstein," Val said. "Let's leave a couch with two rotting corpses for the garbage men to pick up tomorrow."

"Like they'll notice," Eat'em said, "it already smells like rotting corpses, yes. Blech!"

"Why not?" I asked.

"Because," Val said, "what if they fall out when they're throwing that shit in the truck, huh? Or, what if someone comes by before that and goes, *Hey, free couch!*? Could you lower your end? I've got the lower ground here."

I obliged, bending more at my knee than was comfortable, regripping as best I could. "Who's going to take a nasty, stained, reeking couch from beside a dumpster?"

"I don't know," he answered. "Why do people take pee-stained mattresses from dumpsters? It doesn't make sense. But they do. People do it all the time. Lower your end."

"Sorry," I said. "What then? Strap it to the Mustang?"

"You touch my Mustang," he said, "I swear to God... Lower your damned end, Jake. Christ! If I fall down these stairs and land under a pile of zombies, I'm not kidding, I'm going to kill you and find someone else to help me lose three bodies."

"Dude, I'm sorry," I said, "it's kind of hard to keep it that low, V. My back..."

"Your back?" he said, "I don't give a hot damn about your back. You're the idiot that made the idiot decisions and now you have to live with your idiot consequences and lower your end. I'm not kidding."

"Well, I was."

"About what?"

"Strapping the couch to your car."

"No shit," he said. "We're not leaving it by the dumpster and we're not strapping it to my car. You're a regular Columbo. Maybe you'll devise a plan through process of elimination."

"Well, what are we doing?"

We reached the bottom of the stairs and stopped for another rest. Slices of purple and orange began to paint the horizon.

"We," Val said as he once again took a seat on the cushioned skulls of the two dead men, "are going to the park. I almost fell asleep in the damned car while you were sitting out there earlier and I thought it would be the perfect place to hide your body when I was done with you."

"Seriously?" he'd been on my case as soon as I finished my

emotional breakdown. Sure, I was glad he saved the day, but I wasn't particularly happy about his new attitude toward me.

"Seriously," he said. "It's big, quiet, and empty. If we're lucky, the government shutdown will last a while. And if not, we take it to the woods, and we flip it over. We let nature run its course and pray nobody happens by and if they do maybe they'll think it's an abandoned couch and leave it alone."

"We just leave it there?"

"Yes!" Eat'em said, "But we light it on fire!"

"Yeah," Val said, "we leave it there."

We grabbed the couch again and headed toward the park, my back to the rising sun. A single early commuter drove by before we crossed the street, but they paid us no mind. I began to relax, even as my arms strained to keep the couch at Val's preferred height, my stress melted away and I felt lighter. Val was more than an uncle now. He was a friend. An ally. He was someone I could actually trust. Someone I could vent to that wasn't a foot-tall invisible imp. A burden lifted and I felt a smile pinch at the edge of my lip.

"What are we going to do about the apartment?" I asked.

We lifted the couch over the small gate into Arlington Memorial Park, climbing over one at a time.

"You're not going to worry about it," Val said.

"Well, I am," I said. "Fingerprints, DNA, hairs, whatever they find in there. It'll lead them to me. They'll eventually find this too. Maybe not tomorrow or even soon, but they'll find it. I'll be all over the place."

"Crime scenes don't happen in a vacuum, Jacob," Val reassured as we rounded the pond, dragging our feet as we heaved the couch inch by inch. "I'm sure there's enough hair and DNA and fingerprints in there to make the APD suspect half the city. You don't need to worry about it."

"No," I said. "Remember, I told you, the place was spotless."

"Right," Val said. "Neat-freak zombies. I hate those."

Eat'em said, "Me too."

"Look," Val stretched and let out a yawn, found a better grip and kept tugging me along, "we're going to dump the couch. I'll take you home. I parked around the corner and followed you most of the way on foot. Sleep in. Tomorrow you'll go to school and I'll figure something out."

"You're not going to school?" I said. "I'm not going."

"Yes," Val said, "you are. I'm not going because I have a disastrous nephew to clean after. You're going, and that's it."

I nodded a quiet agreement.

"I'd appreciate if you stop fighting psychic zombies for a few days…" he said. "Or you know, forever, would be nice. Get your grades up. Be a normal human being. We can go to a concert or something… a movie. Something not so violent."

"Boring!" Eat'em burped.

"Whatever," Val continued as we climbed into the woods, searching for a clearing to dump the couch. "I don't care what you do so long as you're going to school." He was silent for a moment but finished by saying, "I'm keeping this shirt, by the way. I plan on wearing it to your trial someday."

Chapter 30

Big Mike brushes by a group of prison guards prepared to escort me from the small lockup to the trial. He straightens each piece of his suit they touch as he squeezes through without so much as an excuse me. His chubby face lights up when he sees me, as it always does, his red cheeks burning brighter.

This is the most embarrassing part of each day. I'm in a small enclosure unfit for a rabid beast. My bunk has a small plastic coated mattress; my bookshelf has novels by Dean Koontz, Steven King, Christopher Moore, James Dashner, and several others; as well as books on the philosophies of Plato, Leibniz, and Thoreau; dangling from the ceiling are a multitude of sticky flytraps and car fresheners intended to conceal the unpleasant aroma from the squat stainless steel commode in the corner of the cell. The scent ranges from slightly tolerable to absolutely humiliating. Today it's tolerable.

"Jacob, baby," Mike says with a toothy grin, "how are they treating you, pal? Good? Good! I've got good news."

"Good news is good," I say. "And I'm fine. The hospitality is more than gracious."

"Yeah right," he peeks into my cell. "There anything you need? More books? Smelly stuff?"

"Movies!" Eat'em says. The little demon ascends the cage in a mock cirque du soleil routine, his tail whips from one bar to the next, pulling him from a lower platform to a slit in which food used to be delivered before the new expansion was complete.

Outside my micro-domicile lies a cafeteria style dining facility with proper cooks and a fully staffed kitchen, there's a gym with fitness coaches and a theater that plays films only a few months out of regular circulation. These amenities are the result of men like Mike who have a certain political power, which forces the state to throw tax payers' money at facility improvements as opposed to fattening the pockets of those who'd mistreat all the poor murderers and rapists keeping me company.

"And…" Eat'em continues, "a vending machine, yes! With rip its and RockStars!"

"The only thing this place is missing," I say, "is a sauna and an Olympic size pool."

"Can't do anything about the sauna," Mike says, "but word I hear, there's a big push for a swimming pool, so that one ain't so much a stretch. Tell you the truth, you hang out here long enough,

I'm sure I can get you that sauna too. Which brings me to why I'm in such a good mood. Did you notice?"

"Sure didn't," I say, "You're always a bundle of joy."

"Shut up," Mike says. "I got wind that this here is going to be a while. You got the media attention on you now, boy, and that's going to make ol' Gomey want to take his sweet ass time on this one. With the world watching, he's going to want to impress. He'll be coming swinging now."

"This is a good thing?"

"Hell yeah it is!" Mike snaps at the cluster of guards. "You going to let my client out or just sit there like a damned fool? Andale amigo. Jake," he turns back to me, "I told you, all we got to do is outlast this guy. Patience. The longer this takes the better for us. The district attorney will be grasping straws now to keep this thing going. And the more details he can convolute this thing with the more these guys are going to forget what matters."

"What matters?"

"The facts," Mike smiles. He wraps his big arm around my shoulders as I'm let out and handcuffed by a burly looking guard with eyes a colorless grey; silver under the flickering fluorescents. Mike says, "The law don't care if you're motivated by this or that, heroism or psychopathic episodes. Don't care. But they don't know that. The longer we keep this ball rolling the more time we have to convince them we need you."

Eat'em rides behind my head, a foot on each shoulder. He grabs my hair and leans back, singing as we walk the row of cells filled with higher morale than any prison in the country.

"We're going to take every tragedy from now until that final verdict and we're going to tie them into this infection of yours," Mike says.

"I wish we wouldn't."

"Oh, but we will, Jacob. From now until 'not guilty.'"

The courtroom is my red carpet. Outside this place I'm plain as any person could be. I never wore a suit or a tie or attended a poetry reading in a cardigan with a scarf or ascot, nor have I ever been the life of the party, the center of attention, the guy that everyone wants to be around. Valentine carries that role among the Brook boys, and I take my place in the corner of the room, where nobody pays any mind. Here, I'm a vaudeville act. I'm Velma Kelly of the musical Chicago. I'm a sensationalized killer on display for gawkers and admirers.

Nobody cared about this case months ago, but something changed. Perhaps the killer of the year already faced their sentence. Maybe whatever high profile trial that normally draws the public eye is in the wings or the verdict hit and the people are now bored, need something new and exciting, and somehow I'm it. I am the corrupt ball of light the world cheers and jeers. The newest flavor for the ravenous palate of public scorn.

Mike guides me through an entourage of flashing cameras and steely reporters hidden beneath a smorgasbord of cosmetics to make them standout on a camera. They scream questions at me and accusations. Anything to get my attention. Mike warned me it would be chaos. Chaos is organized compared to this.

Eat'em poses and waves as we press through the crowd. One statement halts my step: *They say you're the devil!*

"Let's go," Mike says, pushing my back with one hand as he waves off the reporters with the other. I'm led, unchained, toward the same comfy front row seat to the play that will decide my future. Mike sits beside me.

"Who says I'm the devil?" I ask. It's a stupid question, but the accusation brings an icy chill to my veins. Sure, for months I've known the world thinks of me as a criminal, but now the frenzy of vindictive citizens set on sacrificing me to alleviate their disdainful hearts – it casts a shadow on my life I don't know how to handle. Even if word spread that I told nothing but the truth, I would still be considered the cause. And with my only true witness being an aloof demon, how am I to react to being the devil? Had my sidekick been a seraph would my circumstances be any different?

Mike scratches his nose as he leans in and whispers in my ear. "Things have gotten a little weird since more folks are starting to watch this thing. People are seeing little glitches in the footage when the camera's on you. Say it looks like film blur, something stupid, it's asinine. Some think it moves around… conspiracy theory shit. It's nothing. But people want to see it like it's a big deal or something."

"I told you…"

"Shh, shhh, sh," Mike says. "Enough of that nonsense. All you have to worry about is that it isn't part of this case. The district attorney can't use it and even if he could, he wouldn't. He'd look like a damned fool, like he was trying to convince us of aliens."

"But what if…"

"We're not bringing your imaginary friend into this case, Jacob," Mike's forehead creases with a raised brow. And I wonder, what *if* Eat'em had been an angel? Mike says, "Let them conspire. Drop the demon. The case will win or lose with this virus of yours. If we can make it real to them, we can get you out of this mess. The demon will land you in a straight jacket and a padded cell."

Gomes looks far more presentable than he has over the past few weeks. The steady decline in his level of give-a-damn shot up overnight. He's dry-cleaned, clean-shaved, and clean-cut. A file that's downright encyclopedic has replaced the thin folder he brought to the last session. He sets up for a presentation as Judge Brentt stifles the spectators in a method that's more "Shut up" than "order in the court."

"Gomes is going to go over crime scenes," Mike says. "He hopes to start this fiasco off with some grizzly imagery to get the mob in a lynching mood. I don't want you making a face. Not one emotion better come out of you. For you, these aren't crime scenes; they're the fields of battle. And warriors are disciplined. Keep that in mind, huh?"

I nod. The commotion fades to a few stray whispers.

Mike pats my shoulder, almost smacking Eat'em's hind end, resulting in a shrill "Watch it, yes!" from the demon as he scrambles to higher ground.

"Don't worry about what he does," Mike says as he rubs the tension from my trapezoid. "Tonight, we're going to show them exactly what your eyes can do."

Chapter 31

Val danced around like a court jester, his deceivingly muscular arms swaying back and forth as he stared at me with a grimace not even a coward would fear. He wore a blue and white wrestling singlet, which he barely fit all his body parts into, and a set of ear guards that could hardly be seen beneath the wild fire mop of hair growing off the top of his head. He looked like an overconfident cartoon, but beneath the goofy outfit and the so-freckled-he's-kinda-tan skin was a scrappy little fighter who had put embarrassed me in a fight on more than one occasion.

"Come on, Orphan," Val said, "It's time to show me exactly what you can do."

I didn't know what was more embarrassing, Val's wardrobe or mine. Not having the middle school wrestling outfit Val held onto for this precise moment, I wore thigh-high bright yellow running shorts and a black and white ball tee that had gone out of fashion only moments after it was ever in fashion. Then I wore tube socks since I didn't have the right shoes for match.

This would be embarrassing enough if we were somewhere secluded, but no… Val found it necessary to drag me out in public for this humiliating display.

We were in the school's basketball gym, which doubled for an assembly center. In the corner of the room were a few mats, so old the edges rolled up and peeled. They were stiff and not much better suited for floor exercises than the wood gym floor. A few weight machines and a punching bag on a rope took up even more of the space we needed. And at this very time of night, a time Val promised me we'd have the gym to ourselves; there wasn't an area not in use.

Some guy punched the bag, some others rotated on a squat machine, a game of five on five took up half the gym and the other was being used up by a couple kids playing horse. To top it off a second floor running track circled the entire court, and there were a number of very pretty girls staring down at us with the completion of each and every lap.

"I'm serious, Jake," Val said. "If you're going to break into peoples' houses in the middle of the night with your mind set on some vigilante justice… bare-handed, I might add… then you at least need to know how to fight."

He grabbed my wrist and I shrugged away. I was a bit more

concerned about appearances than a guy with an invisible demon should be, but even someone regularly accused of talking to himself still has his pride.

"Because, if you think I'm going to dawn a cape and follow you on a spree of violence," Val continued, "you've lost your mind."

"Oooo," Eat'em turned from a mirror used for aerobics exercises. "We should get capes, yes?"

"Could you not speak so loud," I said to Val.

"You afraid someone's going to hear me?" He asked.

"Yes. Kinda."

Val grabbed at my wrist again and I pulled away again. "I could show these guys a video of you killing someone with your bare hands and they wouldn't care enough to watch it."

I tugged at the crotch of my shorts. Every step I took was another inch they crawled up my thighs. If I didn't change back to my pants soon, I'd be leaving the gym in dental floss.

"I'd watch it!" Eat'em said. "But I wouldn't believe it."

"This is stupid," I said for the fiftieth time since Val told me he wanted me to show him how to fight. "I don't need you teaching me how to wrestle."

He grabbed my wrist again.

This time when I pulled back, he dropped to one knee and swept his other leg around me in an arc. Using my momentum and slippery socks against me, Val pushed me headlong over my feet. I landed hard on my back and my scrappy uncle climbed toward my head and grappled me into what felt like some sort of self-inflicted chokehold. He wrapped my arm around my head so tight that I felt like I was about to break my nose with my own bicep. Before I had a chance to react, Val squeezed the air out of me, forcing me to breathe through the sweaty fabric over my armpit.

I had my head turned one way, my arm pulled the other. My legs twisted uselessly searching for some sort of leverage to shake my redheaded uncle off.

Worse yet, the musky uncirculated gym air felt cool as it rode up my shorts where I undoubtedly gave the giggling trio of girls running on the upper floor a show nobody paid to see.

"Is this how you're going to fight, Jacob?" Val asked.

"He wishes he fought like that, yes," Eat'em laughed. He pounded on the mat three times and shouted, "Ding! Ding! Ding!"

Though, I was the only one who heard Eat'em announce my defeat, I was certain by the awkward silence and muffled laughter that the rest of our audience agreed. Val had my head cranked so far into his chest that all I could see was the white and blue spandex as it faded into blackness.

"Alright!" I tried to scream. "I get it."

Val loosened his grip. "What was that?"

"I get it," I coughed, "okay. I need to learn to fight."

He tightened his vice-like grip until my right arm wrapped so snuggly around the front of my head that I could bend my elbow at the back of my head and just about hook my finger into my lip. He had me bent up like a practiced contortionist. Except, I wasn't a practiced contortionist, and it felt like my arm was a pound of pressure away from snapping in three different places.

I tapped the mat rapidly with my other hand, hoping for Val to relieve some pressure so that my last breath on earth wouldn't be a whiff of my own underarm.

"Weak," Eat'em said.

"You're an idiot, Baby Jake," Val said. "This isn't about learning to fight."

He let me go and all the air rushed back into my lungs - repugnant, but beautiful.

"This is to show you, you can't fight."

I rolled to my back and cautiously looked over my shoulder, expecting an audience. Nobody seemed to care.

"You're not a fighter, man," Val said. "If I can get you in a hold like this…"

"I wasn't ready," I said.

"And what if you aren't."

"What if I have to be?" I sat up and plucked my shorts from my thighs.

"At least be prepared," he helped me to my feet. "Use a weapon or something. A gun. A taser. Pepper spray? Anything."

"Maybe pepper spray," I said before Val put me on my back again. Again, because I wasn't ready.

"You need to wake up, Jacob," Val said.

Chapter 32

The sound of gunfire startled me awake. I thought it was gunfire. The loud "BLAM!" blended so perfectly with my dream. The retired lineman held his hands up in a plea for mercy, "Whoa!" He said, "Jacob you don't want to…" I aimed the pistol at Parsons' nose and pulled the trigger. I awoke in a classroom to the hush of suppressed laughter.

"Jacob, yes?" Dr. Reeder loomed over my desk. His arm ended in a balled fist, squeezed so tight that the freckles on the back of his hand made his flesh look like a crinkled page of connect the dots. "Usually I don't mind my students take a nap in my class. It's your grade, after all. But even I won't be interrupted by snoring."

"Yes sir," I said. "Won't happen again."

I lifted my head from the notebook I'd been sketching in to

keep awake. So much for that.

Eat'em chimed in, something about my ruining Karl Marx, and when I turned to Dixie, she quickly looked away. I felt her stare return to me as I rejoined the classroom.

"We're discussing the needs of the many versus the needs of the few, yes, Jacob?" Reeder said.

"Sure."

So badly I wanted to speak to Dixie, but what words would I have to offer? Lies were impossible to come up with and the truth would be impossible to believe. I kept my distance from her between classes and resented Val for making me come.

My mouth opened as she silently followed the herd out of biology, but voice refused to part from my chest. She walked away without a word, as I expected. As I deserved.

"Jacob," Professor Kempter startled me. My heart chased Dixie out the class, but I weakly lingered behind unable to do anything but watch the door shut on me and the teacher.

I slumped onto a maraschino cherry colored stool by Kempter's desk, dropping my book bag with a thump on the cracked linoleum tiles. My day-to-day life quickly became tolling on my emotional wellbeing. I've shot a man and I stabbed two more. I witnessed the death of a beautiful blonde, who'd come back from the dead only to tear some poor homeless man's throat out and be shot down by police. The only reason I wasn't in prison was because a couple other folks broke into Parsons home to eat the man for whatever reason. Lucky that. Dixie wouldn't talk to me. I couldn't talk to her. And Eat'em... for all that is good and holy in the universe... recently discovered masturbation.

Which he did.

Frequently.

In spite of my reasonable requests and offers of reward.

Kempter either didn't notice my heavy mood or didn't have time to express empathy. She hobbled to the door, peaked outside, and locked it before returning to her desk. Usually, she moved rather gracefully despite her large shape, but as she sat on the large leather chair, she seemed exasperated and out of breath. She opened the bottom drawer of her desk and pulled out the familiar bloody Deftones shirt.

"Where'd this come from?" The question might have come off as accusatory, but it didn't. Perhaps it was because she was a woman of science, or perhaps I naively trusted her, but her demeanor was that of someone genuinely curious, maybe even concerned. Definitely not threatening. "It's not from a dog, Jacob. Is it?"

"I can't say."

"Whose is it, Jacob?"

I looked into Kempter's deep brown eyes. They weren't the same color as my mother's, but they reminded me of them. The shape and softness behind her look. I felt compassion like that from only one other person. And I missed her.

"I wish I could tell you," I said. "But the truth is, I don't really know. That's why I brought it to you. I was hoping for answers, myself."

"Jacob," Kempter's voice lowered to almost a whisper. "I want you to know something. Whatever is in this blood is dangerous. I don't know if it's a plague or a curse, but you need to avoid it.

"Its more than just an infection," she chewed on her thumbnail before continuing. "I don't fully understand how it works yet, but I can tell you this – I discovered – you discovered a new type of parasite. I can see it in the blood. Some kind of micro-organism. It latches onto the cells and seems to organize them. It acts almost like a stem cell would. It gets the body to start creating cells it needs. Muscles become stronger. Fast twitch fibers are improved. Fat tissue is broken down. Weaker cells are eliminated. The parasite actually attacks cancer cells. This is why you observed the rapid healing properties. Its amazing. Unlike anything I've ever seen."

"I thought you said it was dangerous?" I asked.

"Yes," she shifted uncomfortably. "Those are just the side effects. It is doing something else. Something bigger. I'm still trying to understand it. The parasite seems connected. Like some kind of neural network. Even spread across multiple hosts, the parasite stays connected."

"How do you know they stay connected?" I became increasingly curious. Despite sounding like the medical find of the century, Dr. Kempter's observations had the potential to explain not only why the infected were so hard to defeat, but also how they seemingly knew who I was before we'd even met.

She continued, "I'm getting to that. This is why I believe the infection is potentially very dangerous. You already know that I used the shirt to give the infection to mice. Well actually I only used it to infect a single mouse. A male. That mouse bit a female and infected her. The parasites are blood born and can be passed by ingesting infected blood or from the bite of something already infected. After several days, the male escaped. I put a trap out and found him the next day, back broken, still alive. The female was also acting strange. She wouldn't move, wouldn't eat. I released the male from the trap and within thirty minutes it was as if it never happened. He was fine, fully recovered. The female too."

"She was sympathetic?" I asked.

"No," Kempter sighed as if about to lift a large weight. "She was dying. The pain seemed shared. So, I decided to make the experiment a little more morose. I killed the male."

"What happened?" I asked.

"She became feral," Kempter said. "Attacking anything. But she also forgot the things she'd learned, including the maze – she no longer cared about the maze or the rewards. It was like hitting an off switch in her brain."

I couldn't help but picture the blonde. The newscaster went over the grizzly attack again and again. And the curly haired roommate of Trevor. Is that what I'd seen?

"The female," Kempter continued, "what happened to her was a result of losing the consciousness of the one that infected her. It's like traumatic brain-rot. Once infected, either you share the same mind as all the others, or you have no mind at all. Those are the only two options. Breaking the chain… only seems to create aggression on both sides of it."

As she spoke my heart began to race and her room opened up to me. Once again I found myself with no peripheral vision. One hundred-eighty degrees of clarity in all directions. Every stain, crevice, and texture became focused. I could read every word on the chalkboard over Kempter's shoulder at once and simultaneously see every pore on her face. My vision grew perfectly crisp. Then I blinked it away.

"Jacob," Kempter snapped her fingers. "This parasite, if it's able to infect people, it could be worse than the plague. It could be worse than any natural disaster humanity has ever known. If the same goes for the mice and the chain is broken, everyone downstream would do the same thing she did."

I stood and grabbed my backpack. My stomach churned as if I couldn't digest this new bit of information. Like the knowledge had gone sour and my body fought to reject it. I asked, "Is it possible for memories to be transferred through a bite?"

"Memories, ideas, consciousness, I don't know," Kempter said. "I don't know if it could be passed to humans, but if so the effect could be disastrous. Were you ever able to find the girl that was attacked by the dog?"

"YES!" Eat'em shouted. "Jacob, let's go!"

"Jacob, this is not something to mess around with. If you know something we have to report it."

Easy for her to say without blood on her hands.

Chapter 33

Clouds rolled across the open sky like a heavenly mountain range. Twenty minutes earlier the campus was under lockdown for a tornado watch and a malevolent shield of scorched atmosphere blocked the midday sun. Hail pelted the earth with unfaltering hatred. Electricity rippled from one cloud to another as a premonition to a storm that never came.

Now I sat under a sky so friendly it was almost impossible to imagine the darkness that came and went. Students flooded from the buildings behind me as if in anticipation of more chaos. Though, this time of year, chaos was typical.

Every person that walked by was another of Kempter's mice. My mind went wild with the thought of them turning to me, revealing their darkened eyes, judging me for what I had done to disrupt their unit, whatever it should be called. Family. Cult. Colony. I pictured them as fire ants and I kicked their pile.

Val said he wasn't going to school, and I figured he'd have been by to pick me up already, but still I waited for his Mustang to round the corner into the school's parking lot.

"What is this?" a notebook slapped against my lap. My notebook. My sketchpad. Dixie stood at the other end, pointing down at a picture I drew during our philosophy class.

The picture was of Dixie sitting on her bed and myself with my arms flung wildly over my head. Dixie's finger pushed down on the pad, extended in the direction of a little character I'd drawn on the floor, looking up at me with large sorrowful eyes. It was Eat'em.

"What is this?" she said again, not a hint of emotion in her cadence. "This thing right here. You drew it. I want to know what it is."

"It's nothing," I said, snatching the book from her, closing it and shoving it into my bag.

"It doesn't look like nothing. It definitely didn't sound like nothing. So what is it? Some sort of gremlin?"

"I am not a gremlin," Eat'em screeched. He climbed my pant leg and stood at the edge of the bench where I waited for Val's car. He pointed to her with a long bent finger and said, "You can't feed a gremlin after midnight! You can feed me anytime you want to, yes. Tell her, Jacob!"

"This thing," Dixie said. "This is what you were yelling at. What is it?"

"It's nothing," I said. "Look, it's no big deal, okay."

"Not a big deal?"

"No," I said, "it's a metaphor."

"I'm not a metaphor!" Eat'em said. "I hate you both!"

"This is not a metaphor," Dixie reached for my bag, but I pulled it away and tucked it behind myself. She jabbed me in the chest. "You weren't yelling at a metaphor. What were you yelling at? Tell me. I deserve to know."

"Nothing," I said. "Myself."

"Yourself?"

"Yes," I said, "myself. I was yelling at myself."

"For what?"

"For, I don't know. For not kissing you back."

"Oh that's just adorable," she didn't sound like she meant it. Whatever word she substituted with adorable was probably four letters and rarely uttered by nuns. "Scoot over."

I made room and Dixie sat beside me, forcing the demon onto my lap.

"I kept your secret, didn't I?" Dixie said. "Even from your uncle, by the way, who's quite the little interrogator, you know? I think I deserve to know what's in your little drawing."

"No," I said, "no, no, no. I'm getting a little tired of everyone asking me questions all the time."

"Can we get donuts?" Eat'em asked, pointing across the parking lot to a bakery that just lit up with a sign reading *Hot Donuts Now!*

"No!" I yelled at Eat'em.

"See!?" Dixie said, "What was that?"

"Nothing!"

"Nothing? You just yelled at your pants. What's on there?" She swiped her hand over my jeans and Eat'em rolled to the side, letting out a "What the? Hey!"

At the risk of Dixie's frisking, I stood and stepped away from her, keeping myself between her and the demon.

"Why are you afraid of me?" she asked. "You told me you were involved with a murder that's all over the news, and did I go to the cops? No... No I didn't. And when Valentine grilled me did I tell him? No."

"Why not?" I asked. "Why haven't you? Because you like me? What happens when you don't anymore?"

"What?" she shoved me. "Because I like you? And when did you become so full of yourself? What happened to Mr. Humble? Mr. Uninteresting?"

"He's still uninteresting," Eat'em said, keeping cover.

"For your information," Dixie continued, "my not telling anyone has nothing to do with whether I like you, which I don't know why you would still think I even do after you stormed off on me and haven't spoken to me in weeks."

"What then?" I asked.

"Well, stupid, let me think about it for a second. Maybe it's because I believe you."

"Do you?"

"Sure," she said.

"That's reassuring."

"Look, honey, why shouldn't I believe you? It's not like you're the only one in the world who's seen weird things."

"And what have you seen?" I asked.

"I saw a grown man breakup with an invisible gremlin once," she said.

"He's not a gremlin." My cheeks burned bright with embarrassment. I wanted to reach out and grab my words, put them back into my mouth and swallow them forever.

I sighed and took a seat once again on the bench. Dixie sat beside me, closer now, and said, "Then what is he?"

"I don't know," I said.

Eat'em climbed onto my lap and extended his hand in the international gesture for a handshake. "I'm an Eat'em, yes!"

"He's a demon, maybe," I said begrudgingly. "His name is Eat'em. He's been with me as long as I can remember."

"A demon?" Dixie asked dryly.

"Yeah, but not an evil one," I said.

"Of course not."

Eat'em cleared his throat and thrust his hand out further.

"He wants to shake your hand," I said. I felt stupid. Like I was introducing my imaginary friend to my crush.

"Of course he does," she said, "where is he?"

"He's standing on my leg."

"Well, nice to meet you, Eat'em," she said reaching out,

greeting the air like a lunatic, pretending to shake with the demon four inches from her hand. "I'm Dixie."

Eat'em grabbed hold of her pinky. "Nice to meet you."

"Oh my god," Dixie's face turned pale beneath her heavy rouge. "He's really real."

Chapter 34

"You're an idiot," Val stormed through the living room like a hurricane. He ran his hand through his copper hair, further devastating its already hacked appearance, then he grabbed a glass from the coffee table and threw it into the wall.

"Whoa!" I said.

"No, don't you whoa me! You're a damned fool. Why would you tell her? Of all the stupid things you could possibly do. Why in the world would you tell her?"

"I'm sitting right here, you know."

Dixie and I were sitting at the dining table. She sat in Val's chair and I sat in my usual. We were on forced timeout. After working his magic in Trevor's apartment he finally came to pick me up a couple hours behind schedule. I invited Dixie over for dinner and figured I'd let Valentine know what I told her. All except for the demon, which I still hadn't gotten around to letting Val in on. He listened calmly for what it was worth, but the moment it was his turn to speak he turned into Mt. Vesuvius.

"I see you are," Val said, "Whoopdy freakin' doo! Maybe you can be a good girlfriend and tell my nephew here what an imbecile he is. Oh, that's right, because you encourage his maniacal behavior. Yippee freakin' dee!"

"Whoopdy dee!" Eat'em shouted gleefully. He'd found a new perch on Dixie. I was still mind blown it didn't bother her. He must have felt like a poltergeist. I'd never seen him warm up to someone else. Truth be told, I never let him.

"What," Dixie said, "and you don't?"

"Absolutely not," Val attempted to strangle her using some Jedi force trick and then returned to stomping around the small room. "No! If someone you care about starts killing people you don't tell him to keep doing it."

"That's a little obtuse coming from the person who just cleaned up after him."

"Oh ho ho," Val said. "Look at the big vocabulary on her, would you? I bet she knows other words too. How about *informant*? Huh? Or *snitch*? How about that one?"

"Shut up," she said. She squeezed my hand. "Is he always like this?"

I shook my head. "Only when I've been killing people."

"Great, Jake-tard," Val said. "Just great. Nothing like a little levity to warm you up for the standup routines you'll be doing on death row. Do you have any idea how stupid you are? Any at all? I hope you plan on freakin' marrying this girl because she's a one way ticket to a gas chamber if you don't."

"You're being absurd," Dixie said.

"Am I? Am I? Because, what? I'm smart enough to think of shit doughy eyes don't?"

"No," she said, "he did think about it. He asked me the same stupid questions you did."

"And it's not like I wanted to tell either of you," I said.

"But you did," Val said, "because you're an idiot."

Val plopped down on the couch, propping his legs up on the coffee table and burying his head in his arms. He mumbled almost inaudibly, "I'm going to jail."

"So that's the problem," Dixie stood from the dunce table. "You're selfish."

"Selfish?" Val stood. For a moment they're in one another's faces and I can feel my leg twitch as I hold myself from joining in the fray. Val's words come out in splashes of saliva, which Dixie does nothing to avoid. "Do you have any idea what I did for that little bastard today? Selfish!?"

"Yeah, selfish!" she spit back.

"Since when is self-preservation selfish? Furthermore, since when is protecting my nephew selfish?"

"It is if the rest of us depend on him!"

"Depend on him for what?"

"For fighting these things. For... I don't know... postponing the apocalypse or something."

"Oh, yeah," Val scoffed. "Oh, okay, yeah, well, how about, you know what... Screw you! Screw you both! Jacob, I hope you're happy with her because this chick is going to turn you into a little Charles Manson."

"Quit belittling him!"

"Who?" Val pointed at me as he veered toward his room, pausing at the door. "Wicker Man Jake-Nasty? Him? Maybe he needs belittling. Did he ever tell you where those gnarly looking scars came from?"

It was a rhetorical question.

"I figured you would have seen them already," Val said. "Know this—Jacob got them the first time he tried to play vigilante. See how that turned out for him. He lost his mom and dad and almost lost his own life. And Jacob couldn't remember anything but his mom's face and that the room seemed to breakdown into trillions of magical little particles. That's what happens to vigilantes. Eventually they die. I hope for your sake he doesn't take the rest of us down with him."

Val glanced toward me before finishing. His eyes filled with something too heart sickening to be rage and too wrathful to be sorrow.

Val shut the door on us, closing himself off in his room.

Dixie yelled behind him, "And what about what you saw?"

Muffled but still clear enough for the words to resonate, Val answered back. "I saw a blind man who wasn't ready to die."

Chapter 35

With what little I learned from Professor Kempter and what I learned for myself over the following months, my vision became ever clearer, yet remained agonizingly convoluted. My tormentor was a microscopic bug, an infection capable of spreading the experiences of one person to another without need of passing it down either genetically or through any amount of time required to learn. Confined to one body, instead of many, I only had one set of experiences to work from. And from what I could tell, I wasn't up against a group of monsters. They were more akin to super powered cultists. They contained the singular belief that people don't have a right to their own lives.

Making matters all the more unsettling, in death their progeny *did* become monsters. I saw it first hand with the curly-haired roommate of Trevor Schrekengost. Or what had been Trevor Schrekengost. The only way for me to come to terms with my actions since first running into Louise Parsons in the planetarium restroom was to acknowledge that the three people I killed weren't the three people they were supposed to be. They were doppelgangers of real people. Like the film *They Live!* they were merely shells of who they once were. They were harbingers of something dark and evil. And with the possibility of creating an army of feral cannibals by killing whatever infected individual loomed at the top of their peculiar food chain, it was too much a risk to kill'em all guns blazing.

Reality seemed grim and strangely oblique. At no fault of my own I became aware of something that might just be the end of humanity. Or at best the upheaval of uniqueness. I wasn't privy to the concept of a soul, as to whether one existed or if human cognizance came from a physical part of the brain, but I knew whether mind or spirit, the infection replaced it with something else altogether.

Val knew it too now. He didn't want to admit it but he knew as well as I did what he saw, and when Dixie left for the evening he finally came out of his room and told me. He even went as far as to offer his help the moment I was over my head. Which, of course, was a moment that already came to pass.

I told him I needed to start from the ground up. Work at the bottom of the chain and make my way toward the top. If I only struck the most recently infected I wouldn't have to worry about causing an outbreak of something much worse. I needed to avoid 'breaking the chain' as Kempter had described it.

Parsons was the first I'd come into contact with. Schrek came a few weeks after. Before then the only thing I had to worry about was feeding an insatiable demon and appeasing my uncle's education requirements. If the parasite was in its infancy, I guessed there must have still been dozens out there, and counting. The longer I waited, the more there would be. Dixie hypothesized there might be hundreds if not more... possibly countless. Val insisted I consider having already done my part, though I knew he couldn't believe that. And, needless to say, Eat'em said he could hardly tell the difference between one of us and one of them anyway, so we might as well embrace our new Grotesque overlords.

And that's how we came to start calling them Grotesques. It caught on with Dixie and Val. And before long we started getting together and imagining how I would go about saving the world.

They'd ask me how they could determine for themselves whether someone was infected. But I had no idea myself. The two I'd seen for sure had large pupils, inhumanly large, but they didn't stay that way. There were definitely moments that their eyes retained their normal shape and coloration. They looked dull, without reflection, as if they absorbed all the surrounding light, but to get close enough to see that would put them at risk. I'd only ever seen the two... there wasn't much telling whether that was a trait in all of them. Other similarities were in the irregular pulse beneath their skin. As if their blood flowed faster and harder than what would be considered normal. Again, the only way to notice such a thing would be to get up close to someone. I tended to see things from afar that most couldn't see if held directly in front of their face. My stellar eyesight wasn't constant, but at least it seemed to work when I needed it to.

I suggested they stay away from people that can jump across buildings and run as fast as a wildcat. To this Val said, "Great, I tend to do that already."

We started to have regular meetings where we would discuss the infection. None of us had any idea how long the infection had been around or where it had originated. There was no way to know how many Grotesques could be out roaming around. So we began the exercise by observing. Throughout our daily lives we would people-watch. Try to notice strange behavior. They would bring me lists of people they thought might be infected based on the symptoms I had discussed with them. Sometimes they were correct, sometimes it was just a strange soul that while not infected probably presented a threat to someone. We began trying to piece together a hierarchy based on how the people were connected. Some of them were easy, it made sense that Trevor had been infected by the gas station manager. Parsons was a little harder to figure out. Eventually we were able to track his infector to an ex-girlfriend. This took a combination of questioning acquaintances and using social networking websites to put the pieces together. Once we were confident that we had the hierarchy correct, I would act. Finding new and creative ways to rid the world of another parasite-ridden host.

The troublesome part was that it was much easier to climb up the hierarchy to discover who infected a particular target than it was to know how many others that person may have also infected.

For instance, it was easy to figure out that the gas station manager had infected Trevor, but it was difficult to know how many others the gas station manager might have infected. Through due diligence, in most cases we were able to track down each existing branch from the infected. However, occasionally mistakes were made. It would usually turn up in the news several days later. Another 'zombie-attack' would show up and the police would inadvertently clean up my loose ends. I justified it as collateral damage in my attempt to save many more innocents. And so we did our best to postpone the apocalypse.

Chapter 36

Lieutenant Bellecroix bites at the bristles hanging from his upper lip. The nature of court is redundant; they've asked him the same series of questions over and over, varying from script just enough to drive one as mad as Bill Murray in *Groundhog Day*.

Bellecroix takes to the cameras like a dying man takes to chemo. His anxious hair pulling, mustache eating and nail biting would make him bald, bare and nubby in a matter of days. He chews on his lip as Gomes questions him.

"Describe what you saw when you walked into the home of Trevor Schrekengost."

"No victims were present, of course," Bellecroix says. "We had a missing persons report, same kid who picked a fight with Mr. Brook. 'Course we don't know that yet either. All we know is some convenience store clerk ain't showed up for a couple weeks and suddenly he ain't paid his rent. So a couple our boys showed up to investigate and called in that the apartment smelled an awful lot like a morgue met a zoo. And by the time I get there that's what it looks like, too. Animals are all over the place. Squirrels, raccoons, rabbits, a fat little coyote, a few possums, cats, birds, some snakes, frogs and flies. Some of them are alive. Most are dead. As you can imagine, at first the food chain worked its magic, then starvation began to take the remainder.

"And I ain't no entomologist so I can't really tell you all the what's been in there nor for how long," he rattles on, "but they'd been in there for a good damned time. Far as we can tell, someone let the things in through the kitchen window. Everything else was locked tight.

"You've never seen a bigger mess of malnourished creatures living ankle deep in shit. Most of the things still living did it by hiding from everything else."

"At what point did you know you were dealing with a murder?" Gomes asks.

"We didn't. In fact, most of us thought it was an act of vandalism," Bellecroix says. "Figured he destroyed the place and ditched out. That's what it looked like. The bodies weren't in the apartment. We didn't find the bodies until weeks later. By that time there weren't much bodies to be found. They were stuffed in an abandoned couch in a nearby park. It took us a while to tie the bodies to the apartment. Had to go off dental records to identify them on the account of not having DNA samples to simplify things."

Later, Big Mike asks what evidence, if any, the lieutenant has that I was involved with Trevor's death at all. It's a moot point, since I've already confessed to most of the charges brought against me, but Bellecroix still answers by once again bringing up the convenience store footage, making me the last person to see Trevor alive. It's circumstantial, but tied with the confession, I fail to see how it's help for my cause.

Mike tells me the DA wishes to represent me as a liar, so creating doubt only benefits us.

Am I a liar or a hero?

Mike says, "Why not both?"

On stand, Lieutenant Bellecroix covers more of my alleged crime scenes. In addition to creating a bio dome out of the apartment, other bodies were found buried, burned, covered in isopropyl alcohol and soaked in paint bought at a variety of home repair depots. One house the lieutenant described looked like a macabre Marti Gras. Another body was fished from Joe Pool Lake. Two more had been dragged into a field where they were dumped, each holding the other's murder weapon, in a bizarre attempt to make it appear like they'd killed each other. The injuries sustained were such that neither could have survived the assault long enough to repay the debt, and even still, the trail leading to the display clearly showed a third person's footprints, which Mike is quick to point out came from neither shoes I owned nor shoes that fit my enormous feet. What kept police from tying all these together was a lack of modus operandi in either the killings themselves or in the overly thought out methods in which they were covered up.

It is the first time I am made aware of exactly how much effort Val has gone into keeping me out of prison. A parade of techniques that I am sure he learned from watching too many forensic television shows. It is also apparent in Bellecroix's dopey expression that nobody cared to hypothesize the existence of a partner in my proceedings. Which by the subtle thumb up Mike gives me as he returns to his seat is great news for us.

Chapter 37

The first few times I took a life it was in self-defense. Whether a court would see it that way was another story, as I had broken into the homes of those I was forced to kill. Still, I could hide behind the guise of self-preservation. That excuse could no longer defend my actions. I no longer cared to defend myself as much as I wanted to destroy the Grotesque infection. Needed to destroy it.

I became the plague's blight.

The bane of the curse.

In acknowledging my role as the scourge of the infection, I accepted a bleak fate. To rid the world of the parasite, I would have to die.

Heroes live on because they have an enemy that opposes them. I wasn't after an enemy. I was after a greater corruption. I stood for the eradication of a disease that threatened to strip people of their very essence. I was pesticide. At best a pesticide preserves the crops from the epidemic, which is certain to bring upon destruction if gone untreated. Things never workout for the pesticide though. Its fate is sacrifice.

As surely mine would be.

I'd killed six people since committing to the cause. After Schrekengost and his curly-haired roommate there was Trevor's manager from the gas station, a security guard at the Parks Mall, a Juggalo with a hatchetman tattoo, a fry cook from a hole-in-the-wall western flair restaurant called Pico Mundo, a woman sinking her teeth into the throat of her husband who was pulling weeds in their pristine garden, and the husband whose indecision in eating either me or his deceased bride gave me the split second advantage needed to bring him a swift death with the sharp end of a gardening spade.

Val reluctantly picked me up from each excursion. He shared my pessimistic outlook. Searching for death, I would inevitably find it.

I found a hiding spot behind a three-foot wall of white stones, which enclosed a farmhouse amidst a large grove. At the southeastern most part of Arlington city limits, where Grand Prairie and Mansfield came to a head, much of the area was either rural farmland or untouched woods. This part of Arlington laid about a two-hour jog from our old apartment in the central part of the city, where the university, bars, and sports stadiums flooded the streets with surges of traffic on a daily basis. Here the dirt road lie deserted, surrounded by tall oak trees fenced with barbed wire meant more to keep in livestock than to keep out trespassers.

Unmanaged foliage and a barn in ruins provided evidence that the sagging fence hadn't been necessary in some time. Further down the dirt road Interstate 360 was incomplete. Beyond that was the more affluent part of Mansfield, with million dollar houses equipped with fully stocked bars, personal movie theaters and grand swimming pools designed to look like natural lakes and private sanctuaries.

From my cover behind the dilapidated wall, I could neither see the freeway nor the hidden wealth beyond.

Eat'em and I followed a Grotesque to the abandoned farmhouse. He was a long-necked fellow with a pronounced Adam's Apple, giving him a closer appearance to Ichabod Crane than to the Headless Horseman. Either fit suitably into the setting of the foreboding wood on the outskirts of society.

"This is the end for you," Eat'em said. I watched him dig into a nostril with his tail. "No longer will you impose on my ability to breathe, yes! Vile. Corrupt. Blockage of my sinus cavity. Prepare to face your doom!"

A strand of snot followed the tip of his tail from his face as he cleaved it in my direction and plucked the trail with two lengthy fingers.

"You know," he said as he slurped the strand of tyranny into the smiling mouth of justice, "if you jumped around like they do we wouldn't waste so much time in disgusting nature."

"Thanks for the advice," I said.

I peaked over the wall, seeking my quarry. Ichabod-Grotesque disappeared up ahead, traveling in the direction of the vacant farmhouse, which he more than likely squatted from. I'd made a habit of tracking the infected before confronting them. Our short conversations ended with the death of Trevor. I'd learned everything I figured I would learn from talking. My new tactic was to keep to the shadows. My latest target was the next link in the chain connecting to Parsons. Parsons had been infected via an ex-girlfriend that took a French kiss a little too far. However, she had been infected by Ichabod. Ichabod was a graduate assistant at the university that taught her lab class. Apparently she had stayed late for some extra credit.

"Seriously, yes," Eat'em said. He followed me over a fallen branch I used to climb over a dip in the barbed fence. "You never train. Not once."

"It doesn't work like that," I said.

I walked slowly across fallen leaves. Any chance of a stealthy approach was betrayed by the harsh whispers of Fall. Each step crinkled and each crinkle revealed my encroaching presence.

"No amount of training could enable me to do what they do."

"So you're not even going to try?" Eat'em walked beside me on a low branch, swinging to another as I moved from tree to tree.

"What do you suppose I do?"

"Best way," Eat'em said, "climb to the top and jump."

"Jump from the top?" I asked. "Do you know what a forty foot drop would do to me?"

"If there's no chance of failure, you'll never do it, yes."

"Makes sense," I said. "I think I'll stick to the ground."

"Wuss."

Situated in a clearing was a shack encircled by refuse and broken tools from the lot's previous owners. From there I could see the house the Grotesque entered. There was no front door and most of the windows were smashed and boarded up. Before barging into the front unarmed, I decided my best bet was to check the back for any other ways in or out.

I crept around the side of the shed and was greeted by the business end of a double barrel shotgun.

Chapter 38

"Give me one good reason not to put a round of buckshot into your skull," said a man as equally opposing as the shotgun he pointed at my face.

His sunburned arms were tattooed and matted with silver hair, trailing up toward a muscular physique scarred with what might have been crudely removed tattoos or possibly the result of a severe burn. His ashy cheek pressed tightly to the stock, squishing his face toward eyebrows that at any moment might erupt with the emergence of a majestic butterfly.

"I can't think of one," Eat'em said, always the optimist.

"Well," the presence of the double barrel put my brain at a standstill, "with the looming economic decline, and the increasing cost of ammunition, it might be more financially sound to beat me to death."

No parasite corrupted the old man. Aside from the cancerous cells built up in an angry looking scab on the bridge of his nose, and a yellow cataract in his non-shooting eye, he was healthy as an old man gets. Definitely not the possessed sort I sought in the farmhouse I assumed was abandoned.

"What's your name, wiseass?" he said.

"No, sir," I said, "that's not it."

"What's not it?" he asked.

"Wiseass, sir. It's a fair guess, though. Good as any."

He shook the gun to remind me that in his index finger he controlled the fate of my head and all its contents.

"My name is Jacob," I said.

"Well, Jacob, you're trespassing on private property," he said. His voice sounded like it was the result of a two-pack-a-day Marlboro diet for the last century. Picture Sam Elliot, but homelier, and far less Hollywood.

"I didn't know it was private property," I said.

"Does this look like the mall, pretty boy?"

As flattered as I might have been to receive such a compliment, it felt a bit blemished, as if the class dunce were to praise my intelligence.

"No sir," I said.

"You going to tell me what you're doing out here, boy?" he snorted and hacked up a glob of phlegm. "Or you going to 'yes sir, no sir' me till I grow tired and shoot ya?"

"My advice," Eat'em whispered, "go with the latter, yes. Ten-to-one he doesn't have the guts."

"To be honest, um…" I held my hand out palm up, a gesture intended to ask for the old man's name.

"Terry," he said. He kept the weapon trained between my eyes, but his brow softened.

"To be honest, Terry," I said, "I followed someone out here."

"You followed someone?"

"A lanky fellow," I said. "Maybe you've seen him? He's sick and he forgot his medicine."

"I don't right care if you got a sick friend or not," he lowered the shotgun to my abdomen. It was a start. He snorted and hacked up a black glob of chewing tobacco. "You and your friend can get off my property."

"No sir, he's not my friend."

I considered grabbing the gun, but didn't think I'd win a scrap for it even if one of his scarred arms were tied behind his back.

"What he's got," I said, "there's no cure for."

"Thought you said he forgot his medicine," Terry said.

"Yes sir," I flashed a glance at his gun, which he promptly brought back to eye-level. "The kind of medicine you undoubtedly mean to give me with that there buckshot of yours."

"You mean to kill him?"

I nodded.

"Ain't nobody killing nobody unless it's me," he spit

another wad of tobacco.

Eat'em yanked on my collar. He said, "Ask him if he has more of that black stuff, yes!"

"Well, sir, I wouldn't have any objections to you curing the guy yourself," I said, "but if it isn't too much to ask, I'd prefer not to succumb to the same treatment."

He kept the weapon trained on me as he rummaged through the pocket of a shredded pair of jeans that might have gone for a hundred-fifty dollars if sold at the right outlet. It suited the gray-haired, one-eyed, tattooed monstrosity more so than the adolescents that seemed to think pre-worn outfits were more-or-less in vogue.

"Probably the best treatment for you'd be an institution," he said without so many consonants and an added word, which seemed to suggest the institution he referred to consisted of gratuitous sexual acts. He pulled out a cell phone – the kind that flips and couldn't be purchased anywhere in the last ten or so years. It actually had buttons, which he had to press to dial. "We'll see what the boys in blue gotta say about a couple trespassers wantin' to kill each other on my land."

"That won't be necessary," I said, holding my hand up for him to put the fossil back in his pocket.

"Boy, you take one more step forward and I'll be calling a coroner instead." The type of coroner he mentioned was of the spiritually forsaken sort.

"I bet you wish you'd listened to my advice on training now," Eat'em said. "Yes? Then we wouldn't have to listen to this stupid human's vocalizations anymore. He'd said, 'blah blah blah.' And you'd been *ZIP!* Running on leaves. Now you're going to have to go to prison. You know what Val says is in prison, don't you, yes? That stuff you do with Dixie, but with dudes! Ugh... My suggestion, yes. Plug those cavities with a couple phalanges, bob and weave. I've only ever seen you use much of one hand anyway, yes. Waste for the other to even be there."

"Hello, police," Terry spoke into the phone.

I didn't think the old man would do too much shooting if I cut tail, but I still needed to get a look in the house. I could outrun him and be hidden in the shadows of the woods before he could get a clean shot. No need to sacrifice a hand.

Before I could turn away or heed the demon's advice, my opportunity was lost. He dropped the cell phone and the gun all at once. Blood oozed down his dirty tank top. Ichabod Grotesque had rounded the corner of the shed faster than I could react. He sank his teeth into the old man's neck.

Chapter 39

On further inspection, Ichabod didn't look much like Ichabod at all. Other than the defined Adam's Apple, his hair, which I earlier mistook for the dark brown locks of the hero of Sleepy Hollow, was actually a sandy blond coloration. He was also a good foot too short to play Crane, who, if I recalled, stood quite higher than six feet and some odd inches.

Still, I'd much rather have faced off with a horseman than an acrobatic cannibal. For one, headless horsemen in particular, tend not to have spectacular eyesight. Horses themselves have a decent blind spot directly in front of them. And headless people don't seem to see much of anything at all.

If what I knew of Grotesques was true, they managed to see through the eyes of many, and weren't at all limited to the same nearsightedness disembodiment often came with.

This Crane looked more like a beach boy. His brightly colored outfit reflected the apparel of a Californian youth. I'd never been to the state myself, but I imagined them wearing the same floral patterned board shorts and three-sizes-too-loose T-shirts as the almond-eyed man-eater.

He winked at me as he dropped Terry to the ground with a thump. Then he wiped a trickle of blood from his lip and licked it off his palm for effect. I assumed it was for effect anyway, as he had a whole body still at his disposal if he was still feeling famished.

"Jacob," he smiled. "It is so good to see you again."

"Likewise," I said, in spite of never having seen nor talked to him prior to the night. A tremor climbed up my legs, which I fought to subdue.

"One of you is lying," Eat'em said.

"I've been meaning to talk to you," Crane said, popping a squat next to his victim, who writhed in a violent spasm before letting out a horrid breath that should have been, but wasn't, his last.

"I think you're the one lying, yes, Jacob?" Eat'em said.

"The set of *Friday the Thirteenth* seems like as good a place as any, right?" I said, failing to conceal my shudder.

"Yeah, well, it didn't always look like this," he held Terry's head as a fierce convulsion wracked the old man's body. "I used to live here. Long time ago. It was nice then."

"I bet," I said.

"You don't believe me?" he asked. His nostrils flared in

casual bewilderment. He acted as if we weren't having this conversation over the twitching body of the current owner.

"I believe you just fine," I said, "but when you say you lived here..."

"No, no, not..." he pressed a hand to his chest. "I did, however. The me you seek, I presume. I lived here with my wife and two children."

His eyes dropped and his face grew more somber.

"It was a long time ago," he said. "This place looked quite different then. Not like the dump it is today. My wife kept a very clean home. She was a great homemaker. You look at it now, though. This..." he gave Terry a smack on the cheek. The old man had fallen unconscious once again. He looked dead. The Grotesque continued, "I'll just say the house isn't up to my wife's standards."

"What happened to your family?" I asked.

"They died."

I didn't care to press the surrogate infected for further information because I felt sorry for him, but I hoped some small detail would provide insight to where I should go if I happened to survive the encounter. I was hopeful that I was getting close to the top of the hierarchy.

"They couldn't live with what you'd become, I'm guessing," I said, hoping against hope he wouldn't take my jest as enough reason to end the conversation prematurely.

"What I'd become?" he shook his head. "I couldn't live seeing the world through their eyes."

"That's some scary stuff, Jacob," Eat'em tugged at my ear. "Spoiler alert in case you didn't catch that, yes. Ugly here just articulated he exterminated his family. No less, after turning them into uglies. He's going to do so much worse to you, yes. My guess? Some sort of impalement." Despite the elementary lesson from Eat'em, I had gathered that at this point I was not speaking to Ichabod; rather, he was some sort of conduit from whom I spoke to whatever self-proclaimed deity existed at the top of his hierarchy.

"I would like," the Grotesque carried on, "if this wasn't necessary for everyone, you know. But this world, Jacob, this world needs fixing. You see it. You see it too, I know you do. You think you're so much different than me, but really we're not. We're one in the same. That's why I want to keep you around, but sonofabitch if you don't stop killing me. You could be there in the end if you just leave it alone."

"The end?" I asked.

"Yes, Jacob," he said, "the end of humanity's madness."

He stroked Terry's hair. The old man's body was twisted in much the same way I remembered Schrek's roommate just weeks ago. His limbs contorted in impossible directions. The wound on the man's neck had begun healing. The cataract faded from his bad eye. The scars on his arms and neck faded into the rest of his skin. He began looking younger and more vibrant.

"You take what I'm doing as the breaking of some sort of ethic law," the Grotesque said as he continued to run his hand through the old man's hair, which peppered with more black as it had before. The silver remained, but I swore he lost ten or fifteen years of age. Ichabod went on, "I have never killed anyone, Jacob. Can you say the same? I give life. You take it. Such is the balance of things. But I'm not mad at your misunderstanding, see, because you also just want the madness to end. And it will. Give it time and you'll see. I want you to see. I want you to be there when I have created peace. People are capable of utopia. They just need the right guide."

"Guide?" I asked. My eyes fell to the gleaming stock of the discarded shotgun. It lay under the old man's mangled legs. "Is that the right word? *Control* sounds more fitting."

"What's the difference?" the blond looked up, a subtle grin at the edge of his lips. "God said give your hearts and minds to he who gives you life. Matthew knew he wasn't the one living in his own flesh. I'm no different. Neither is he."

He shook Terry, who blinked and shifted both of his perfect eyes in my direction.

"I am the giver of life," they said together.

I dropped to the ground and grabbed the shotgun from under Terry. I scrambled on my back, rolled and held the shotgun like I'd seen done in the movies a hundred times. I didn't know whether to pump it or if there was a safety nor where to find it if there was one. So I held my breath and pulled the trigger.

I am the giver of death.

Chapter 40

Ichabod collapsed in a splash of gore. The pointblank range of the shotgun turned his head inside out and scattered infected bits of brain and bone and tooth and tongue all over the side of the shed, piled trash, and dried leaves.

The weapon's kick was almost enough to knock me clean out. And already I could hear Eat'em complain in my ringing ears about firing a gun so close to his face. Also, he was ticked I'd jumped to the ground without warning him first, but warning my demon of my plans never seemed to bode well when others were present to hear them too.

The farm's new landlord didn't fair well either. He didn't have an exploded head like the one who 'gave him life' but he was back to his spasms and was now vomiting waves of dark bile. In less than a minute he would be mindlessly trying to eat whatever was in his destructive path, which I didn't so much care to be on, so after a quick apology I pumped the empty shells from the chamber, aimed at Terry's head and again pulled the trigger. This time, instead of a bang, I was greeted with the dull *thap* of metal smacking metal.

If there were more rounds, Terry had them, and I was fairly confident he wouldn't give them up without a fight.

I ran.

Twigs and dead leaves cracked with my every step as I sprinted back into the woods. The bumbling brute just as quickly took off in the same direction. His grunts and screeches, more than the foliage underfoot, gave ample evidence he was gaining more ground than I could put between us. He was clearly not as fast as Crane or Trevor or Parsons, but he easily outpaced me.

I didn't turn to see just how much he outpaced me, but by the sounds he made I knew I wouldn't make the freeway before he was eating my face and washing it down with my insides.

A case could be made for the stupidity in the decision, but I figured higher ground would be safer than running through the unfamiliar trees, hoping to lose the beast at my heels.

I leapt to a low branch of a split oak with relative ease and barely struggled to climb to the second and third. My only hope was that the high-jumping, tightrope running capabilities of the infected were cut-off whenever the link was lost. If not, I hoped I could climb high enough that the fall would kill me and I wouldn't have to experience being Terry's midnight snack in the middle of the shrouded grove.

I pulled myself to an upper branch, about fifteen feet from the ground and looked up toward the canopy. The limbs thinned considerably, much faster than I thought from the ground. Only halfway up the tree and my footing already bowed. It wasn't nearly as high off the ground as I figured it'd be either. Maybe thirty-five feet total, possibly forty. High enough that I'd be in considerable pain if I fell to the ground, but not so high that I wouldn't be conscious when Terry's yellow teeth ripped into my windpipe.

Still, I lifted myself once more and grabbed a branch overhead so narrow that my hands wrapped entirely around it. As luck sometimes wins out, Terry stopped at the base of the oak inefficiently clawing at the tree instead of climbing it, I didn't have to worry about fighting Spider-Man for the high ground after all.

I sat on the highest branch I could reach and stared out at the sky. Killing didn't weigh on me as it had the first few times. I didn't think I'd be doing it for much longer with the course of things, but at least I'd be able to get a full night sleep before I inevitably fought my last fight.

I swung my legs around the branch so I straddled it and gave Valentine a call.

He answered groggily, "You better be dying."

"About to," I said. "I could use a ride."

"You're kidding me. It's almost four in the morning."

"I can call Dixie," I said, "but if I recall you wanted me to call you when I was in a jam first."

"Yeah right."

"I'll buy you breakfast," I said.

Eat'em answered ecstatically, "Pancakes!"

Before I could give Val directions, a hand wrapped around my ankle. Apparently, Terry figured out how to climb.

I dropped my phone and hoped the sickening *crack* wasn't enough to break it completely. Terry's teeth sunk into my shoe and I kicked him hard with my other foot. I stomped over and over until all I could hear was whistling and the meaty *thump* of my shoe smacking against his forehead repeatedly.

The beast dropped, crashing into several branches on his way back to the earth.

After hitting the ground he ran in the direction of the whistling and I realized they were sirens. The police must have been able to trace Terry's phone. Or maybe someone else called when they heard the gunshot. Nevertheless, they were at the property and Terry, himself, was running toward them with insatiable hunger on his mind, and my shoe in his hand.

I remained in the tree, glad I hadn't given Val the address before our call was rudely interrupted. He'd be mad tomorrow, but for now, I had the safety of the Texas oak. I wrapped myself around a sagging limb and ignored gunshots and wailing sirens.

I slept.

Chapter 41

Sergeant Cameron, a twenty-something year old cop with a sparkling complexion and teeth that belong in a toothpaste commercial, corroborates a nonsensical story about how Terry's death was an accidental shooting. Cameron's the face of the APD, some golden boy that helped the lieutenant bring me down, Terry's death is a mishap, and the whole story's a giant steaming pile of bunk.

The dead are so easily made martyrs.

Bellecroix mentioned the man's killing as if collateral damage was expected out of police officers. Like a magician revealing a mark's selected card, he manipulated the crowd into believing death is merely an illusion the prosecution is capable of pulling off. And for his next trick, please bring Sergeant Cameron to the stage.

He has oily black hair, slicked back, requiring constant

grooming to keep from clumping or falling to the side. His eyebrows are cherry blond, so I imagine black isn't his usual hair color. It works in opposition of his uniform as most of the officers grouped in the back of the courtroom have clean buzz cuts, flat tops or fades.

"He came running out of the forest like he was being chased or something," Cameron says. That's about where his credibility ends. "He had his arms up and was screaming. We didn't know he was screaming for help until it was too late. You know. Some of us thought he might have a gun. We didn't know he was the one who called it in. He came running out holding something. I thought it was a gun. Looked like a gun."

"What was it?" Mike asks.

"Like L.T. said," Cameron points over my shoulder toward Bellecroix, "it was a shoe."

"Who gave the order to shoot the man wielding a shoe?"

"Nobody specifically. I saw the shoe. I opened fire. He was holding it like this," Cameron holds his hand up as if he's pointing a gun. He twists so the jury can see his imaginary shoe. "I knew I'd done wrong. So did we all know. But it was an honest mistake. In the dark, he could have been armed."

"Did you yell a warning for him to stop?"

"Hell yeah we did," Cameron says, "but all that's already been brought up back in April. I said it then same as I'll say it now, we thought he had a gun. It may have been an error in judgment, but I don't think it was, lives might have been saved. Especially, you know, had it been a gun."

"And not a shoe."

"It looked like a gun."

Earlier in the year, a case went public regarding the State of Texas vs. the Arlington Police Department. No suspects were found outside of the two men involved. The case settled as a public dispute between one Terry Lee and the headless trespasser. Police, then, said Terry was crazed, had shot the victim while on the phone with dispatch and then ran into the woods to wait for first responders. They called it 'suicide by cop' and the case was pretty much a farce.

Finding the second shoe at my home upon my arrest drastically changed that first case. Terry became a victim. His guttural screams of rage became frantic cries for help. The police acting in self-defense became a tragic accident.

"Anyway," Cameron says with a silky Texas twang, "we didn't know at the time Mr. Brook'd ever been present. You can gather all that from what was said back in April. We'd only known of the two men and that's all. 'n' everything changed in light of new evidence from what we learned about Mr. Brook being there and that he'd killed some other victims too."

"Allegedly," Eat'em says. He chimes in every so often, but has mellowed significantly since the start of the trial. I think we're both ready to accept whatever fate comes our way. "I don't recall you killing anybody. And I've been with you the whole time, yes. Put me on stand, I'll clear things up."

If Big Mike hadn't already shot down the request, I might have entertained the idea. Unfortunately, my lawyer already stated, putting my 'imaginary friend' on stand was about the dumbest idea he'd ever heard of.

"I've got manuscripts from this spring's trial," Mike says as he opens his manila folder and searches a stack of papers. "You said then that no rational man would have considered Terry's actions as anything less than an attempt on Officer Denman's life. You said he was crazed, carrying a weapon, and he tried to bite another officer. Is that so?"

"I don't remember saying that."

"You did," Mike shows Cameron a sheet of paper, "right here."

"Ah…" the officer stalls, tapping the page and nodding as he does. "This. I do remember saying this. See, the key word here is rational. See, what I meant by that, and what I mean now, is that the events preceding that, those events had taken the rationality out of the situation. You understand?"

"I don't."

"Well, it's simple," Cameron nods. "Real simple really. Mr. Lee… Terry… he suffered from post traumatic syndrome. That's what had happened. He'd seen this horrific thing, which Mr. Brook'd done, and that's why he was acting the way he was. 'Course we didn't know that then. That's why it's said the way I said it. But we know it now. He had the PTS and that's what made me say no rational man."

Mike nods.

"You can't really go off what I said then anyway," Cameron continues. "Memory's only as reliable as the one of us with the worst of it. The evidence is where you're going to find your answers. And's far as I can tell you, all the evidence points to this man, Jacob Caleb Brook, killing them folks."

It feels like a horrible place to end the conversation, but Mike ends it with no further questions.

Chapter 42

Climbing down the tree in the daylight proved more difficult than climbing up at night. Eat'em coerced me to take a leap of faith, but I didn't feel compelled to shatter my ankle upon landing. Instead I slithered down – like a snake competing with vestigial arms and legs – I groped down the wide trunk of the oak, sliding on my chest as I dropped from foothold to foothold, limb to limb.

At the base I retrieved my cracked smart phone from the large tree's discarded leaves. The screen lit when I touched it, but only long enough to reveal a flashing battery to indicate my phone died sometime in the middle of the night.

As I climbed back over the dropped barbed wire and followed the dirt road toward the freeway, I peeled off my dirty shirt and used it to wipe away what little blood that stained my skin from the previous night. My scarred torso might be enough to terrify passersby, but it seemed the better option to running the risk of getting taken into custody, once again, for wearing a blood-stained t-shirt.

Police staked out the farmhouse overnight, but they were gone by the time I woke up forty feet above the ground. Surely, they would be back, but I took advantage of their absence while I could.

Eat'em's long fingers clung to my collarbone as he swayed back and forth on my upper back. His prickly skin felt warm even compared to the midday sun, which kissed my forehead, creating beads of sweat.

I wondered if I would have a demon shaped suntan line. The thought never crossed my mind before, mainly because I never made a habit of being shirtless, but now that I considered it, I almost wanted to laugh at the preposterousness of trying to explain it.

In the past I've spent a good amount of time trying to conclude whether Eat'em is somehow stuck between two realms or if he's even tangible at all. I know he must be, because where light hits him he creates shadow. If I were to have only imagined him, I wouldn't have also imagined his ability to manipulate the world around him, especially the way he is subject to light and darkness the same as any other physical object. Even if my mind were creative enough to manifest such a creature, there was no way I could also warp my perception of the physical world to compensate for his presence. Also, as Dixie had demonstrated time and again, she could, at the very least, feel Eat'em on the occasion he was brave enough to touch her. She compared it to having the sixth sense of being watched, that something else is present. She felt an extra electricity in Eat'em, though she couldn't perceive him in any other way. Similar to a ghost story in which a wispy figure is briefly caught on camera, just enough out of focus to question its very existence. That's how she explained Eat'em. The way the hair on the back of your neck stands up and you knew something was near though it can't be placed. That was Eat'em. Yet to me, he was as real and tangible as ground beneath my feet.

He hummed joyfully as I walked to Val's apartment, ignoring the hot pavement beneath my sweltering feet.

"Where have you been, neighbor?" Isaac greeted me as I came through the door. He looked as tired as I felt, as Val often called me, a bag of smashed ass.

"Camping," I said. "Where's my uncle?"

"He went looking for you, dimwit," Isaac said. He loaded dishes into the washer, organizing them as he spoke. "Val woke me up last night and said you were missing and he thought you might be in trouble. Asked if I would wait for you here and call him if you showed up before he did. Sounds like you're in trouble."

"I'm fine," I said, "I just need to get cleaned up and changed. Mind texting him for me? My phone died or else I would have called."

"Ugh…" Eat'em belched as I grabbed some fresh clothes and dumped my dirty shirt and shoe in Val's hamper. "It smells like a potpourri convention, yes. Where's the scent of pizza crumbs and Monster and Red Bull and perspiration? Where's the charm?"

I closed myself into the bathroom and shouted through the door, "Did you tidy up or did Val?"

"I did," Isaac said, "I don't know how you two live like this. It's an armpit in here."

"Yeah," I said, "well, I hardly live here anymore, so you know, whatever."

"That's right, how's the girlfriend?"

I turned on the shower for me and ran the sink for the demon. It took some training, but he finally bathed on his own. Though, he didn't use much more than water, and even then, he wasn't the biggest fan of getting wet. Maybe nobody else had to smell him, but so long as I did, he'd bathe.

"She's good," I yelled. "Busy doing something community service related. I forgot what it's called. Like Big Brothers, Big Sisters, but that's not it."

"You don't know the name," Isaac laughed, "of where your girlfriend works."

"No, I do. I just forgot it."

"That's fine," he said. "I'll just ask her tonight."

"What do you mean, you'll ask her tonight?"

"Ah yeah," Isaac's voice grew louder and less muffled, as if he pressed his face to the bathroom door. "You know Dr. Reeder?"

"Yes," I said.

Eat'em said, "Yes! Yes! And Yes! Monads!"

"Well, one of his students is in some band," Isaac said. "Asked Reeder if he wanted to go to a concert. So he's making a shindig out of it. And I thought I'd invite y'all."

"You hang out with Dr. Reeder?"

"Yeah, man," he said, "I told you, I love philosophy. You think you'll come?"

I dried off and threw on my fresh outfit, a pair of shorts and a white tee.

"I'm fairly sure Val's going to be too pissed off for me to want to go anywhere," I said, opening the door.

Isaac greeted me with a toothy grin. "No, man, I already talked to him about it. He's cool. I told him it'd be good for you to get out and be normal."

"Normal?"

"Well, whatever?" Isaac said. "I don't know what the deal is. You stress him out. Maybe he gets stressed easily. Doesn't matter. I asked if he wanted to tag along and told him to invite you and Dixie. And since you're here before he is, I figured I'd go ahead and ask you."

"Do I have to dress up?" I asked.

"I'd look nicer than that," he pointed to my clean clothes. "I'm not going to get caught dead in what I'm wearing. But, I guess it doesn't really matter for you. You don't got to impress anybody. Val and I are the stags."

Eat'em shook dry as he sauntered into the living room. He took a detour toward the kitchen and hollered for me to open the fridge. I obeyed and grabbed a water for myself.

"I guess I'll go," I said.

"Alright," Isaac said, "in the meantime you ought to relax. Your impromptu camping trip looks like it's did you in. Now, that you're here and Pat's on his way back, I'm going to go rest, myself. But I'll see you all tonight. Good catching up."

"Likewise," I said as Isaac left.

"That evil scumbag!" Eat'em yelled from the kitchen.

"What?" I asked.

"She's back!"

"Who?"

"Who do you think?" Eat'em asked. "Jemima!"

Chapter 43

The band played to a sea of swooning girls and various punk rock wannabes that sang along to every word. It wasn't the kind of environment I figured Dr. Reeder would be comfortable in. Even with his philosophies spanning the spectrum of human existence, I thought surely an independent pop-punk concert wouldn't be his venue of choice, especially considering how far out we were from Arlington.

Aside from a slight buzz coming from one of the massive floor speakers, the acoustics in the converted basement were decent quality. I could make out every frantic drum beat and every crass lyric. A flurry of spotlights tore through the audience before finally joining together at the foot of the stage, where the lead vocalist poured his heart out to a flock of cheering women.

"You're a pretty little thing but your love is like a pocket knife," he sang. "Fun to play with up until you get your finger sliced. They don't make bandages to cover up the wounds that you left me with, yeah baby!"

"No!" Eat'em belted out from his perch on my head. "No, no, no! Kill me! Kill me now! I will not be the sufferer of such a cacophonous racket. Human! Let's go. Take me somewhere less awful, yes. The end of all that is good is in this room."

"Shut up," I said as we made our way through the crowd with Val and Isaac at my flank.

"Shut up? Shut up?" Eat'em said. "Oh how easy for you to say. You just say whatever you please, yes. Eat'em, shut up! Yes. No! I have done many things for you. I have saved your life from much turmoil. And yet, it is I that must do what you say? No! I will not have it. I'm no dupe. You remove me from this enclave at once or I swear to you, you'll face the full force of a demon's wrath!"

"And what wrath is that?"

"I'll eat all of your food, yes!"

"You do that."

"Then the silent treatment. I will not speak to you from now… until… five minutes from now. Starting now," he paused and I could feel him holding his breath. As he exhaled he lamented, "Is this what you want? I'm not bluffing! Five minutes of pure unfathomable silence… aside from this mournful garbage. Tell me, yes, is that how it has to be?"

"I guess so," I said.

"Well, I won't have it!" Eat'em bellowed. He grabbed my hair and yanked it back and forth, trying to turn me back toward the exit like a jockey rides a thoroughbred. "Turn around, you oaf! This is worse than the infection! This, yes, this is what you should be trying to expunge from existence."

"They're not bad," Val screamed over the crowd. "What do you think?"

"I like it," I said.

"No!" the imp on my head pulled and thrashed. "No, no, no, nonononononono, NOOOoooOOOOoooOOOooo! Do you hear me!? NO!!!"

"What's the name of the band?" I asked Isaac.

"Jamie something," he said. "Maybe, Hello Jamie. I think that's it. That guy," he pointed toward the long-haired guitarist. A guy in his thirties, maybe; he had some chin scruff and long highlighted bangs. Isaac nodded to the beat as he pointed him out, "he's the one from Dr. Reeder's class."

"How do you know?" I asked.

"I met him," he said.

As we pressed through the crowd toward the front of the stage, I saw Dixie in one of her trademark sundresses. She smiled as we approached and waved to introduce us to a gathering of her friends.

"Jacob," she grabbed hold of my hand in both of hers, "these are some of the girls I work with."

Val leaned in and whispered in my ear, "you better

introduce me, Orphan."

"This is Valentine," I pushed my uncle toward the girls with my free hand and then nodded back at Isaac. "And this is our friend, Isaac. He's our neighbor."

Dixie pulled in close to me as Val and Isaac joined the rest of the girls.

"This is so exciting," Dixie kissed me on the cheek. "How long have I been telling you we need to go to a concert?"

"Don't know," I answered.

I gave into the bobbing of the crowd and ignored the screaming demon as the music spread through my core. I wouldn't say I danced. I was never much of a dancer. But I swayed gently, Dixie clinging to my side, and watched the throng of Hello Jamie fans as they sang along with songs I'd never heard.

As my troubles began to slip away into the harmonic dissonance, my weary eyes finally caught sight of Dr. Reeder. He stared at me. Eyes black as coal.

Chapter 44

I pushed through the dancing mob, leaving Dixie and the group behind. The realization suddenly hit me. Reeder, the great philosopher, was at the head of the infection. That's how they knew me. It all seeded from his classroom. He wasn't merely spreading his beliefs, but also his very existence. He brought me here as some sort of showcase to his power. And now, I had the opportunity to end it.

He disappeared into a hallway lined with instruments and bands waiting for their turn to perform. I just had to reach him before he found a way to disappear for good.

"Finally," Eat'em said, "We're getting out of here."

Entering the hallway, I found a waiting area with drums and guitars, and large portable sound equipment. To my right was a large bay door, almost like a garage. Tour vans and buses could park on the other side so the bands could more easily load and unload their instruments before and after each show. It opened to a long ramp, which led to the street. As I exited the building, I stopped amidst a group of hipster teens, smoking cigarettes and drinking illegally. Across the street were more buildings, painted with murals that emulated popular graffiti artists and urban taggers. Beyond was another venue, alive with music. Country music poured out somewhere in the night, though I couldn't tell if it was from a live concert out of eyeshot or if someone blared it from the radio of a parked car.

I walked around one side of the building where Hello Jamie sang, "Gonna tear that ass up like I just got out of prison." The lyrics resonated as being oddly appropriate, though I'd never been to prison. Still, if and when I found the doctor, my intention very much was to tear his ass up.

I didn't know what that would do to the possible swarms of infected beneath him, but it didn't matter. The police were more than willing to put down the infected once they became brain-dead shambling beasts. Once the mayhem unleashed, it wouldn't be long before authorities brought it to a halt.

After determining that Reeder hadn't gone around the building, I went back to the garage entrance where the band started a new song. Something about vampires.

If he'd run from the building at top speed someone would have noticed. Eyes would have been drawn in his direction. But if he had a car parked out back, nobody would have bat an eyelash. He could have hopped in and driven off without alarming anyone.

He had to be there.

Reeder relished in our conversations and the idea that I was a step behind at every turn. I knew he watched me. Wherever he was, he could see me.

A truck pulled up and a band began trickling out of the bay, loading their cases and stands and rolls of cable. I stepped out of their way and caught a glimpse of an alley hidden by the base of the loading ramp. I hopped down and stalked through the narrow walkway.

Heeding Val's advice, I reached into my front pocket for a small can of pepper spray. It was that or a concealed gun license, in which case I'd be traceable. Pepper spray was cheap and easy to find.

The safety pin snagged on my belt loop and as I tugged it free, I inadvertently sprayed myself in the face.

Imagine jalapenos, cayenne peppers, and ghost chili powder – all mixed with a handful of sand and rubbed in your eyes.

Eat'em laughed at my shrill scream for mercy.

I braced myself on a brick wall and attempted to get a hold of myself. Keep myself from coughing and gagging. Opening my mouth made it worse. My eyes burned and face began to sweat and leak from every opening.

Everything went black. I couldn't open my eyes. When I forced them open with my fingers, my vision went nuts. Bricks opened into porous structures that looked like sponge. The ground grew ever closer, transforming into an ocean of molecules weaving in and out of each other. Air converted from an invisible substance into swirling elements orbited by electrons and protons. I attempted to blink it away. Blink the world back into structure and sense. But everything continued to break apart.

I could hear Eat'em laughing hysterically. "God, that was funny, yes! Brilliant! Brilliant!"

His voice came from a world of infinite depth. My head screamed. I knew I had to will myself to see straight, but I couldn't.

I waved my hand in front of my face, trying to see it, but all I could make out was the chaos of cellular life working together and fighting to be free of the imprisonment of my body. My skin became molecular structures as seen through a microscope with an infinite field of vision. As if I dissolved into a microbiological mosaic. Parts of me became the wind and the wind became me. Until all the world was all at once united bedlam.

Rubbing my eyes made it worse. My hands felt solid, but looked anything but. All they managed to do was spread the burning sensation to my cheeks and then my nostrils. I couldn't breathe past the scorching snot that dripped from my nose. My lips felt like they'd kissed the sun.

The icy sting of steel against bone shocked me back to Earth. A knife stuck into my chest, reopening a wound that had long ago healed.

Chapter 45

The ragged blade dug through the muscle on the upper left part of my chest. Almost a decade had come and gone since the burglar had stuck the sharp end of a fireplace poker into that same spot. The overwhelming sensation of hot and cold burned through me the same as it once had.

Except this time, the heat was from a pepper spray misfire and not from the blade shattering my shoulder blade. Instead the knife prodded the inside of the bone, sending ice through my entire body. The blade twisted in Reeder's cruel grip and I struggled to remain on my feet. My entire body wanted to collapse.

"Hit the spot, Jacob?" Reeder asked. His dilated eyes shrank and a malevolent pulse rose up his neck, beneath the flesh on both sides of his face. "Feel familiar?"

I tried to speak but only managed throw up. My tongue felt a couple sizes too big for my mouth.

"Yeah, that's it," Reeder said.

He pulled the knife from my shoulder and wiped the blood on my shirt.

I jerked, managing to knock the knife to the pavement, and in retaliation Reeder shoved me hard against the wall. He grabbed my throat with one hand and buried the thumb of the other into the fresh hole he created with the knife.

"Do you know how many times I've experienced death?" he asked. "How many times I've died for you? At your hands alone, how many times must I die? Ten? Twenty? Thirty? For what? You know, I told you before I liked you. But you're really starting to piss me off."

He pressed his thumb deeper into my shoulder. I dropped to one knee and he lifted me back up by the bone.

I screamed, quickly stifled by a closed fist and another clinch from Reeder's menacing grip.

Part of me hoped my short cry would be heard over the noise of the surrounding bands, but nobody came to my rescue. Another fist hit me in the abdomen. The air escaped my lungs and refused to return. The sweet taste of blood filled my mouth, cooling the fires started with the pepper spray.

"Shut up, will you?" he said. "Do you care to know how many pairs of eyes I have making sure nobody comes to your pathetic little time of need? Do you know how many opportunities I've had to kill you?"

"Why haven't you?" I managed to choke out the words.

"I'm no killer, Jacob," he said. "For God's sake. I mean, really, there is no other species on this entire planet so dedicated to the complete eradication of their own. We cry out for peace and pray for the lives of our loved ones, and yet we're determined to destroy the lives of countless others. It's ridiculous, isn't it?"

"This is gibberish," Eat'em tugged at my pant leg. "Quit toying with him. Put him out of his misery."

Reeder pulled me away from the wall and turned me toward the street beyond the alley. He wrapped his arm around my shoulder in faux-affection, keeping his grip firmly on my left clavicle to remind me of the bitterness behind the gesture.

"I am the secret to everlasting life, Jacob," he said. He waved toward the rest of Dallas, hidden behind the veil of surrounding clubs and music halls that ensnared us. "You want to take that from people? Why?"

"There's no such thing as everlasting life," I said.

"Sure there is. Through each other, we live forever, no?"

"No," I said.

"Am I not evidence enough for you?" he spun me away from the road and pinned me to the brick wall once more. "Have you not tried to kill me on numerous occasions now?"

"Not yet."

"Then what have you been doing, Jacob?" he said, "Explain it to me."

"Killing a parasite," I said. The pain in face and chest gave way to light-headedness. I was losing blood, less so with Reeder's thumb blocking the wound, but enough that I felt consciousness fading in and out. Acid built up in my throat and the throbbing in my skull subsided, only to be replaced by a peppery nausea. I couldn't tell what my most pressing need was – cry, puke, or pass out.

"A parasite?"

"Yes," I choked. "You're infected with a parasite. You're spreading it to your victims. That's all I know."

He buried his thumb deeper into my gaping shoulder. Flashes of red obscured my vision. My knees softened.

"Explain it to me!" he said.

"I can't," I coughed. "I don't know. Just. It increases the immune system. Makes you stronger somehow. Faster. Shared consciousness."

"And this is worth killing for?" he said. "Dying for?"

He tossed me to the ground. The world closed in around us.

My head tilted toward my dearest friend. The little demon sauntered across the alley, carrying in his curled tail my only chance for salvation... the knife.

Eat'em moved as stealthily as only he could. The knife skittered and bounced behind him, leaving little divots in the gravel with his every step. I returned his smile as darkness began to enclose the three of us.

Reeder sat on my chest, his knees bent.

"I can heal your wounds," he said. "With me, you can live forever."

He leaned in, mouth open, his breath hot and sour.

"I don't want to live forever," I said. "I just want to live."

I thrust the knife into his heart, turned my head, and puked.

Chapter 46

"What did I think as the blade entered the heart of Dr. Reeder?" I repeat the question. Gomes nods for me to go on. "I thought it was over. I thought it would be the catalyst of an outbreak nobody would deny. I thought the police force would put an end to it. But I didn't think this. I didn't think I would be stuck in a never ending trial for the rest of my life. I didn't think that."

Never ending is more hopeful than anything else. The truth is, the trial is coming to a close. The audience has grown restless. The lawyers have run out of reasons to postpone the inevitable. I'm on the stand for presumably the last time. One last time to be made a mockery. One last time before judgment.

"I spent my life with the ability to see things others can't," I said. "It wasn't some magical ability I could control, nor was it some superpower that arrived at puberty, I was simply born with miraculous vision. At times it's been a curse. I'd be on a date and suddenly I can't tell where my fork ends and my food begins. A distraction. Other times, it's a blessing. I never lose my car keys, for instance."

"Funny," Gomes says. "Where are you going with this?"

"A few years ago," I say, "I stumbled into a bathroom, and I saw something nobody else could see. A man, Louise Parsons, biting into the neck of a woman. Carrie Gerberich. When I tried to find out why I saw this, I was forced to end Louise's life in order to save my own. How do I share the burden of something only I can see? Sure, Professor Kempter ran experiments. Nobody believes her either. That's my only corroboration. My family. My friends. If they take this stand, they risk their lives. And for what? More stories nobody will believe. There's got to be a bad guy, and that role has fallen on me. All I ever wanted to do was help. But as you said, I'm here for what I've done, not what I wanted to do."

"That's right," Gomes says. "And what you've done is confessed to a series of murders. And you're only real argument for doing so is that you can see things others can't."

"Can I show you a couple magic tricks?" I ask.

"I don't know if I care to entertain this idea," Judge Brentt says. He gives me a stern look. The kind that suggests he is a couple headaches away from beating me half to death with his gavel.

"It's I who wish to entertain you, Your Honor," I say. "It's nothing quite so incredible as pulling a rabbit out of a hat, and I assure you, if I had a disappearing act, I would have done it long ago."

"I've got a disappearing act," Eat'em laughs.

"Make it quick," Judge Brentt says. "And if I find this act of yours to be as irrelevant as I think it's going to be, I swear I'm going to add contempt of court to your charges and start stacking your time in lockup."

"Is that charge worse than murder?" I ask. The judge's face drills a hole in my spirit and I drop the attitude. "Alright, it's a two-parter. First, I need Lieutenant Bellecroix."

The lieutenant's face turns beet red. He sits at the back of the auditorium. He's been trying to hide from me for a while.

"Lieutenant," I say, "I need you to do two things. First, give Officer Cameron your handcuffs. Not your keys. The keys, I want you to lie down right in front of you, so everyone can see them. Officer Cameron, if you would, please come up here and put the cuffs on my wrists. Nobody freak out, okay. Neither of the kind policemen are infected."

I hold my hands in front of me and wait for the sergeant to cuff me. I flash a quick smile to Big Mike, who's mouthing something like "What are you freaking doing?"

As Cameron locks the cuffs to my wrists and tightens them a couple clicks too tight, I turn my attention back to Bellecroix. "Now, Lieutenant, as he's doing this, I'd like you to find a dollar bill. It doesn't matter if it's yours or someone else's. I just need you to hold one up nice and flat so everyone can see it. Any denomination."

He removes a money clip from his breast pocket and dramatically unfolds a dollar from it. He rubs it on the pew in front of him and holds it up.

"Alright, you ready for this," I say. "The serial number is A86998541G. It's dated 2006. On the back is a 'Where's George?' stamp with the URL circled in red ink. In black ink, written under the stamp, it reads 'Georges dead.' There's a missing apostrophe. Someone tried to erase it with a pink eraser from a number 2 pencil. If you hold it up to the light you'll see the microscopic fragments stuck in the bill's threads."

Bellecroix flips the dollar and examines it. He grunts and puts it back into his money clip, sliding it into his pocket as he does so.

"How'd I do?" I ask.

"You weren't even close."

"Are you sure?" I ask. "I have a feeling nobody is going to believe you."

"Why's that?"

"I'll tell you if you unlock my cuffs," I say.

"Not a chance," Bellecroix says.

"Why not?" I ask. "Don't you have the key?"

In front of the lieutenant is a set of handcuffs. It's the same set that was on my wrists. Eat'em had replaced the lieutenant's key with them as I described his dollar. The same key I held in my outstretched hand.

"Pretty cool trick," I said. "Wouldn't you agree?"

Chapter 47

Val overreacted. I didn't need to go to a hospital. As much as I refused, my dependence on my uncle's Mustang prevented me from having my way.

I laid down in the back seat with my head on Dixie's lap and a dirty rag pressed to my chest. Val grabbed it from the trunk. It smelled like oil and added a bitter taste to my coppery blood. Surely, it poisoned me, but as I pulled it away, Val reached back and smacked my hand.

"Keep it on the wound, Jake-ass," he said. "If you get blood on my upholstery again I'm going to lose my mind."

"It's not even bleeding that bad," my voice sounded faint.

"Yeah, well, it's bad enough you're going to need some stitches. And that's only if you didn't puncture a vein or an artery or something. Christ, Jacob, this is pretty messed up."

"Ugh," Eat'em said. He banged his head against the center console. Neither of us were hospital fans. He hated them ever since he discovered they weren't giant warehouses for what he thought were special edition ice cream trucks marked ECNALUBMA. He groaned before saying, "Do we have to ride in another Ec-na-lub-ma? I can wait in the car, yes?"

"Yeah," I said. It was more a response to Val than the demon, though I really didn't care if he came in or not. He saved my life. That was enough to ask of him for one day.

"Why you so afraid of hospitals, anyway?" Isaac asked from the front passenger seat.

"I'm not afraid," I said, "I just don't like them."

"Why's that?"

"Who does?"

"You got a point," he said, "but for a guy with the tendency to get bloodied up and get into knife fights, you sure hate them more than most."

I dabbed a build up of bloody saliva from the inside of my mouth, regretting it immediately. Peeling the rag from my chest felt like ripping out a hot coal from an open sore and worse yet, the rag tasted like the inside of a Jiffy Lube.

"Well, Isaac," I said, "I don't exactly have a great experience with doctor visits."

"Sensitive to needles?"

"Nope."

"You weren't…" he turned around and gasped dramatically, "touched… were you?"

"No, Isaac," I said, "the last time I was in a hospital was the day my parents were murdered."

Sick patients galore filled the waiting room. A child cuddled on her mother's lap, a man with rash, another with a broken arm, chest pain, headaches, a woman with ankles so large and misshapen she was destined to spend the rest of her life in a wheelchair.

The air smelled like sickness. Coughs and moans drowned out any potential of happy thoughts. The implementation of universal healthcare brought all walks of life for all illnesses severe and imagined to the Emergency Room. One guy looked nothing worse than hung over. One had a runny nose. One sat cross-legged on the floor, playing a shooting game on a handheld device. Which was great, because I had nothing more I wanted to do than spend the rest of my evening in a room with sick people and poor air circulation.

"Next," a cinnamon-skinned clerk called me to the sign-in window. She kept her face buried in her computer and asked, "What are you here for, sweetie?"

"Busted lip," I mused, peeling the rag from my shoulder. I wanted to throw up.

She looked up from the screen and said, "Oh, honey. That doesn't look good. You shouldn't play with knives."

My heart skipped a beat.

A pulse ran from the bottom of her neck, up her cheek, and

through her left eye, briefly dilating the pupil.

"Never mind," I said, backing up. "I'm fine."

"Nonsense," she flashed a wicked grin. "Something like that needs to be seen right away, Jacob."

My heart racing, I rushed across the room where Val and Dixie waited with Isaac. "I can't be seen here. We need to go."

"What are you going on about?" Val said. "Did we not just go through this?"

"We did. I can't. Let's just hit the pharmacy on the way back. I'll grab a suture kit."

"You can't stitch your own shoulder," Dixie said, her face contorted in confusion.

"I can," a stinging pang of fear rolled up my chest. A peppery ball of panic, built up from my ribcage, formed into a tangible beast, spiked with fear, the color of dread. It clawed its way up my throat, pushing serrated talons into my flesh as it ascended. It lifted itself into my mouth and bored deeper into my skull until the acidic buildup behind my eyes grew uncontainable. Tears slid down my cheeks. I attempted to shake the feeling and said, "I can't be here, Valentine. Dixie. I can't. I have to go."

Dixie softened and nodded understanding. "Okay, Jacob," she said, "let's go. We'll drop by the pharmacy, get some gauze, antiseptic, whatever. I'm sure I can stitch you up. It's alright."

"You're serious?" Isaac scoffed. "Look, I don't want to belittle your traumatic experience, or whatever, but you sew that thing up wrong or don't clean it right and you're going to make it ten times worse."

"Val," I said, "I can't see a doctor here."

"Come on, Isaac," Val said, "I'm sure Dixie can figure out a needle and thread."

"Jacob!"

The three of us turned toward the entryway to the ER. The male nurse holding the door open looked like a young Keanu Reeves, his stubbled jowl drew back in a forced grin.

"You're up, buddy," he said.

I shook my head.

"Dude," Isaac nudged me, "it's not that big a deal. As much as I'd enjoy watching your girlfriend mangle you with a fishhook and a pair of pliers, don't you think you'll be much better off in the hands of a professional?"

"No."

Val gestured for the nurse to wait a second longer and said, "Jakester, it's alright. We'll be right here."

Chapter 48

I clinched the rag, wet with blood and oil, so tightly I felt warm liquid drip from my knuckles. I drudged down the hallway, following the Keanu-cool nurse at a distance. We passed medic after medic with the same dead-eyed stare. The same shark-toothed smile. The mind-rotting parasite.

Each hungered glare stalked my every movement. Like the lenses of an asylum they monitored me, tracked me, prevented my escape.

The nurse led me into a room in the center of a forked hallway. Emergency exits flickered at the end of three of the corridors. An Operating Room and group of elevators stood toward the back of a fourth hall behind a reception desk guarded by two more infected medical personnel. Finally there was the way I came in.

All equal distances from the small room with a plastic cot adorned with paper sheets.

"Go ahead and have a seat, Jacob," the nurse said, holding the door for me. "The doctor will be right with you."

I halted outside the door, too stiff to move.

"It's alright, buddy," he said. "Ain't gonna bite you."

His smile bore an uncanny resemblance to an angler fish. The illumination of a deathtrap. Yet, I couldn't run. Not with Dixie and Val and Isaac at risk in the waiting room. I could only hope this room wouldn't be my final resting place.

And what would they do to my uncle and girlfriend and neighbor? Kill them too? Turn them into grotesques?

"We're going to fix you right up, Jacob," the nurse's smile dropped. "Get in the fucking room!"

I did as told and the door shut behind me.

No time.

That's what I had to deal with. Precisely no time. Now I was in the room, they no longer needed the charade. There was no more reason to play doctor, and I had exactly no time to think of a way out of a room with no windows, one door, omnipresent security guards, and the disadvantage of said room being dead center a labyrinth, which happened to be a hospital.

No time.

I pressed my back to the corner furthest from the door. More than anything I just needed my eyes to do their trick. "Come on," I said aloud, "do it."

On cue, the room unfolded in an incredible panorama. From my left: A poster of Audrey Hepburn, Breakfast at Tiffany's, signed; corkboard, notes, calendars, ten thumbtacks, a picture of a little girl, a wife, a family; a receptacle, empty but for one latex glove and a tube of ointment rolled to the nozzle; a red call button, speaker box; a comic strip above the light switch, Blondie, the punch line unfunny; stool; door; counter, sink, hand sanitizer, bar of soap, paper towels, bedpan; glass jar of individually wrapped sterilized needles, lid shut, twists off; cupboards, closed; television, flat screen; chair, green cushion on birch frame, unwieldy; IV drip, metal rod on steel platform. In the center of the room; the bed, pull out drawers, manual recline lever, on casters, wheel closest to me has foot-locked brake applied.

All my focus narrowed to the door as it opened.

"Jacob, Jacob, Jacob," the doctor said as he entered the room. "Privacy at last, huh?"

His chin scruff looked more Grinch Stole Christmas than Wolverine. Same could be said of his eyebrows, which were so dark and drawn so close to his deep eye sockets, I wondered if he could see anything above the bridge of his nose. His head was otherwise bald as if a cruel god pulled what was once on his scalp through the pores on his face.

"I'm Dr..." he looked down at his nametag, "Sri-long-cole, is it? Sriloungkhol... that's a helluva name ain't it? What do you think that is? Puerto Rican?"

"Looks Asian."

"Asian?" he said, looking at his arms. "Am I Asian? Weird. I get mixed up from time to time. Asian?"

"Yeah."

"Asian one minute Puerto Rican the next," he said. "Did you know, I know fifty-six different languages?"

"No."

"That's cool, right? There was a time I didn't even know fifty-six languages existed. Yesterday, I learned Farsi. What an interesting language. I could write in it too, if I wanted."

"You must impress yourself when you meet you at the bar."

He laughed and spun toward the end of the bed, pushing himself away and toward the Breakfast at Tiffany's poster. "See this? Mr. Sriloungkhol tells everyone that comes in here this is Audrey Hepburn's genuine signature. It's not though. This is a manufactured signature. Mr. Sriloungkhol bought this from a used video store for seven dollars and ninety-eight cents for his wife, Mrs. Sriloungkhol. They haven't seen each other in a very long time. He wasn't faithful..."

"That's too bad," I said. "He must have not been himself."

"HA!" he said as he spun himself in a circle. "You're right, Jacob. Mr. Sriloungkhol wasn't himself. He realized he could be anyone he wanted to be."

"I bet."

"He realized he could do anything he wanted to do," he continued. "He realized he could live a life fully without consequences or repercussions or better yet, the fear of death."

"Everyone should fear death," I said.

He stopped the stool and kicked his feet up on the foot of the bed. "Do you fear death, Jacob?"

"I do."

"That's why people come here," he said, spinning in a circle with his arms out wide. "Fear. I am the destroyer of fear. Of death. Through me, they have everlasting life. I am their savior. Do you believe me yet?"

"Sure," I said, "though I'd say pestilence was a better word for you."

"Pestilence?" he smiled. "You know, I do enjoy our chats. You're a smart kid. If only you weren't also demented, because unfortunately, I just can't have that."

"Of course."

"Did you know that I can cure all of them?" He gestured in the direction of the waiting room.

"To what extent?"

"Any extent, probably," he said. "Cancer, heart disease, you name it."

"You?"

"Me?"

"Yes," I said. "Can you cure them of you?"

He drew near the foot of the bed and rested his chin on his elbows. Then he sighed heavily. "I'm not an illness," he said. "I'm not a parasite. I'm a god."

"No," I said, "you're an infection."

"There's no infection!" he said thunderously. A sliver crawled from his brow, across the top of his scalp, disappearing behind his head. "A parasite cannot have a conscience! I am a god, Jacob! I am God."

"Is that why you were outsmarted by a demon?"

He paused. His Cro-Magnon eyebrows raised and with a snort he erupted into laughter. At first he let out a mild chortle, which quickly evolved into a nauseating guffaw. His raucous laughter rattled to the bone. After a moment he composed himself enough to say, "Outsmarted by a demon? You mean you?"

"No," I said, "I mean the half-pint sugar-addicted crimson demon that gave me the knife I stuck in your chest."

He laughed. "I like you, Jacob, I really do, but you see, you're kind of a problem. I can't let you go around killing me and I can't bring you into my little family. So what do I do?"

"I don't know."

"Yes you do."

He meant to kill me. I represented some sort of loose end… I was the threat.

"If you kill me," I said, "you're going to have one very upset demon on your hands."

"Does this demon have a name?" he asked.

"Eat'em."

He laughed again. "Eat'em. Eat'em. Eat'em. What a name! I remember you mentioning him before. Does he eat people? Does he eat their souls?"

"Candy."

"Ha!" Dr. Sriloungkhol said, "Where is he?"

"He's behind you."

He twisted the stool around and I moved all at once.

I stomped the brake on the bed, yanking it toward the doctor's back. The momentum threw him headlong into the trashcan and onto the floor.

The jar. I knocked the IV over as I sprung from one side of the rolling bed to the other, grabbed the jar and threw it across the room into Audrey Hepburn. A shower of glass and needles rained down on the doctor. He was on hands and knees.

Again with the bed, I rolled it into him, knocking him off balance.

No time.

He still blocked my passage to the door.

With haste I grabbed two packaged needles from the shattered remnants at my feet.

The doctor lifted himself to one knee and shoved the bed back in my direction. I jumped and rolled over it, banging my shoulder against the metal frame as I did. I ignored the sting and thrust both needles into the doctor's face, without bothering to tear the plastic off first. One hit below his right eye, the other embedded into his cheek, piercing his gums. He roared and grabbed his face. He would heal.

Stumbling over him, I threw open the door, flinging myself into the hallway.

The receptionists were up before I was out.

One defied gravity, racing across the ceiling on all fours. Her hands and feet were both split down the center, gripping ceiling beams in much the same way a chameleon grabs onto a branch. *They were evolving...* The other ran with an inhuman intensity, covering distance at half my pace.

I took off the way I came, sprinting with all my might toward the waiting room. Doors flung open as I passed them as others joined the chase. I slammed into a door that opened to my left, I juked right, grabbed the handle of a second door and yanked it open as I ran past without missing a step.

Halfway there.

My legs pumped faster as the infected drew nearer. Fifteen yards left.

Their feet clomped right behind mine.

"Val!" I yelled. "Isaac!"

Ten yards left. Nine.

"Dixie!"

A hand grazed my wrist. I yanked forward and picked up the pace.

Five yards.

Four. Three. Two.

The beast on the ceiling dropped behind me, inches away.

I shoved through the door, running with all my might.

I screamed, "RUN!!!"

Chapter 49

"Run!" I yelled again. But this time, my voice trailed off and dropped into a murmur.

Standing with Dixie, Val, and Isaac was a black-haired officer I'd never seen before. His gun trained on me ready to fire if I made any sudden movements. All the sick people in the lobby were cleared out. I had nowhere to go.

I held my hands above my head. My left arm drooped ever so slightly due to the pain that shot up from my shoulder. I anticipated a horde of Grotesques bursting in from the ER doors, but they didn't come.

Someone grabbed my hands from behind and yanked them behind my back. It was Lieutenant Bellecroix.

"Jacob Caleb Brook," he said, "you're under arrest for the

murder of Emerson Reeder."

Cold steel clasped around my wrists.

"You have the right to remain silent," he said. "You have the right to an attorney. If you cannot afford an attorney one will be appointed for you by the court of law."

The words barely registered. One way or the other, it was over. The Grotesques were no longer my problem. I did what I could. I tried to stop them.

Dixie's eyes swelled up with tears. Valentine's hands balled into pale fists. He wanted so badly to be the all-powerful uncle. I couldn't help but stare at Isaac. He almost seemed emotionless as he rubbed the muscle below his eye.

"You need to get out of here," I said as the lieutenant escorted me past. "It's not safe."

They let me put my personal affects in Val's Mustang before they tucked me into the back of the squad car. Really, all I cared about was retrieving my pipsqueak demon.

I shifted on the hard plastic seat, scooting my hands under my butt for the small amount of comfort they were worth. Eat'em curled up in my lap and flashed a solemn look of reassurance. For what it's worth, the little red devil often surprised me with the compassion he was capable of. The small flash of empathy reminded me why my life was improved by having traded his servitude for a bottle of antacids.

"What happened to your shoulder?" the black-haired cop

asked.

I stared out the window without answering. We drove by the Ranger's Ball Park and then the newly built Cowboys Stadium. Arlington was a flat city. Without these monuments one could see for miles. I could stare out the window of the police car and see the curvature of the earth. If I looked to the east I could see a golden future rising over the vast landscape, and to the west was the blood red past. Trails of violet streaked from horizon to horizon as Lieutenant Bellecroix and his partner drove me toward a future that wasn't so bright, away from a past much more grim.

"Not gonna talk, no?" the cop said, "I gotcha. That's alright. I figured you would just say its self-defense. You know. Ain't nothing illegal 'bout self-defense."

We were on side roads now. Streets wound up from old horse trails from a hundred years past. Then much of Texas was still considered the Wild West. People rode bareback and carried six shooters on their hip. Many citizens still owned weapons, but the state had laws against 'open carry' now. No longer did the west harbor the great cowboys nor was it home to the likes of Billy "The Kid" or other outlaws. No. Instead it had invisible plagues and a red-eyed man with a pet demon.

At the station, I was processed and given a piece of paper with my name and social on it, along with other identifying numbers and a date. I held it up for a photo to immortalize myself as a criminal.

They hosed me off and a medic assessed my wounds. I was

grateful not to be seen by some super powered freak of nature. What a great ploy, spreading the infection to those who are already sick. Maybe my detective skills needed work, but I would have never guessed.

My first night was spent in a community cell with other lowlifes like myself. After that I received my own room. The room was long enough for a single cot, wide enough for a toilet, and deep enough for a bookshelf.

This is where I expected I would spend the rest of my life.

Chapter 50

I'm not superstitious. I realize the contradiction in saying such a thing – that someone whose very existence should stand as testimony for any number of religious revelations – but it's difficult for me to see the things I do and not wonder what logical explanations might explain them. Yet, the truth is, I don't know if there is a logical explanation, and if there is, I doubt I'll ever know it.

Now, I'm a victim of superstition. What I thought would explain my actions put me at the heart of the nation's fears. My spontaneous presentation of incredible vision and handcuff picking demons results in a fervor of religious zealots. They haven't arrived to support the man whom protects humanity. They arrive to watch the witch burn.

The angry menace surrounds the courthouse in droves. Big

Mike escorts me with a team of bodyguards. We drive through the gathering of hissing, spitting, screaming vipers. They curse and spite me. They swing Bibles and Korans and Torahs like clubs and maces and protective shields. My safety derives from a few muscle bound jocks that would just as soon join the throng as keep me from falling victim to it. And I have Mike. And I have a little red demon that spits back at the crowd and laughs at the mania gleefully.

I don't know if Eat'em doesn't comprehend my dread or doesn't care, but he finds enjoyment in the uproarious horde. He chants along with them as I am shoved into the courtroom. "Murderer! Murderer!" is the sweetest of their hateful cries.

Armed officers keep the protestors from following me into the building and through a set of metal detectors.

We continue toward the auditorium where I will receive my final judgment in a few more days. Mike pulls my chair for me and says, "That stunt you pulled… Yeah. That backfired."

The final witness before closing statements is called up by the state. It's Isaac.

"The call was made last minute," Mike says. "I don't know what the deal is, but by the hush behind this thing, they're trying to say they got something big."

"My neighbor?" I say. "What's he got?"

"I don't know, Jacob," Mike says. "What does he *got?*"

"I'm not going to pretend he's my biggest supporter, but it's not like we've ever talked about much. He's a coffee shop philosopher. We talk about the meaning of life. Dumb stuff."

"Maybe he's a character witness," Mike says. "I know as much as you do. You sit through this and closing statements and then it's up to a jury to decide. That's it. But after that hocus pocus you pulled yesterday... you saw. People aren't looking favorably at you."

"I don't get it," I say.

Isaac swears in, pressing his hand to the Bible. He wears a sweater vest beneath a dinner coat that looks like it came from a period in which the only public court cases dealt with women's suffrage or the constitutional repeal of alcohol consumption. Isaac looks like he initiated the Hipster movement.

"They're scared of you," Mike whispers before cowering into his seat and sinking into the posture of the defeated. He chews the back end of a silver pen.

By the looks of it, Mike fears me too. The entire lot of attendees fears me. Compared to yesterday the courthouse is morose – filled with downturned chins and upturned eyes. The room oozes a melancholy so thick that not a muffle can be heard through the fog. Not a single sniffle or cough or sneeze tears through the silence. The only person in the building who doesn't look like his dog just died is Isaac. He takes his seat at the pulpit, flashes me a look neither friendly nor reticent, and turns his attention to Gomes with a smile so coy you'd think he just accidentally bumped into him at the grocery store.

"If it isn't Stinky the Stench, himself, yes?" Eat'em says as Isaac goes through a series of preliminary questions, confirming his identity and relationship to me. Eat'em sticks out his tongue, making a fart sound. "Let's rally these sad saps and beat this fool with soap on a rope. A public bleaching, yes. Waterboard him with pine oil."

For the record, Isaac doesn't smell that bad. Maybe he has a slight musk, like the dryer lint trap of a pack-a-day smoker, but not as ghastly as Eat'em makes him out to be. Still, Eat'em never liked Isaac's scent. For whatever reason, he hated it.

The District Attorney turns his back to the jury. He clears his throat and asks, "Have you ever known Jacob to possess magical properties?"

"What do you mean *magical properties*?" Isaac asks.

"Well, has he ever spoken to you about having enhanced vision or anything of that nature?"

"No."

I shake my head and Eat'em mutters, "This is so stupid." Putting Isaac on stand is a waste of time. It's as if they're intentionally dragging this thing on as long as they can. I share Eat'em's sentiment, the trial has gone on long enough and I'm ready to accept whatever follows. It wasn't as if I could ever convince anyone we needed to carpet-bomb a hospital. And by now the plague would have spanned outside of my reach. My only hope was to cut off the head of the thing, and that did nothing.

"What have you spoken about?" Gomes asks.

"Mostly school," Isaac says. "I really like the kid. I kind of see him as a protégé. He's got his head on his shoulders."

"When you spoke with me earlier you mentioned another

conversation," Gomes says. "Would you be so kind to tell the court what you told me?"

"Yeah," Isaac says, "I didn't want to say anything, you know. I like Jacob and I'm a friend with his uncle, Patrick. It's weighed heavy on me after hearing some of what's been said here. I watch the trial, you know, because I'm rooting for Jacob. I don't think he deserves the wrap he got. But at the same time, if people are in danger because of me, I wouldn't be able to live with myself.

"Not after what I've done."

Chapter 51

"A year ago," Isaac says, "before Jacob's arrest, I confided in him a couple things I don't typically talk about."

"I don't know what he's typically talking about now," Eat'em says. "Is he going to pin this whole thing on himself or not. Because I want to get out of here, yes. I'm going to need quarters and a vending machine."

My mind draws a blank too. Isaac has hung out with Val and I quite a bit over the time we've known him, but we've never been sentimental. Nor has he ever given me reason to believe he'd willingly be a fall guy if I were to ever be arrested for multiple counts of murder.

Isaac bobs his head like a turkey as he talks, almost as if he's trying to reassure himself of his own memory. He says, "I told him my wife had left me…"

"Wait!" Eat'em interjects, "Someone married the Reek Face?"

"…and she had taken my kids…"

"And copulated with it?" Eat'em belches, "Yuck!"

It's news to me too.

"It was a tough time in my life," Isaac says. "I lost everything. I lost my job. I lost my money. My car was repossessed. I lost my house."

"We never talked about any of this," I whisper to Mike. "He never told me he was married before, nothing."

Mike shushes me. He leans back and folds his arms across his chest.

Gomes signals for Isaac to go on. He does.

"I was venting. And I figured I've talked to Jacob a lot. I trusted him. He's a good listener and he'll hear me out. And he does, so I don't think anything of it.

"But then," Isaac continues, "a few days later, Jacob asks me more questions about the house. Where it is? Who lives in it? He asks me a lot of questions about it. I don't think much of it, but I at least ask him why he's so curious. He told me not to worry about it, and said he knew a way to get my house back."

Eat'em flicks his tail back and forth. He lets out a tiresome groan and says, "What is he prattling on about?"

"How did he plan to do that?" Gomes asks.

"He didn't say. That was pretty much the end of it."

It makes no sense. Why would Isaac volunteer as a last minute witness to make up some story about a discussion that never happened? My stomach is in knots. What am I supposed to make of this?

The silence agonizes. Everyone else seems to follow the story just fine. Gomes looks like he just uncorked the biggest mystery of them all. Mike now carries an invisible weight even more unfathomable than what he carried before. I, and I alone, sit completely in the dark.

"Why did you feel compelled to come forward with this information?" Gomes asks. "Can you tell me again what made your home so significant?"

"The person who bought it after me," Isaac says, "was Terrance Randall Lee. That's the man who was shot down last year on the property. His son, Nicholas Lee, was shot there as well. Police said they found Jacob's shoe there."

My heart leaps to my throat. For the briefest moment, Isaac's eyes turn an unholy black. It's not an unconscious reaction to light. It's as under his control as the focus on a lens. He wants me to see it. He wants me to see how badly I failed.

"It's him," I say and Mike takes the pen out of his mouth long enough to hush me again.

"I have the deed to the house," Isaac says. "Well, the old deed. The deed from when I lived there with my wife and children. I just couldn't believe it's a coincidence."

Gomes hands a piece of paper to Judge Brentt. The

auditorium remains silent as they read over it and all I hear is the pounding in my chest. *Thump! Thump! Thump!*

Two guards with 9mm handguns stand at each exit to the room. There's more guarding the doorways behind the pulpit than there are to the double doors in the front, even though that's the way out and the doors behind the judge only lead deeper into the building. There's a couple holding cells there, but they're more for recesses than keeping criminals for prolonged periods of time. The jailhouse and prison aren't in the middle of Arlington city limits, in spite of the courthouse being there, so there's less concern about me making a run for freedom than making an attempt on someone's life.

And that's all I can think of doing.

"This form says you purchased the house in 1886," Judge Brentt says.

"It's a mistype," says Isaac. "When I said the deed was old, I didn't mean that old." He smiles his shark-toothed grin, baring all of his teeth, top and bottom. His awkward smile looks even more predatorial now. It's the menacing visage of a cackling hyena. The hungry snare of a Great White. The mug of the bloodthirsty. Not the friendly smile I once mistook it for. Behind Isaac's smug face is a taste for power and a hatred for humanity. He says, "I tried to resolve it for years, but I didn't see the point after it went up for auction. I figured they'd fix it for the new owner."

The fiendish Isaac turns his head toward me. He thinks he's won. He thinks he has dominion over me. Over everyone. He thinks because I'm a fool I will allow him to continue his veiled corruption of humanity.

I won't. The demon won't allow it.

"Please," Eat'em says, "for the love of all that is good and holy in this world, yes, will someone please shut him up?"

"I will," I flow like water. I slide over the table before me, grabbing the pen from Mike's mouth all at once. I'm through the partition. It's just me and Isaac.

The world fades. I cross the threshold before a gasping jury. A demon yells from behind me, "Get'em!"

I am a meteorite colliding into a planet long overdue for extinction. I am a Red Dwarfing Sun! I am the Crimson-Eyed killer!

I fling myself toward the pulpit, Grotesque-fast.

Ten thousand volts of electricity really hurts.

Chapter 52

And that's how I almost saved humanity... desperately clinging to an ink pen, contorting madly on the floor, soiling my pants in front of all those who tuned in. I writhed and twisted and screamed. I put up as convincing of an argument as could be expected from a man with an invisible talking demon. And as I curled into the fetal position and frantically guarded my face from a flurry of unnecessary batons, I reminisced of the first moment I met Isaac. Eat'em told me if I cared anything for the human race I would dispatch Isaac.

I don't know if killing him then would have saved me all the trouble. Maybe I would have never run into Parsons. Maybe I wouldn't have ever killed anyone else. Maybe I wouldn't have pooped myself after being tased on national television. Unfortunately, I'll never know. Because later that afternoon, after a forced recess, which included a hosing that Eat'em found hilarious, I had the distinct pleasure of listening to a jury of my peers declare me guilty for multiple counts of first-degree murder. The deliberation was short and sweet and the courtroom almost lit up in a hooray. Had it not been for the overemotional demon, one might not have thought anyone cared about me at all.

My heart broke as I was led out of the courtroom in cuffs by the same guards that beat me senseless hours earlier and I finally brought myself to acknowledge Dixie and Valentine. Their eyes were red as mine and sadness brought them together in an embrace that I so much wanted to share.

Alas, hugs are reserved for those found innocent.

I sat in the confines of my cell. The last place on Earth. Not even Eat'em could cheer me up. Though, I will say he provided an excellent candy smuggling service, as his confinement was more-or-less on a volunteer basis. He snuck out to find treats and trinkets, but he always snuck back in. And yes, I did consider my key trick, but getting out of a cell is not the same as getting out of a prison. The cell was for my protection; the prison was for my confinement. At least, that's how I figured it, anyway. I didn't know what I'd do if I somehow managed to break out. Maybe I'd kill Isaac. Soon enough all the world would be Isaac anyway. So, it didn't matter.

I flipped through the pages of a book Isaac got for me. It was a leather-bound print of the original Bram Stoker's Dracula.

Complacency led the people of London into self-destruction in the wake of several murders by a blood-sucking vampire. How subtle, Isaac. How subtle.

But at the end of Bram Stoker's Dracula, Dracula dies. At the hands of a Texan, no less.

If you want to live forever, prison is the place to be. The countdown to death was agonizingly long. The year I spent waiting to be judged and sentenced lasted longer than the combined twenty-two years preceding it. The only hours that go by quickly while imprisoned are visiting hours.

"Jacob," a familiar voice resounded as the mustachioed chief of police, whose name was Benjamin Milan, approached my cell. "You have some visitors."

"Visitors!" Eat'em yelled, "YES!"

Two other officers were with the chief. Bellecroix and Cameron. Behind them was Isaac.

"No..." Eat'em said. "Lame."

"What's going on?" I asked, putting down my book.

"I don't get why we're here," the lieutenant said. "The judge ordered us to come see you. Said it was imperative. That chief Milan bring myself and Cameron specifically, and to bring this guy. Don't know what strings were pulled, but here we are."

"How are you holding up, Jacob?" Isaac asked.

"I'm great," I said, "you know. Just waiting to die. Here to gloat?"

"If I'm to be honest," Isaac smiled. Chief Milan and

Cameron smiled too. Bellecroix had the same stupid look on his face I imagine I had. Isaac, Milan, and Cameron all said in unison, "kind of."

Cameron and the chief grabbed Lieutenant Bellecroix from under each arm.

"What in the Hell is going on?" the lieutenant said as they hoisted him against the bars and Isaac unlocked my cell. They tossed the senior officer onto the floor beside me and locked us in together. Bellecroix's voice cracked. "Are you serious? Are you fucking serious? You better open this thing right the Hell now, Cameron. I kid you not! Chief! What's going on here?"

He reached for his holster to find it empty. Isaac held up his sidearm.

"I don't know who you think you are, but you just made the dumbest decision of your life," Bellecroix said, "Damn it, Chief! Cameron, you better open…"

"SHUT UP!" the three said as one. Then Isaac stepped toward the bars and spoke alone. "I'm not subject to your threats, Hershel. You are more inconsequential than nothing. Jacob," he smiled, "how stupid you must feel.

"I've been around for a long time, kid. Long enough to see my wife and children grow old. I tried to make them young again, Jacob. Who wouldn't? But there was none of them left…"

"What are you talking about?" Bellecroix asked.

Isaac pointed the gun at him from the other side of the bars. "It is not your turn to speak, Hershel. It will not be your turn to speak until I am gone. And if you speak again, I will shoot you.

"There was none of my wife and children left, Jacob," he continued, "because all that was left was me. So, you see, I didn't kill them. I gave them life. And in effect, I only killed the part of myself I couldn't live with anymore."

"Jacob, what's he...?" Bellecroix said before a gunshot dropped him to the floor. Blood oozed from his thigh as he screamed, drowned out by the aftershock of the blast.

"Again and I kill you, Lieutenant," Isaac said. "Nod if you understand."

Bellecroix nodded.

"Good," Isaac looked over his shoulder as if waiting for response to the gunfire, and turned back as soon as nobody rushed into the bay. "I fought in World Wars One and Two. I died in every battle. I've experienced death many, many times, Jacob. Undoubtedly, I will experience it many more times. It's maddening. But I know how to create a life without death. It's my destiny.

"You thought you were working your way toward the top of some chain," Isaac scoffed. "Jacob, you weren't even on my radar. You were some kid to talk to, that's it. I've been doing this long before you were born. You don't even have a clue as to how long the chain goes nor do you know how many chains I've started. But I'll give you a hint. Here's one..."

Isaac lifted the gun to Chief Milan's head and pulled the trigger. Another shot rang out. Blood and teeth, fragments of skull and chunks of brain exploded into the air. The behemoth fell. The lieutenant held in a scream.

As if in reaction to the chief's sudden departure, Cameron began to twitch uncontrollably.

Black liquid poured from Cameron's mouth. Blood dripped from his eyes and nose and ears. He collapsed and seized violently, an intense growl broiled up from his heaving lungs.

"I wanted to cure humanity from death," Isaac said, "but through the perverse nature of some evolutionary trait that created you, it's now clear to me that humanity wants death. Humanity craves death. Humanity somehow needs death. Well here it is. My gift to you. And I've given you front row seats out of the kindness of my merciful heart. You wanted to start a war. Nobody has more experience with it than I do."

He turned and walked away.

"Wait!" I yelled. "What happens next?"

He paused. Without turning back he said, "Enjoy the show."

After he disappeared out of sight, Bellecroix finally coughed. "What was that, Jacob? What was that? Christ on a Cross! You were telling the truth? Tell me what's going on."

"I don't know..." I said.

"Were you two not paying any attention?" Eat'em chimed in. "Must I explain everything?"

"It's not good, sir," I said. "And it's about to be worse."

Outside the cell, Cameron climbed onto his hands and knees. He lifted himself up on the bars and pulled himself to his feet.

A hollow howl escaped his ragged windpipes. It echoed through the bay. Other howls followed. From inmates. From guards. From outside the prison walls.

The world faced an epidemic, as I remained locked behind bars with the man who put me there, listening to the events leading to this predicament as narrated by a small red imp.

Epilogue

*D*ear survivor,

Firstly, good on you for spitting in the face of the apocalypse. Civilization has come to a big bloody finale and it's time to sit back and relax with a book. Why not, right? The world's gone to Hell, hope is all but lost, Internet is down, cable's out, how about a good read? I wouldn't blame anyone.

I lost hope when the newest *Star Wars* got canceled just months before release. I lost hope again when all the movie theaters started locking their doors. I lost hope when all the power went out and never came back on. Sure I kept what faith I could that maybe someone out there would have an old BluRay player and an HD TV and a power generator or something so we could watch movies, but I guess not everyone has the same priorities when the news anchor tells them it's too dangerous to go outside before signing off for the final time. People started biting and killing each other the world over. I lost hope.

The post-apocalypse isn't nearly as bad as I thought it would be. Perhaps, I'm guilty of having seen too many post-apocalyptic movies, and that's why I expected some *Mad Max* kind of nonsense. I figured there'd be gang wars and violence, people struggling to survive, that kind of stuff. That hasn't been the case. In fact, food is readily available and the people whom were able to wait it out are all pretty friendly.

I guess we all just kind of have stronger stomachs now. When everyday's a funeral, it's kind of hard to be rude to each other. So we shuffle down roads lined with abandoned vehicles, and we always say hi to one another. On occasion people group together and help each other out, but not always. That said – I haven't seen anyone fight since the end. I've seen people walk into an old CVS and take just what they need. One guy even stayed in the store for a while, helping people find medicine and food and such, almost like he worked there. But nobody paid him and nobody took more than they needed.

Granted, it's really easy to share when almost everyone is dead. I never thought about it when things were normal, but as one of only a few hundred people left, nobody wants the reputation as the guy that horded all the children's Tylenol and is shooting people for formula and diapers.

Back when people swarmed cities there were plenty of shootings for cases of *Enfamil*. Gang bangers were having baby gang bangers they couldn't feed with welfare checks spent on booze and cigarettes. Now, there's no reason to be forced to choose. All the gang bangers are reformed… or dead. It's nice.

To be honest, I kind of prefer the way things are. People

aren't as judgmental and now that the world has ended I'm not so afraid to die. I mean, that day… the day people were screaming and death cascaded upon the Earth to punch the collective society's meal ticket… for me that was almost a relief. It was a relief. A huge burden was lifted off my shoulders, really. I'd put a lot of effort into postponing the post apocalypse and all it did was end me up in a short line to be strapped to a table and injected with God knows what. Dead. Me. And I would have made that exchange to save the people we had to bury. Gladly I would have taken the needle to keep everyone else from the grave, but I couldn't. It's a huge weight on your shoulders to know Death is sitting there on his black stallion and you're the only one doing anything about it.

My favorite part of surviving any tragedy is finding out where people were when it happened. Everybody does it. "Where were you the day…?"

As the rest of the world collapsed, I was in a prison cell with the one man who hated me more than anyone else on earth. Lieutenant Hershel Thibodeaux Bellecroix. Some sergeant named Aaron Cameron chomped on the bars to the cell like it was some sort of snack. He chewed the thing until his teeth broke out his mouth and he gummed it until someone outside the cell disrupted his thinking with a magnum round.

I'd like to say it was my Uncle Valentine or Dixie or even Big Mike… someone cool and pertinent to my life somehow. But our rescuer was just some cop that happened to be fighting his way through the prison one bullet at a time. Unfortunately, it was his last bullet, and an orange-clad maniac tackled him seconds after getting the key into the lock, and commenced eating our shining hero as I helped Bellecroix step over the smorgasbord.

See, because Bellecroix had been shot earlier by the guy that started this whole mess. Yeah… him.

Anyway, I helped the lieutenant out of there. It was the right thing to do. And then I headed off to search for my friends… Valentine and Dixie. Not Big Mike. He died. Because he ate. Not because he was eaten.

Diabetes.

I'm on a tangent. The point is. You're alive… Yay!

Yes, yes, I know it's a crapstorm. But I'm trying to keep optimism alive. Because without optimism, without hope, without *Star Wars*, what is there really?

When I started writing this, I meant it as a rally. Like, "Hey, we're alive. Meet us here. Let's do brunch." That kind of thing. But, we've decided not to stay here.

The one who caused this is still out there. He's still alive. This isn't over. And I want to leave this as a promise to you. Whoever you are. You will feel safe again.

Wherever he hides. In whomever he hides. I will find him. And I'm gonna Get'em.

Jacob C. Brook

In Memoriam

A special thank you to those Immortal few who have sacrificed to make this book possible. These individuals have contributed to the making of Eat'em, either financially or through their time and energy. They deserve my sincerest gratitude and have earned recognition in the pages of this story.

Financiers:

Lisa Fuqua
Ronnie Monroe
Chelsea Mirelez
Dallas Webster

Sherri Jo Morris Webster

Deborah Ahlstrom

Trey Kegley

Na Lo

Amy Dominguez

Cameron Webster*

Travis M. Webster

Mark Bauer

Brentt Morris*

Nikki Kube

Matthew Deo

Trevor Dyllan Schreckengost*

Mike Morris*

Terry Webster*

The band *Hello Jamie* for their likeness and lyrics to the song *Pocket Knife* as read in Chapter 43:

West Albaladejo – singer/songwriter

Ronnie "The Rooster" Monroe – guitarist

Jordon Lennon Downes – bassist

Mark Mirelez – drummer

Early contributors:

Mary Duncanson

Von Jocks

Darrell Morehouse

Amanda Stone

Jace Roscoe

Becky Crook

Natasha Smith

Author Photo:

Darryl Erby

Test Readers and Editors:

Dallas Webster

Terry Webster*

Jason Boyd

3D Render Eat'em Art:

Jaime Bengzon

Cover Artists:

Milan Jovanovic*

Benjamin Roque*

Friends and Encouragers:

Patrick Valentine Rivers*

Caleb Fonville*

Dale Gomes*

Shannon Ramsey

Benjamin Cheng

Nick Scharold

Lee McLendon

Derek Flagg

Kristian May

Byron Talley

Oren Hammerquist

David House*

Webster & Morris family

There are many others whose kind words and encouragement have helped guide me through the five year journey of creating these characters and writing this story. These are the names of people who specifically helped make this story what it is, whether through their kindness, generosity, or brutal honesty. Some of them impacted the story directly, and some of them had a more subtle impact on myself or the inspiration within these pages. All of them, however, are owed a debt of gratitude.

*Denotes only the most faithful of contributors, whose generosity has earned them a character specifically named after them within the pages of this novel. Sure, most of them died, but it's a small price to pay for immortality.

Coming Soon

Get'em

The drive to my old home was uncharacteristically quiet. I sat up front with Val, while the lieutenant slept in the back seat. His chest rose and fell rhythmically, each breath a trial in and of itself. Every so often one of Bellecroix's inhalations would catch and for a moment it appeared as if he wouldn't breathe again – but he did – his airway would open with a choppy gasp and he would fade right back into a drawn out lungful of air.

Valentine drove with the window down. His shaggy copper hair whipped across his face as we soared through deserted roads, weaving between one accident and the next, heading south on residential streets calm and panicked all at once.

Eat'em lay across the dashboard in front of me, poking his

tail through the cracked window, watching it bob against wind current like a lure swaying from the bow of a fishing boat.

The cab was reticent. Hope dissipated. The world outside reeled in shock from sudden pestilence. My heart swelled and I fought back the tears, which scratched at the back of my crimson eyes, threatening to make them redder.

"Can we listen to some music?" I asked. "The quiet is going to drive me mad."

Val clicked on the radio without a word. The omnipresent gods of irony controlled the airwaves today. *Down with the Sickness* by Disturbed tore into my eardrums, as my uncle's thousand dollar speakers burst to life.

I turned it off with the same immediacy, but the damage had been done... within seconds, Eat'em began to hum the tune as if the song were still playing. I could almost hear the words "Madness is the gift that has been given to me." It was the worst song I could think of to get stuck in the pint-size demon's head.

Dixie still lived in the same apartment. It was the same one she lived in when we met, and the same one I moved into before getting arrested for the homicide of Dr. Reeder. The small single-room domicile wasn't anything to be excited over before, but in recent history it'd fallen to the destruction of vandalism as much as time. The words "Devil's Bride" were spray painted across the door in bright red. Windows were cracked, some shattered out completely, spatters of dried egg spotted the side of the building.

"When's the last time you checked in on her?" I asked Val as we helped Lieutenant Bellecroix up a small set of stairs leading to the front entry.

"A couple weeks ago," he said.

"And it was like this?" I knocked on the door, overwhelmed with more emotion than I could handle. I was exhausted and saddened, but excited to see my purple-haired beauty.

"Not like this, no," Val said. "But we haven't exactly had a large following of fans due to your dumb ass."

"My dumb ass was trying to prevent this," I knocked, ready to embrace Dixie the moment she opened the door.

"Good job that," Val said. "You might as well have jumpstarted it."

"He was our neighbor for how long?" I said, "You could be like them. You could just as easily have been added to his army of freaks."

"But I wasn't."

I knocked again.

"A little gratitude would be nice," I said.

"Gratitude?" Val said, "Ha! Okay... How 'bout, thanks Jacob, great job on ending the world early. Thanks Jacob, life is so much better now I'm one of the most hated men in America. Yeah, telling women I'm related to the famous Jacob Caleb Brook really does a number on their panties."

"I get it."

"No, no, no," he said, "Least of all let me say this! Thanks

Jacob, the death of my friends, and teachers, and coworkers is going to do wonders in conjunction with all the hard work I've done for the degree I will now never receive, because even if all the great and wonderful things Jacob Brook has done for the world, somehow... by the grace of Jacob, of course... smooths itself over, I'm sure every university nationwide is going to jump through hoops to have me attend their campus. So, pardon me for not expressing my immediate gratitude to you for placating my most deeply desired hopes of being loathed amongst the few survivors of your insipid fantasies of grandeur. Forgive me for not praising your heroics when all I've done is put myself and everything I care about at risk protecting you. How could I be so selfish?"

"Dude," I said. "I'm sorry,..."

We stood in silence on my old doorstep for what felt like ages – each of us under one of Bellecroix's limp arms as the officer drifted in and out of caring about our loving feud.

"I didn't know, Val," I said. "I'm just trying to do what's right."

"Yeah, well me too."

Bellecroix mumbled, "I've never wanted to die this badly." To which, Eat'em added, "Amen, yes."

I knocked one last time before checking the handle.

The door of the Devil's Bride opened to an unthinkable nightmare. A mosaic of blood and gore strewn about in a physical rendition of madness. Bloody scribbles combined together on the far wall to create a giant collage, which when observed from the front doorway formed a three letter word.

WAR

Are you worried your loved one has succumbed to the Grotesque Infection? Use this quiz to find out:

1. What color is your loved one's eyes?

    a. Blue, brown, green, or hazel

    b. Blood red

    c. Jet black

2. Which activity best fits your loved one?

    a. Play video games or watch television

    b. Play baseball or other sports

    c. Clean obsessively

3. Whose your loved one's favorite philosopher

    a. They don't care about philosophy

    b. Wilhelm Gottfried von Leibniz

    c. All of them

4. Describe your loved one's complexion:

    a. Old and wrinkled

    b. Young and smooth

    c. It's like something is living under their skin

    d. Red and covered in quills

5. What did your loved one eat for lunch

    a. A sandwich

    b. Three energy drinks and some antacids

    c. Another loved one

ANSWER KEY:

If the answer to any of these questions is C there's a good chance your loved one has been infected. If you circled C more than once, you should probably consider leaving their presence as soon as humanly possible. If the answer to number 5 was C, you should call the proper authorities regardless; there is definitely something wrong with your loved one. Seriously.

Writing Eat'em

I started Eat'em more than five years ago while taking a
creative writing course at Tarrant County College SE in Arlington,
Texas. The class, taught by romance novelist Yvonne Jocks, provided
a fertile environment for meeting other writers and networking with
others with similar creative goals.

The year before I began work on Eat'em I had just finished
my premiere novel, LA Fisher, and looked forward to writing about
someone more heroic than my first go at literary fiction. The idea
began with a killer stalking an invisible force through the darkness.
He was accompanied only by a porcupine-like creature with a thirst
for energy drinks. The names of the characters, which came later,
were inspired by the book of Genesis, in which Jacob's twin brother
Esau sells his birthright for red pottage. Esau later has his name

changed to Edom. Similar to the biblical story that inspired it, Eat'em sells him-self for a bottle of Pepto-Bismol and furthermore is given a new name.

It was the relationship between these two characters that drove every aspect of the story.

Of course, there are many other things that go into a writing a story than a good idea. So what else went into Eat'em? A lot, actually. Five years, four rewrites, three test readers, two cover designers, one awesome editor and countless drafts later and the dream I had in 2009 is now a reality. That's a long time to be writing a single story. In that time I went from a college student to an airman, and from a bachelor to a husband and a father. As I changed, Eat'em changed too. Not only as a result of honing my literary craft, but also as a result of the many works of fiction that went into inspiring it.

Here are some of the books I read during the time it took to write Eat'em:

Odd Thomas by Dean Koontz
A Dirty Job by Christopher Moore
Rant by Chuck Palahniuk
Divergent by Veronica Roth
Maze Runner by James Dashner

This is by no means a comprehensive list of books I read, rather it's an example of the books and authors that inspired different aspects of my own writing. I also read books by Stephen King, James Patterson, and many other authors during the last half-decade. It's my firm belief that in order to do something and do it well, you must first look to those who do it better than you.

The inspiration behind Eat'em's bizarre behavior:

When imagining Jacob's foot-tall companion, I looked no further than Sigmund Freud's philosophical teachings of the id. The crimson demon is single-mindedly focused on his own desires. While Jacob may be in danger, Eat'em is still concentrated on fulfilling his own selfish desires, whether it's to be entertained or fed. Finding the perfect voice for Eat'em was difficult. That is until my wife and I adopted our own little devil. Our dog, Tibby.

Tibby is our Labrador/heeler and is in every way Freud's definition of id. For the last two years he has provided my wife and I (and now our year-old daughter) an endless source of entertainment. And I can't help but narrate the dog's every action and pretending to be the voice he would have if he only had the anatomy to use it. It wasn't long before my voice for Tibby found itself on the page as my voice for Eat'em. The demon's innocence, mischievousness and charm are a reflection of the lives I am surrounded with every day.

The infection:

The Grotesque Infection has changed more than any other

element of the novel. When I sat down with the first draft, I imagined the infection being something more paranormal, and the cause was a shadowy creature much like the Bodachs in Dean Koontz's *Odd Thomas*.

Having grown up a fan of zombie movies, vampires, and tales of apocalypse, I began merging the ideas into something that better resembles what it is today. I experimented with using real life infections such as Toxoplasmosis and Cordyceps. Eventually, I settled on something more ambiguous, as to allow for changes as needed. The concept of combining the terror of zombies and the intellectual hive-mind of vampires developed with each draft.

The story became less about whether the infection was feasible than how we would react if it happened. The tireless story of the coming apocalypse has been at the forefront of pop culture for decades, yet we are quick to alienate those who see it as anything more than a source for the next Hollywood blockbuster. This is why Jacob needed to be isolated in his fight against the infection. Though he has allies, only he is aware of the possible ramifications if he were to fail.

The future:

Jacob and Eat'em's journey will continue with *Get'em*, set to release this winter. I began the follow up immediately upon completing Eat'em. It will pick up where this novel ends and just like Eat'em it will be filled with twists, turns, and plenty of Jolt Cola.

About the author

Chase Webster was born in Germany and grew up across the United States. He wrote for the Shorthorn Newspaper and is the author of *LA Fisher* and *Eat'em*. He is currently an Airman in the US Air Force and specializes in munitions storage and maintenance. Recently he served in Operation Enduring Freedom.

Chase lives in Texas with his wife Ornanik "Nikki" Webster (Bug), his daughter Olivia "Little" Webster (Monkey), and their dog Hershel Thibodeaux "Tibby" Bellecroix (Bubba).

SURVIVAL NOTES: